CW01638436

Love You Too Special Edition

A SMALL-TOWN, ACCIDENTAL PREGNANCY HOCKEY ROMANCE

STACY TRAVIS

FTP
FAST TURTLE PRESS

LOVE YOU TOO

STACY TRAVIS

Cover Design: Wildheart Graphics

Copyediting: Erica Edits

CHAPTER *One*

BEATRIX

"Beatrix, can we squeeze in a large party tonight at the restaurant? It's for the mayor."

Check!

"Can you make a decision on the fabric for the lobby chairs at the inn? And approve the menu changes at the café? And choose a stain for the floors, but make the work happen while we're closed?"

Check, check, and OMG, check!

I am the queen of multitasking, the grand dame of juggling, the duchess of details. Really, I should have a crown.

Or a big, fat pillow because I'm freakin' exhausted.

There's no crown or flower wreath with ribbons hanging down my back. No long sundress. No casual, easy, relaxed vibe. Design and construction are moving at the pace of an injured slug, and I'm a frazzled, hot mess.

"Will the inn be open in time for my wedding?" My younger sister, PJ—short for Penelope June—twirls her dark, wavy hair around a finger and blinks meaningfully at me as I bury my face in the foam of my latte.

So. Not. Check!

"Hey, do you see that butterfly on the wall over there? Isn't it pretty?" I point, and her grimace says she's not falling for my distraction. Her question has only one answer, so I nod and smile, rather than force myself to lie.

Stress etched on her face, she stands in my office above Butter and Rosemary, the gourmet restaurant at our family winery, Buttercup Hill. Her wedding is set for early January, five months from now, and the inn on our property is in shambles. Water damage from a faulty fire sprinkler system ruined furniture, floors, and paint, so we had to shutter one of our best revenue sources. I had the idea of using the repairs as an excuse for a full-scale renovation to make the place a vineyard haven, a gem in the wine country.

Totally on-brand for me. My plate is already full, but I can't resist a new project. Can't fight the shiny glimmer of a design challenge.

My hair pulls at my temples in a tight ponytail that's already giving me a headache. It looks professional, with a couple of intentional loose pieces framing my face to make me appear softer. Kinder. Less likely to bite someone's head off for placing a fork at the wrong angle next to a plate in our Michelin-starred restaurant. Less likely to bark at my sister, who doesn't deserve my ire when she's just stressed and worried about her wedding. Though I do wish she'd have a little more faith in my ability to pull off the wedding of her dreams at the inn.

"Don't worry, sweetie. I've got it covered. Go hug your sweet fiancé, and I'll talk to you tomorrow." My sister leaves, reassured, and I head toward the conference room, where linens are splayed out in a colorful fan of paisley, damask, and ikat prints on the large plank table. The rep for our fabric vendor stands a few paces away, holding her breath, waiting for me to point to the prints I want for draperies, sofa coverings, and pillows. With thirty-five rooms to decorate, the decisions will result in thousands of dollars in fabric. I can't afford to make mistakes.

"I like these." I point to a family of pale blue and sandy brown tones that will offset the natural wood I selected for the refurbished suites. "And let's do some kind of accent for the bathroom tile in this blue shade," I tell my assistant, Julie, whose superpower is her ability to appear when needed. She makes notes in a binder, which doubles as my lifeline—the flimsy tether between the ideas in my head and their eventual execution. I'm too busy thinking three meetings ahead to remember what I've decided in the present, so Julie makes sure I have records of everything jotted in color-coded pens. Then she blinks up at me, looking awake, bright, and ready for the next challenge. She's my other lifeline.

"Blue tile—check. I'll order samples."

On a side table in the winery's main conference room, stacks of Italian- and American-made pottery sit on display. There are plates and bowls painted with colorful images of farm animals, more classic porcelain, and handmade earthenware from a local potter in Sausalito. Each year, I try to change the dinnerware at Butter and Rosemary because returning guests say the design elements are as important as the food. Heaven forbid we just use something for several years in a row, and I maintain a little sanity. Not to mention the sheer wastefulness of starting from scratch.

"I'm tempted to keep what we have," I tell Julie, feeling the wave of exhaustion that comes with making too many decisions. "We can call it a return to classics."

"You mean boring."

I love that Julie doesn't mince words, but sometimes I wish she wasn't right about everything. Her messy blond hair, untucked oversized tee, and face devoid of makeup give her the aura of someone who should be skipping among the vineyards, not keeping my to-do lists, but she has a great memory for details, and she works her tail off.

"Fine. Let's do the one from Sausalito. We can play up the local angle. I'll feel better about buying new dishes if we're supporting a Bay Area business."

Julie makes more notes and dismisses a few more of the vendors she's assembled for our design meeting. A few minutes later, we're in my car, headed into downtown Napa, where cute shops line the small streets bisected by the Napa River. Our destination is the Oxbow Public Market, where I want to make sure the jams from Buttercup Hill peaches are prominently displayed in the artisanal section. And going into town will give me an excuse to look around for design inspiration, which I desperately need.

At a stoplight, I rub my temples, trying to ward off an impending migraine. My jaw aches with tension, and my body feels shaky, running mostly on caffeine. I hate the sense that I'm not in control of my emotions, my temper fraying over tiny inconveniences like a woman on her cell phone who doesn't see the light turn green. I honk and hate myself a little for my lack of self-control.

"Have you eaten today?" Julie's blue eyes hit me like accusing pinpricks.

"I had coffee."

"Yeah, that's not food. You need fuel. You also need to get laid."

I startle at the non sequitur and then glare at her.

"What?" she asks, matter-of-factly. "You're thirty-two years old, and you have nothing in your life but work. You need to get out, be impulsive for five minutes, live a little. Otherwise, you'll stay wound up, and that's not good for anyone."

"I do live life. I'm right here, living life, trying to work against the clock to make everyone in my family happy." She's not necessarily wrong, but I don't have time for this now.

"Not what I meant." When I glare some more, she relents. "At least eat breakfast."

"I'm not a big breakfast person." I wait for a pedestrian to cross against the light and fight the urge to honk.

"It's after two."

"Guess I'm not a lunch person either."

We have this exchange daily, as though it's brand-new information. I act surprised and grateful to hear Julie remind me that food is fuel, knowing I'll ignore it again the next day. Julie slips me a handful of almonds from her purse so I don't get cranky, and I eat them to stave off feeling hangry for another hour.

"Thanks," I say, crunching through a mouthful and steering my green SUV into the parking lot behind the market.

Julie zips her purse and points to an empty spot. At thirty-five, she's only a few years older than me but worlds away in lifestyle. Each morning, she leaves her tiny blond two-year-old daughter with her husband, who works evenings at the Dark Horse pub in Calistoga. She likes to start early and finish in the afternoon, so her family has time together before the pub shift.

They seem to have everything figured out in a way I can't fathom. All of my multitasking is directed toward my job. No husband. No cute kid. No real life outside of work. The screen goes blank when I try to think beyond today.

Falling in love isn't even on my radar. I had my heart smashed to pieces one time, and it was enough to cure me of any urge to date for a long while. Been there, done that. No reason to put myself through it again, so instead, I let my work be my true north.

It's worked well for me so far. I'm a career woman, and with three brothers, I've never felt like male energy was missing from my life. I can't imagine being with anyone who could understand the time and energy my job requires, and I'm so tired at the end of each day that I can hardly keep my eyes open, let alone have enough energy for an orgasm.

After an hour, I've snapped some photos of decorating ideas and sourced a supplier for vintage artwork made from old wine crates. Julie's husband, Ed, waits for her in the parking lot. I allow myself a thirty-second break to coo at her toddler, who scampers out of her dad's grasp and runs toward Julie, arms outstretched.

"You need to eat something real," Julie calls back at me before lifting her daughter to the sky and kissing her belly.

"I will, I will."

"Except you won't. You know how you get when you're obsessed." She holds her daughter out to me so I can squeeze those fat cheeks. I do so because it's what's expected of a woman at child-bearing age, even though my own biological baby clock is on pause while I work on my career. A tiny thought wiggles through the chaos in my brain and tells me that those cute baby cheeks have taken my stress level down a couple of notches. But I can't think too hard about it.

"What's that supposed to mean?"

She doesn't take her eyes off her daughter, kissing her belly while fumbling through her purse and shoving a granola bar at me. "You make impulsive decisions you regret later on, you blurt things out when you should think first, and you snap at the people you love."

"I do not!" I snap.

"Just do me a favor and eat something, please. And get fucked, for heaven's sake," she whispers, cradling a hand around her daughter's ears. "That will take the edge off for sure." She knows my refrigerator at home is empty, and I can't remember the last time I ate a meal. It's either snacking on the go or not eating at all. As to the getting laid part, it's about as likely as having the inn renovated by tomorrow.

"That ain't gonna happen anytime soon unless you have a man in your purse."

She laughs. "I'll work on that."

An hour later, I'm running on fumes. I fish around in my bag for Julie's granola bar, but my mission is disrupted when the sales clerk returns with my swatches of fabric. She smiles, tucks her long silver bangs behind her ears, and adjusts her wire-rimmed glasses so they sit higher on her nose. "Here we go. I threw in a few extra color palettes in case you want to try it a different way." She always stashes away new fabrics she thinks I'll like before other customers see them.

"Oh, you're sweet. I'll probably come back with a whole new color scheme after I try the alternates."

"Not trying to make it harder," she sings.

"You're not. I love options."

Her smile widens, and she pulls out a bag from beneath the counter. It's practically big enough to hold the fabric swatches *and* her. And the counter. "Sorry. We only have giant bags for some reason."

"It's okay. I don't need a bag."

I tuck the pile of fabric under one arm and resume the hunt for a snack. The granola bar has somehow slipped into the purse abyss, never to be found amid useless pennies and old lipsticks. Tin of mints? The only one I have contains change for parking meters.

My stomach grinds from the coffee I guzzled on an empty stomach. I don't think I can wait until I get back to the winery to put something in my system, so I detour to the bakery. As I stare at the glass case filled with golden croissants, berry muffins, and little fruit tarts, the only challenge is to choose just one.

"Blueberry bran muffin and a coffee with cream. To go, please." I shouldn't have more coffee, but the muffin will soak some of it up, and I need the energy boost.

I balance the folded white bakery bag on top of the coffee cup and adjust the stack of fabric in my other hand. My purse dangles from my shoulder by a skinny strap, and I navigate past the cheese counter and a display of pretty packaged chocolate.

Passing a wine shop with floor-to-ceiling bottles of local vintages, I notice the owner hasn't ordered the recent crop of cabernets from Buttercup Hill, but that's a problem for my older brother Archer to solve. I have enough to focus on today with restaurant decor and reopening the inn.

The late afternoon sun shines so brightly that I squint to find my car in the parking lot. I sort of remember where I parked. It was near a tree. At least, I think so. I'm busy looking into the distance, so I don't see what's directly in my path. Or rather, *who* is directly in my path. Not until my knees hit a brown ball of fur, and I lose my footing for a second.

That's all it takes for my bakery bag to topple from the lid of my coffee. "No, no!" I beg, but it obeys gravity instead of me. I lunge to grab it without spilling the coffee, my purse sliding to the ground and dumping its contents. The tin of coins opens and sends rolling quarters in all directions. Tampons fly. Lipsticks scatter.

The ball of fur decides my little catastrophe is a really fun game and begins leaping toward the coins and pawing them to the pavement. The dog is medium-sized with fur like a brown shag rug and warm cocoa eyes. "Where's your leash? Who owns you?" I mutter, glancing around. All I see is bright, glary sunlight and pavement.

I manage to grab the muffin bag before the dog gets to it, but I'm gripping my coffee cup too tightly, so the lid pops off, and the life-giving drink sloshes down my arm.

"Ow! Shit, shit, shit." I suck air through my teeth, shaking liquid from my scalded arm while I scramble on the hot pavement to retrieve the lid and gather my stuff. So very ladylike.

Note to self: always carry snacks. Never balance things on coffee lids. Conceal tampons in some sort of a pouch. Advice I will ignore the next time I leave the house.

The dog chooses my moment of vulnerability to charge at me like I've just yelled "go." I lose my footing and roll backward, coffee spilling again. The dog seems to think this is a game and starts licking my face with glee.

Listen, I am a dog person. I think they're cute. I willingly pet them. I've even toyed with getting a dog. But right now, in this moment, I am not feeling the love.

Well, maybe a little bit. The dog's rough little tongue tickles as it laps at my cheeks and chin. It feels like an apology for the chaos. "Okay, buddy. I know. You just want to play. Not your fault your human is a dumbass."

I hold the muffin bag under the dog's nose for a good sniff and then toss it a few yards away. Predictably, the dog chases after it, and I cover my face with both hands to block out the infernal sun for a few merciful seconds.

That's when I finally hear a deep shout in the distance. "Truman. Tru! Stop. Sit. There. No. Stay."

Even I know that's too many commands for a dog to understand and obey in a single moment, but at least someone is claiming responsibility for the fur monster. Truman bounces around like he has pogo sticks for legs, his curly fur glinting in the sun, tongue hanging out one side of his open mouth. Pure joy.

As flustered as I am here on my back, I start to laugh. I haven't sat down all day, and apparently this is how I need to accomplish it—by getting flattened by a hyperactive dog on the sidewalk. The whole situation is so ridiculous when I realize I'm jealous of a dog and his zest for life. Not to mention his freedom from deadlines, fabric swatches, and stress.

The air around me cools as the sun is blocked by a cloud. I wrench my hands from my eyes and open them.

Only it's not a cloud blocking the sun. It's the broad shoulders of a tall man standing over me with a confused expression. With the sun behind him, he's hard to see clearly. "Geez, sorry about that. You okay?" he asks, raking a hand through his hair.

"You really should keep your dog on a leash." I sound like a crotchety old lady, but this is about animal safety. "Cars barely stop for humans, let alone dogs. Give your guy a fighting chance, at least."

He lets out a long exhale and unfurls a leash from his hand, so it dangles in front of me. "That was the plan. But the little trickster escaped before I got it on him." He rubs a hand over his chin, where a few days' worth of stubble catches the sun. I still can't get a clear view of his face because of the glare, but his voice sounds familiar. He's a local or someone I've run into at Buttercup Hill.

"You sure you're okay?" Something snags his gaze, and he spins around to yell, "Tru, what the heck are you doing?"

"I'm good." I push myself to a sitting position, noticing the scattered coins around me and the tampon squeezed in my fist. I quickly shove it into my purse. Then, a hand comes into my field of vision. It's large, strong-looking, and extended toward me. When I look up, I see that the man is offering to pull me to standing. I wave him off.

"Thanks, but I think I'll stay on the ground here with my dignity."

He waves his hand, insistent. "Come on. At least let me replace your breakfast."

Grudgingly, I place my hand in his and nearly recoil at the jolt of electricity when I touch his skin. It's like a shock of lightning entering my body at my fingertips, ricocheting up my arm and down my spine. His palm is dry and warm as it connects with mine, flooding me with an unsettling heat. His fingertips rough and calloused as they take a firm but gentle hold. It's jarring because of its intensity but also…familiar. My body reacts to a long held memory.

When I'm on my feet, I crane my neck slightly, taking in the full six feet and four inches of the man in front of me, cataloging his soft brown eyes, chiseled jaw, high cheekbones, lips that have no business looking as soft as they do. My eyes quickly scan his body, noticing the defined muscles of his arms beneath his t-shirt, his thighs pulling at the denim of his jeans.

Guess some things never change. At least not for Dominick Renaldi, star hockey player, gorgeous physical specimen, and champion heartbreaker. Or Ren, as I called him back before he broke mine. Ten years earlier, he was the love of my life. The butter to my toast. The capital O of all my orgasms, which have been few and far between ever since.

And now…a stranger.

Playing hockey clearly still keeps him fit, which is decidedly unfair—the rule when you bump into the ex who broke your heart is that he's supposed to look like a hairy ogre. Oh wait, that's me—covered in coffee, hair a mess, clothes in disarray from being trampled by his dog.

"Trix?" His eyes soften as they go round with disbelief. That nickname. He's the only one besides my family who ever uses it. It sends a warmth of familiarity through my veins before I remind myself I don't feel anything for this man. We aren't friends. We're barely acquaintances now.

"W-why are you here?"

He smiles. Dammit, there go the dimples and those perfect teeth.

"I play for the Otters now. I'm a local. Sort of."

I know enough about hockey to know that means the Oakland Otters, which are just an hour from here. I nod, trying for an air of nonchalance but probably looking like a woozy fangirl instead.

Well, shit.

You know when you want to act like an adult and let the guy who broke your heart see that you're completely over him? Yeah. I want to do that, really, I do. Because I *am* over Ren. I have been for years. I no longer think about him. I barely notice when some picture comes across my social media feed of Ren cavorting with yet another beautiful woman. And when a hockey game is on at the Dark Horse, I barely give it a passing glance.

I am over him. Over. Him.

And yet…seeing him again jars my senses and roils my stomach with something unexpected. My heart starts beating like an amateur drummer in a slick marching band. Loud, discordant thumps that surely can be heard two stadiums away. My face heats with embarrassment—that has to be what it is—because he found me disheveled and flat on my ass, and he looks, well, perfect.

Why does the one man who I planned to never see again have

to be so freakin' beautiful? No, not beautiful. Sinfully, undisputedly gorgeous.

And as good as he looks, that's how angry I suddenly feel. The hurt I had over the way we ended comes roaring back like an untamed waterfall, drowning out any kindness toward his adorable dog. I do not have a warm feeling for Dominick Renaldi, not anymore. I have nothing to say to him now.

Yet here he is, looking at me with that amused smirky smile I used to find so damn cute. I feel my hackles raise and my fists ball defensively. I've never slugged a man, but I'd have no problem making Ren the first. It's been ten years coming and it would feel oh so good.

College sweethearts. Young love. Impossible choices. We were hot and passionate for a full year before the wheels came off. Life happened. Real-world factors came into play, and our romance couldn't survive it. Things went from blissful to finished so quickly that I had whiplash.

I realized in hindsight that we never really had a chance. Before the end of his senior year, he was recruited by a Canadian hockey team and missed graduation because he needed to replace an injured player immediately. I was still a sophomore, still undeclared and uncertain about what I wanted to do with my education or my life.

I offered to follow him to Canada. That's how stupid in love *I* was. But he cured me of that in one fell swoop by dumping me abruptly and leaving the country for his new career.

So I finished college, discovered a love for design and renovation, and figured out I had talents that far outweighed being a puck bunny. I moved to Napa to help out at Buttercup Hill, and here I am, eight years later. Wiser, busier, career-focused. Far too rooted in my feminist ideals to follow anyone anywhere.

My career is my identity, and I wouldn't follow a guy like Ren across the room, let alone across the country. He taught me not to fall for a man whose career is his one true love, and I'll never forget that lesson. And while my heart and mind are content never seeing or speaking to this man again, my treacherous body can't decide whether to slap him dramatically across the jaw, telenovela-style, or grab that pretty face and kiss him silly, showing him what he's missed out on for all these years.

All of these thoughts hurtle toward me at lightspeed. Just seeing him in front of me produces a rip inside my chest. The same feeling of my heart deflating that I felt all those years ago, but now it's tinged with irritation that he's here. In Napa. My territory. With a dog who's clearly as poorly behaved as him.

"Trix, are you okay?" His warm brown eyes are tinged with concern. His lips tip downward as he surveys me with something akin to sympathy, and I hate that he seems to pity me. The frustration turns to anger in my veins, giving me an unquenchable feeling of…

Nope.

I should walk away. Quickly. Before I say something I'll regret.

Gathering my stack of materials from the ground, my muffinless brain goes rogue, and I mutter the one thing that would make me okay. "No. I need to get laid."

CHAPTER
Two

REN

"W-what?" I can't have heard her correctly.

Beatrix looks as shocked as I feel at what she just said. Her face goes peony pink, cheeks hotter than the pavement, and her pale blue eyes round into lakes.

"Nothing."

"Not nothing. You just—"

"No, I didn't," she insists, fanning the air around us as if to dissipate the words. Or cool her skin.

"You—"

"No. I didn't. Let's just move on."

"O-kay…" I'm not sure I can do that, not sure I want to do that. But I also don't want to make her so uncomfortable that she runs off, so I grudgingly let it go. For now.

"Yeah." She smooths her hair, even though it's already perfectly tidy. I take in the totality of what I see before me—the pouty lips, the full breasts outlined beneath her shirt, her curves in all the places I loved to touch.

But now there's more—the spark in her eyes is fierce, unforgiving. The curve of her cheekbones is still soft, but the set of her jaw looks resolute, like she doesn't suffer fools. I want to hate that she's looking at me like I'm the prized fool of all time, but instead, it's a turn-on.

Ten years.

I had ten years to convince myself that the woman I fell for in college was not as pretty as I remembered. And she's not. She's better. More stunning, more effortlessly graceful—even when she was scrambling beneath my dog—and so fucking gorgeous that I'm having a hard time forming words.

A light breeze tugs at her long, dark hair that she's tried to tame into a ponytail. Tendrils spill out, framing her face and igniting the flame in her eyes even more. Her mouth, which I can't stop staring at, is twisted into something between a scowl and resignation.

Beatrix looks like she's about to hit me, which would be a first. Not that we didn't get into it regularly when we were together, but it was always the feisty kind of foreplay that led to the hottest sex I've ever had. Sex I haven't been able to get out of my head, despite a string of fleeting, lackluster relationships with puck bunnies who were more than happy to oblige when the loneliness got to be a little too much for me.

If the salacious tabloid posts about me and various women had anything to say about it, I succeeded. But none of the women I've been with could hold a candle to Beatrix Corbett, and not because she was my first love.

Because she was my only real love.

Ten years of wondering what Beatrix Corbett was up to. Ten years of googling her name to find out. Ten years of wishing I hadn't been the biggest asshole on the planet because then I just might have a snowball's chance of asking for her forgiveness.

But I was, so I don't.

Gave up that hope when I walked out the door at twenty-two to a million-dollar contract that seemed like manna from heaven to a kid with no other skills. I was young and dumb, but that doesn't excuse my lack of explanation. My lack of communication. If I didn't know it already, I see it on Trix's face—pure disdain with a side of disappointment.

That look takes me right back to the days after we broke up, when she refused to take my phone calls and sent barbed replies to my texts. I convinced myself that she was the one being unreasonable, and I actually started to dislike her a little bit. Way easier than loving her from afar and feeling guilty about hurting her. But what they say about love and hate is true—two sides of the same coin. I chose the one that allowed me to sleep at night.

When a guy is lucky enough to find the purest kind of love with a woman like Beatrix Corbett, and then he blows it like I did...well, that guy pretty much deserves whatever miserable fate befalls him after that. It's why I never tried to contact her, never tried to cross paths with her.

Yet when given the choice between a hundred vacation destinations, you bought one in the one town where she lives.

Well, that's different. The deal was too good to pass up, better than any of the other vacation homes my broker showed me. When she told me the property has a working winery in addition to old vines in a sought-after appellation, she piqued my interest. I'd never considered being a winemaker, so I almost gave the place a hard pass.

Then I came to visit. Under a setting sun, the vineyards extended out toward the horizon amid a sea of birdcalls and a peaceful lack of bustle that reminded me of where I grew up in the Vermont Berkshires. I wanted to regain that sense of peace without flying across the country. The commute here takes just over an hour from my house in Berkeley, even in traffic. The main residence was a pigsty and a half, sending me into a fever dream of carpentry projects I haven't had time for, but maybe once I retire from professional hockey.

Right now, that feels like a long way off. The Oakland Otters are a hot mess. Last season, they made every mistake possible on the ice, lost a lot of games, and pissed off fans and investors. The team earned the name Otter Pops because they popped, sputtered, crashed, and burned.

As the new team captain, I'm supposed to have a heavy hand in righting the ship. I've been here a month, and there's no obvious fix. I was the first player brought in during the free agency signing period, and now we have the best roster of players in the league—all the top picks because management decided to throw tons of money at impact players.

And we look like shit. Everyone's playing his own game, and all the star power in the world can't win a game if we don't connect the dots. Fan and investor expectations are sky high, and we're positioned to be unstoppable if I can create some team unity and get us as good as we look on paper. It'll take some strong words and leadership, and I haven't felt this much pressure since I was a rookie player right out of college with everything to prove. I thought those days were in the rearview. Apparently fucking not.

No surprise I've been in a surly mood, with only a couple months before our first game. And now, this. *Her.* The one bright spot in my week. A gorgeous woman who, by her own admission, could adjust both of our attitudes with an afternoon quickie.

But I don't dare touch that one, not when she's scowling at me.

"Just like I figured. Truman's human is a dumbass." Her answer comes with an eye roll and a raspberry, which only serves to draw my attention to her lips. Plump, pink. Frowny.

Great. I'm the proud owner of a multimillion-dollar piece of property I'll never see, not if it means a repeat of the way she's looking at me right now. I get enough pummeling on the ice. The last thing I need is to get my ego stomped on my days off. I need to apologize for my dog and walk away.

"Glad you're smart enough to blame the dumbass, not his dog," I say.

This is you apologizing and walking away?

"Helps that I already knew you were a dumbass, even before your dog stole my breakfast."

"I don't think it counts as stealing when a person throws her breakfast across the pavement."

Her eyes narrow, fire blazing within the pale blue. "It was that or let him attack me."

Truman comes loping over with the remains of the pastry bag and nuzzles Beatrix, tipping his face against her leg and looking up at her with his big, dopey, brown eyes. I defy her to be angry with him, even if he is licking the last of her breakfast from his mouth.

"Labradoodles aren't known to be attack dogs."

She rolls her eyes. "Figures you'd have a designer dog," she mutters. I see her hand flutter as she resists the urge to pet him. I say nothing, just wait for the inevitable to overcome her, and she reaches for his head and scratches him between his curly, floppy ears.

"He knows you're talking about him. Smart boy."

"Not smart enough to know he shouldn't run through a parking lot."

"Smart enough to find the prettiest woman in six counties." I lock eyes with her and dare her to believe I'm sincere, even though I know I don't deserve her goodwill.

"Just six counties?" She retorts. "I'm not falling for your pretty one-liners, Ren. Those days are long gone."

I study her face, wanting to find some sign that she doesn't mean what she's saying. Maybe she doesn't hate me as much as I always presumed she did. She looks serious, frustrated with me. It's a look I remember well, and it brings back the end of our relationship when I insulted her with lame explanations and excuses.

"And you didn't answer my question. The Otters play in Oakland. What are you doing *here*?"

"I bought a place." I point in the distance as though she can see it from here.

Her jaw clenches, and her eyes grow bigger before she looks away. Kicking a toe into the gravel beneath her feet, she brushes some dust from the back of her shirt. Despite her attempt to act casual, she understands that I intend to be here more permanently. Her eyes flit from my face to a tote bag on my shoulder branded with a logo from a fancy paint store.

"Didn't know you were a winemaker."

"I'm not. At least not yet."

She rolls her eyes. Probably seen a dozen of the likes of me, rich guys strolling into town, thinking we can design some cute wine labels and add a vineyard to our collection of toys. She's wrong about her assumptions, but I'm not going to insult her intelligence with my tale of being swept off my feet by a sunset and a few birds. Or tell her the real reason I bought it.

"Well, good luck to you."

Holding her cumbersome stack of fabric swatches against one hip, she tucks a wayward strand of hair behind one ear. I bend down to pick up her spilled cup of coffee and its lid a few feet away because it's the least I can do, but I wish I could say I'm a better guy than that. I wish I could pretend I didn't notice the perfect swell of her hip and the curve of her cheek. I wish I could say with a straight face that the sight of it didn't make my dick twitch in my pants. I wish I could forget that five minutes ago, she blurted that she needs to get laid.

But I can't do any of it, and from the way her face heats when she catches me looking, she knows exactly what I'm thinking. "Stop that." Turning to go, she drops the coffee cup and empty pastry bag into a nearby trash can. Hefting a stack of fabric under one arm, she attempts to move past me. "Bye, Ren."

"Bye, Trix."

Truman's head whips from one of us to the other, seemingly confused about why our encounter is ending.

"You and me both, bud," I want to say. He runs after Beatrix and leaps in circles around her. For a second, I fear he'll trip her, but she steadies herself before turning to glare at me. All the while, she pets Truman and alternates between smiling at him and scowling at me. "Is that leash just for decoration?" She points at the leash dangling uselessly from my hand.

I should have slung it around my dog's neck. Would have, if she hadn't distracted me so much. "Fully functional."

"Use it," she calls, crouching down in front of Truman. She looks him in the eye while talking to him calmly. "You're going to go with your dad here, and I'm going to leave, okay? He's going to get some fancy asshole coffee, and hopefully you can use that trick where you knock it out of his hands. Okay, good boy?" She smiles at him.

"Nice," I say sarcastically. It's my turn to roll my eyes.

"All's fair in love and war."

"Are we really at war, Trix? Come on, it's been a decade. Maybe we can start fresh as adults. I'm not the bad guy you think I am."

"I think I know exactly who you are, Ren."

I smile at her and shake my head. I can't help it. Her feisty streak amuses the hell out of me. The more riled up she gets, the more I want to push her a little harder, even though the woman already looks like she just might choke me with my own dog leash.

"Can I at least buy you a new cup of coffee? If you're anything like me, you won't get far this morning without it."

She peers at me like I'm strange. "It's not morning. That was cup number three for me."

Glancing at the time, I see that it's late in the afternoon. I stayed up half the night drawing up plans for what I think I want to do with the main house on the property, only to rip them up this morning. I'm not further along with all my imagined woodworking projects than I was when our season ended and I started working on the place.

"I think you're the one who referred to it as breakfast. Fine. Let me get your afternoon caffeine fix and a new muffin."

She shakes her head.

"Please?" I add.

It's the *please* that seems to soften her resolve. Or maybe it's the bag of paint samples on my shoulder. She sneaks another look at it and inhales, opens her mouth, then shakes her head.

"Fine. But only because my blood sugar is dangerously low."

She starts walking toward the market while I put Truman on his leash. By the time I catch up, she's holding the door to Oxbow for us, and I brace it with my hand so she can step inside first. "After you."

As we stand wordlessly in the coffee line, Beatrix smooths the front of her beige sweater and brushes nonexistent dirt from her pants. Tucking a few strands of hair behind her ears, she looks at the coffee menu. My hands itch, dying to free the strands. In college, her hair hung loose and free, and unless we were going to a formal, she wore hoodies and jeans. I know she has a career now, so I don't expect to find her in sweats, but there's something else. She seems tense, wound up.

I love that for as smart and capable as she was, she showed me her vulnerable, messier side. I see none of that vulnerability now —just a polished, organized woman with places to go that have nothing to do with me.

Except that ... "Or...we don't need to have coffee. We could go back to my place and..."

Her eyes lock on mine. "Are you serious?"

I shrug. "You said you had needs, and I'm just trying to be helpful."

"You're. Not," she grumbles through gritted teeth.

Busy tapping on her phone, she doesn't notice that the person in front of us has finished. I gently place my hand on the small of her back to urge her forward. For a millisecond, she sinks against my hand. Then she jolts away like I've just fired the starting gun at a sprint. She leans hard on the counter, as if trying to get as far away from me as possible. "Coffee with cream and a muffin. Whatever you have." She waves a hand, flustered. I won't deny that I like seeing her ruffled.

I order a black coffee and a dog cookie for Truman and hold up my credit card. "We're together."

"No, we're not." She rifles through her purse, but I push the card forward, smile at the barista, and nod. She snatches the card, and by the time Beatrix gets her wallet out, I'm finger-signing the iPad screen.

She turns to me, pointing accusingly. "So, the morning starts at three in the afternoon for you? Out partying or posing for photo ops or whatever you do?" She asks me as though the whole idea bores her, yet the way her hands flit around betrays that she cares a little bit.

"No. I was researching craftsman design features and drawing plans. Not that it came to anything. I'm not much of an artist, turns out."

Her frosty demeanor thaws slightly. "Designs for what?" She looks pointedly at the tote bag.

"Renovations. I have ideas for the house, but I can't seem to make them look right on paper. And today, I got sucker punched by paint colors. Did you know that there are about a billion shades of white? I get overwhelmed when I have to choose between paper towel brands."

I know from some casual Google stalking that she's won design awards for the restaurants and inn she runs at Buttercup Hill, but it seems that my project has caught her interest. If I toss out breadcrumbs carefully, maybe I can keep her here longer.

Her eyes soften for a moment, as though she's imagining the glorious blank canvas of a dilapidated house and all she could do with it, but then the focus returns, and she frowns. "It's harder than it looks. You should hire someone to help."

I walk toward a tall round table with two chairs and indicate for her to follow. "I think it sounds like you're offering." She follows me with a huff that says she's not enjoying my company.

"You thought wrong."

I pull the chair out and extend my hand. Shaking her head, she pulls the fabric samples to her chest. "I'm not having coffee with you."

"Okay," I say, sitting down and waiting. Her options are to join me or march out, and I know she's not rude. Beatrix grudgingly puts down her bundle and perches on the chair. She keeps one foot on the ground like she might need to make a hasty escape. "Do you want to see the paint samples? Like I said, there are about a billion, and I don't know what I'm supposed to do with them."

It's a last-ditch attempt to keep her here, and I can see I've failed when she shakes her head emphatically. Then she grabs for the bag. "Let me see what you have."

I feel a secret thrill, realizing I've found her catnip. I seize the small opening when it presents itself. "Go for it. I can't make heads or tails of any of it—seriously, Dutchess Tea Room? Sierra Stone? These are paint colors? What happened to gray and blue?"

I earn the barest shred of a smile. "When all else fails, go with Swiss Coffee. But seriously, it's just a coat of paint. You can always paint over it if you don't like it." In her zeal to search through the bag, she perches more solidly on the chair, leaning toward me. I catch a whiff of jasmine, and it sends a ripple of want through my veins. I never expected to see Beatrix again. I'd hoped to, but even in my dreams, I'd never anticipated how it might feel. I never expected to feel this—the sensation of being drawn to her like she's the source of the air I need to breathe.

"Or if you want…you could come look at the place. It's a zoo of fabric options, furniture catalogs, wood specimens, and paint chips, all rolled up in a disaster of a renovation." I don't deserve what I'm asking of her—a few more minutes of her day—but I'm asking anyway because I can't help it. Now that I'm near her again, I want more. I want as much as she's willing to give.

For the first time since Truman bowled her over, Beatrix Corbett gives me a smile.

"If I come, it's only because I'm interested in interior design. Not…the other thing." She waves her hand toward the parking lot, as if I need a reminder of what's been bouncing in my brain for a half hour—she wants sex, and I know I can more than satisfy her on that front.

I pretend I don't see her cheeks blaze pink again. "Of course," I say. "Whatever you want."

But Is this what I *want?*

If you asked the guy with a twenty-two-year-old heart that never forgot Beatrix Corbett, he'd say that yes, it's what I want. However, the thirty-two-year-old man standing before her isn't so sure that sex is the only thing he wants from this incredible woman. But if that's all she's willing to give me, my greedy heart would ready accept it. My dick would too.

So I walk to my car without turning around. Just hoping she's following me.

CHAPTER *Three*

I DON'T FOLLOW Ren back to his house. I think about it. I think about it as I get into my car and drive to the exit of the parking lot, but I don't do it.

Because it would be ridiculous, and I don't do ridiculous.

I'm not a woman who follows men to their houses just because I need a hookup. And I especially don't follow heartbreaking ex-boyfriends anywhere.

I have an inn to renovate, a restaurant to run, and a list of design tasks as long as my arm. Those things are my focus, not Dominick Renaldi. So I wait behind him and signal to turn left like he does, but once he's firmly headed down the road, I make a hard right and take the scenic route back to Buttercup Hill.

The tall oaks that flank the road to the winery perfume the air with a scent that defined my childhood—the smell of endless summer afternoons, dry earth baking under the sun, crunchy leaves combined with the fruit from hearty vines. A sense of calm washes over me as I drive up the lane to my house on the property where each of my siblings has a home.

Kicking off my shoes and dropping the stack of fabric samples on my white marble kitchen table, I can't dislodge the jarring idea of Ren living nearby. As hard as I try not to think of him, that's how hard my brain forces the image of his muscled arms back into my mind. The one saving grace is that the hockey season is long, and he's new to the Otters, so he'll probably disappear soon enough.

That thought lulls me to sleep after a long day, and by the next day, Ren is out of sight, out of mind.

Two days after that, I'm focused on blue paint. Sometime between three and five in the morning, I had an inspiration for the spiral staircase in the inn—it should be painted a deep marine blue to offset a tiny blue detail in the bold-patterned green wallpaper. For a month, something hadn't been working in the color scheme. No matter what I did, the room looked too much like a forest, with a heavy green and brown emphasis. Dark wood, green walls…boring.

But blue…I could already see how it would be the right neutral to make the design pop.

I rush to the paint store the moment it opens to see if my instinct was correct. Leaning toward the passenger seat to grab my purse, I have one leg out of the car when I feel my ankle covered in…slobber?

No. *No.*

"No!" A now-familiar voice growls in the distance, and I look down to see the contented face of Truman blinking up at me as his tongue takes another swipe at my leg.

A moment later, there's Ren, leash in hand, slightly out of breath. "Sorry."

I roll my eyes. "Are you following me?"

"That's funny. If I was, I'm doing a better job of it than you the other day." It takes me a second to recognize the look on his face because it's so unfamiliar, but I realize that it's hurt. His smile sags at the corners, and the playfulness is missing from his eyes. Like it's not just busted ego, but true disappointment.

"I didn't think we were really serious about…all that." I don't intend to bring up my unintentional booty call, but my face goes hot thinking about it.

He shrugs, eyes regaining a bit of their spark. "Guess I thought you were more interested in design than you are."

My competitive side can't help but protest. "I *am* interested."

He shrugs again and lassos Truman with the leash. "That why you're stalking my paint store?" He nudges me with an elbow, and I don't have time to brace my body for the way my heart races at the tiny touch.

"It's not your store. It's the best paint store in the area."

The owner props open the front door and Ren shudders. "I still have PTSD from all the shades of white." He rakes a hand through his hair, and I can't help but be amused by his fear of paint.

"So why come back?" I meet his eyes and let myself enjoy their calming warmth.

"I'm not a quitter." His jaw flexes and I see determination that I recognize in myself.

I indicate the open door with my head. "Fine, then. Let's go."

Ren sits on the floor of the paint store with about a hundred different paint samples scattered around him like a color wheel. They're all variations on white, and I can barely notice a difference, but to Ren, it's like splitting the atom.

"Which one do you like?" I've already picked the shades of blue I want and have them in a canvas tote bag. Ren looks as green as the Forest Lichen paint sample.

"You're kidding, right?" He looks up at me with glazed eyes I've seen in many of the brides who come to Buttercup Hill for their weddings. I ask them to thumb through lookbooks for decor ideas, and some flip delightedly through while others nearly hyperventilate.

"Should I get an air sickness bag?"

"No," he protests, nodding. "Maybe."

Truman has decamped to a corner of the store, where a bowl of water and a chew toy have kept him entertained for the past half hour.

"When did you become such a baby?"

"When I found out there really *are* fifty shades of gray."

"Exactly. So just pick one."

"Easy for you, you live for this shit."

"I do. And I'll tell you a secret—it doesn't matter that much. It's paint. If you hate it, paint over it."

Ren squeezes his eyes shut and extends his arm with a pointed finger. Then he lowers it deliberately and picks up the first paint sample he touches. Handing it to me, he opens his eyes.

"I should film this, send it to your opponents." I walk over and crouch down to see what he's chosen. "All worked up over Casual Bride."

"Don't you dare." He leans onto his hand to see if I'm telling the truth about the paint color. "Is that really what it's fucking called? I'm not putting that on my walls."

I giggle and hold the sample away as Ren pretends to swat me. He loses his balance and falls toward me, which knocks me onto ver. His hard chest hits mine as I tumble to my back. Ren's hand shoots out to cradle my head so it doesn't hit the floor. His face is inches from mine as we stop moving. I feel a swarm of butterflies in my belly, and a jolt of fire hits my core.

For a second, Ren doesn't move. Our eyes stay locked, and I try to search his for signs of what he's thinking, but his playful grin turns stoic. Then Truman bounds over, deciding that we're having too much fun without him. "Tru…Tru! Sit." Ren pushes Truman off and hoists himself away.

I immediately feel the void where his body was touching mine, and it aches. I don't want it to, but it does.

"I, um, think you're right about just trying out a color. If I don't like it, I'll try something else." Ren picks up a paint swatch and goes to pay for his paint. I'm not even sure it's the one he chose before.

"Rules to live by." I try to sound casual, but my voice comes out raspy.

I dust myself off and get ready to head out when Ren puts a hand on my shoulder, stopping me from leaving the store. "So…I was serious about having you see my renovation. It won't take too long. It's just the main house, five bedrooms. If you're interested."

I can't deny that I'm curious about the place Ren bought. More than curious. "I don't know, Ren. You almost fainted over paint. Five bedrooms is a lot."

"I think I can handle it. And if it all goes well, there's a sixth bedroom in the casita where I'm staying." His eyebrows bounce. He's all smirk—cute and dangerous.

"I don't want to see your bedroom, Ren. Let's get that clear." I keep my voice firm, though I'm not at all clear myself.

He laughs. "I was kidding. Just come over. Look at the house, give me your honest opinion about how much work it needs."

"I can't help but think you're remembering that *other* thing we talked about."

He smirks. "Never gonna unhear it, but that's not why I'm inviting you over."

"Okay."

"But full disclosure, I'm not ruling it out."

I shake my head. "Of course you're not. But you should." I take my bag of paint samples and breeze out the door.

CHAPTER *Four*

REN

Ten Years Earlier

"Don't you have practice early tomorrow?" Trix's pink lips turn up into a shy smile as I trail a finger from her shoulder to her wrist. My thumb lingers at her pulse point, and I rub the soft skin gently as our fingers intertwine. Her soft sigh is a balm to the intense workout I just finished with the team.

I pull her flush against my body and use the side of my other hand to trace the features of her face, grazing her temple, her cheekbone, her chin, her neck.

No wonder I was late for this morning's training, unwilling to pull myself out of her arms. Unwilling to heed my coach's warning about jeopardizing my future.

Trix's head falls back, and I lean closer to inhale the fresh scent of her shampoo and the sweet smell of her skin. My lips drop to her neck and kiss her softly, enough to light up her senses and send a shiver down her spine. She presses into me and tips her lips up to mine.

I want to devour them, but I just barely brush against them, exhaling a long breath. It takes all my self-control not to kiss her hard and deep right here in the hallway outside her dorm, but I know I can build her desire even more by withholding everything I'm dying to give her.

"Ren," she gasps when my lips brush hers once more. I cradle her face in both hands and angle her sweet mouth more perfectly against mine. Then I give her a tiny bit more of what she wants, but not everything. She makes me so damn crazy, and I have no problem working harder to make her feel the same way.

I know I should quickly kiss her good night and go back to my place for a decent night's sleep. She's correct that I have practice in the morning, and I need to put in a good performance. I've been dragging this week after we stayed up all night over the weekend.

But all I can think is that I want a repeat. "I have practice, but I want to spend the night with you."

My mouth takes hers more insistently this time, and her lips part as her body sinks against my chest. She's all soft curves, and I let my hands roam down her back and settle on her hips, pulling them harder against me so she can feel how much I want her.

She sighs, and I slide my tongue into her mouth, tasting her like it's the first time. It feels like I'm falling off a cliff when I touch her, free-falling into a world where nothing else exists. I never want to leave this perfect place, so I push away any niggling thoughts about the future.

I kiss her harder, plunging deeper, losing all awareness of time and space. There could be a full football team and a marching band in the hallway with us, and I wouldn't know it or care. But then I stop, gingerly pulling back and tipping my forehead against hers. Her chest rises and falls in rhythm with my own pounding heart. It's been like this with us since we first sat next to each other in class, a magnetic pull I couldn't ignore.

I'd always kept single-minded focus on hockey, wanted to go pro for as long as I could remember, but there was no ignoring Beatrix Corbett. Impossible.

"I love you, Ren." She whispers the words into my ear as though they're a secret only I can know.

I've been wanting to hear those words ever since I said the same to her—ever since I stopped fighting my emotions and allowed my heart to stray from what was always my one true love—hockey. And now I have everything I could possibly want in the world.

So fuck hockey practice. Well, not really. But I can be tired tomorrow.

A part of me knows I'm fighting a battle against myself, sabotaging what I've worked for, and...a part of me doesn't care. That's the dangerous part. She makes me not care. But I've waded in too deep, and there's a rip current.

"I love you so fucking much, Trix. Promise me you're mine forever." The words rush out before I can stop them.

"I promise." She's breathless, hands coming to my neck and tangling in the ends of my hair.

I shouldn't be talking about forever or anything beyond a few months from now, when I'll graduate and move to Canada. The contracts are all but official, and there's no way I'll be able to have a long-distance relationship and also put in the work required of a rookie player surrounded by the fanfare of being a top prospect.

My coach warned me as soon as he found out I had a girlfriend. My mother warned me as soon as I got my first offer.

I shouldn't be in a relationship because it's causing me to fuck up. I've showed up late to practice so many times after spending the night with Trix that the coach has openly questioned my commitment to going pro. Anyone else would be benched by now, but my coach wants the notoriety that comes from having a player recruited to a starting position in the NHL. I've taken advantage of that and pushed it to the limit because I know the league won't pull my offer now.

Right?

Until I hear otherwise, I'm not changing a thing. Not when the most incredible woman I've ever met just told me she loves me.

I can show up to practice tired one more time. "Invite me in. I'll worry about practice in the morning," I growl in her ear.

She opens the door to her room, and we tumble inside.

CHAPTER
Five

BEATRIX

Present Day

It's absurd.

No more do I have time in my schedule to look at Ren's dumb renovation project than I do to spend time with Ren—a man I shouldn't trust any further than I could kick him with a muddy boot.

And yet, here I am doing both.

I follow him down Silverado Trail and tell myself I'm taking a needed break from working my tail off. Maybe I'll get some design inspiration from his house. Or maybe I'll get laid.

Holy hell, what?

The thought pops into my head unannounced. I could blame Julie for planting it there a few days earlier, and sure, sex would be nice, but not with Ren. Even if the man is hot with a capital H and a gallon of pico de gallo sauce on top. He's always had that boyish charm that made it clear he could commit high crimes and get away with them just by smiling. His eyes twinkled with mischief, and when they were pinned on me…watch out. Cue body bursting into flames.

I drive and daydream about one escapist fling with a guy who looks like that, and I start counting…three, four, five. Not months, but years. Yes, that's how long it's been since I've had any fun with a man. I'm a good multitasker, but my tasks have not included sex in a long, long time.

As I cruise along behind his little roadster and watch his turn signal flash with ample warning to make the appropriate turns, I picture the man inside the car. He looks better in person than in pictures, where he's inescapable on social media. I always have a knee-jerk reaction when an image pops up. I swipe it away as quickly as possible and don't linger on captions detailing who he's dating or what he's doing. It's like a form of fight or flight—I scroll away as a form of self-defense.

Seeing him in the flesh is a different thing. I can tell with minimal staring that Ren is in peak physical form, honed by hours of speed skating and weight training. He was a physical specimen in college, so put ten years of professional hockey muscle on him, and the story is over before it begins. All reasons why I should turn my SUV around and head back to Buttercup Hill.

It's bad enough he's here—in my town—but he's making a home here. It's bad enough seeing him with other women on social media, but I don't want to witness it in person. And the worst part is that as much as I really want to dislike him, I remember all the reasons I loved him.

I hate that I still find him attractive, and I wish I could scroll away from him in person. Instead, I follow Ren up the driveway to the main house, determined to protect my heart and give him sass instead of feelings.

The house is a classic craftsman, and I can see the paint peeling from the front porch and pillars from fifty yards away. The property sits at the other end of the valley from Buttercup Hill, and I don't remember it going on the market.

"How did you get this place? Was it a pocket listing?" I can't help peppering him with questions the second he opens the door to his convertible Porsche, which stuck out among the pickup trucks and Teslas as I followed Ren along the St. Helena Highway. "Is it a tear-down or a fixer-upper?"

His eyes crinkle, and he smiles as he unfolds his long legs from the car and leads Truman across the front seat by his leash. "I've never seen someone this fired up about renovations. You're adorable."

I hate that the compliment makes my heart flutter. I hate that I'm reacting to him at all, when what I want is to be indifferent. I want to be the type of woman who could use him for sex, the type who could effortlessly walk away and forget about him, if only to even the score. I want to show him I'm no longer the same naïve girl, pinning her hopes on a man.

And yet…my eyes rake over him, noting how he wears his hair a little bit longer now. It's wavy and dark, offsetting the two days' worth of beard on his face. He looks more mature now, face more angular, but with those same high cheekbones that could sever a pane of glass in two neat halves.

Moving down, I notice his lightly-tanned skin at the neck of his Henley, unbuttoned at the top. But it's what's underneath the shirt that holds my attention—hard planes of muscle as his pecs give way to abs that cling to the soft material. His shoulders and biceps stretch the cotton to its limit, and it's all I can do not to reach out and wrap my hands around his muscles and squeeze.

Sex with Ren was good. More than good. I need a stern talking to, something like, "Beatrix, march straight to your car, get in, and drive away without looking back. Then, put your head down and get the inn finished. Dominick Renaldi can renovate houses and fling paint samples right up to your door, but you will feel nothing."

"What?" he asks after I've stared silently for over a minute.

"Nothing." I push my bottom lip forward defiantly.

"Not nothing, honey." He casually runs a finger down the

length of my arm, and I wonder if he can tell my skin is ablaze at the barest touch.

"Don't call me 'honey,' Hockey Star," I spit out, taking a step farther away.

He smirks. "You think you're insulting me by calling me that? I know that look in your eye."

My cheeks heat, but I have trouble not staring at his warm, teasing eyes.

"There's no look."

"Trix, I may not have seen you in years, but I know the look."

"I was glancing over your shoulder at the moldings around the windows. They're nice. That's it."

He smirks. "You can admire my…moldings anytime you want, hon."

I refuse to give him the satisfaction of admitting I'm undressing him with my eyes, even if he knows it. "Let's get something clear, Ren. I'm here as a design professional, despite what I said earlier. You should just forget about that part."

He crosses his arms, grinning. "Can't just forget."

"Well, try." I wrench my eyes away from his pecs, and they start watering from staring for so long. "So we should…look at the renovations, yes?"

"Sure."

Ren moves ahead of me to open the front door, extending his arm toward the foyer. His large frame leaves little space in the doorway, and our bodies brush against each other accidentally as I slide past him. A frisson of awareness lights up my nerve endings, and my pulse skyrockets, sending a whoosh of warm heat through my veins.

Ren's eyes fall on mine. The earlier smirk is gone. He's just… looking.

My heart beats so loudly I'm sure he can hear it. Ren clears his throat and glances away, but a lick of electricity hovers in the space between us.

I follow him around as he points out various nooks and

corners in need of help. Mostly, I'm staring at his ass, but I hum and nod as he gestures around the place.

"Ren, this house is…interesting," I say. Actually, it's not. It's a disaster in need of repairs, renovations, and possibly a bulldozer. But I'm impressed that he bought it with no more than a tape measure in his pocket and a dream. "It kind of reminds me of the barn in that Carraway Farm series. Have you seen it on social media?"

"Nope." His hand grazes my elbow as he shows me into a dilapidated library. I shiver and try to play it off with wild hand gestures.

"It's this awesome place this woman bought years ago. It was run-down, kind of a disaster, and she turned it into a working farm. Now, it's the cutest thing ever and she has like a million followers watching her play with baby chickens and pick onions."

"Um, okay. The only takeaway was that you think my house is a disaster."

I tilt my head from side to side. "I didn't say that."

It's worse than a disaster.

We walk the premises—broken, ancient appliances here, cracked moldings and scratched wood floors there. I catch him watching me as I take in each room of the house, and his gaze feels like a breeze kissing my skin.

I pull up some old carpet and send dust flying a foot into the air. He points to a doorframe, and it comes off in his hands. We walk into the kitchen, which has broken cabinets and smells like a combination of mildew and rotting wood. Ren calmly escorts me out, his hand brushing the small of my back. "Don't think we should linger in there." His breath feathers over the back of my neck, and I melt a little.

When we've finished walking through, I turn to him, hoping the pity doesn't show on my face.

"Okay, not beyond hope, but it's a project, that's for sure. The place has good bones, and it doesn't need any real rebuilding. Mainly TLC for the surfaces. Paint, wallpaper, floors, fabrics. If you've hired a contractor, you'll be able to get subs working on several things at once, but everyone wants to be last. Painters, floor people—they all want the last pass at the place, but you just have to tell them to work together. It can be done. What's your timeframe? Because even if it's short—and trust me, I know short timeframes—you can still get people to hustle when things need to get done. Furniture, floors, lighting, all of it can be installed like a movie set. Bam, bam, bam." I motion with my hands like I'm firing a gun even though there's no weaponry required in renovations. He probably knows that.

Or maybe he knows nothing at all because right now he gapes at me until I wave a hand in front of his eyes.

"You okay?"

He shakes his head as though coming out of a stupor. "You're…different than I remember you."

"Yeah? How so?" I have a feeling I know what he'll say. I'm not the impressionable girl who was too naïve to understand that hot hockey stars don't stay with their college girlfriends. Now, I'm cynical and wise, just looking to satisfy my physical needs without strings attached.

"I guess, more driven and goal-oriented? Tightly wound?" It comes out like a question, but he doesn't seem to be searching for a more apt way to describe me. "Like you'd only choose to get a cup of coffee if you needed a caffeine boost, not for the company."

I could be insulted by his assessment, but it's not untrue. I can barely recall the time in my life when I was different. I nod.

I'm this way because of you, I want to say. I'd never actually utter the words out loud, but they're the truest truth. Perhaps it's unfair of me to lay the blame for who I am now entirely at Ren's feet. But when the love of your life sees you as an impediment to his bright future and discards you like dirty gum on his shoe…it tends to leave an indelible mark.

Ren may have been the catalyst for the protective barriers around my heart, but years of isolating myself solidified them into place

My focus, my commitment, my success—all of them are a product of my relationship with Ren. More specifically, they're a result of the way Ren walked away without looking back, leaving me to pick up the pieces of myself and figure out what to do next.

The idea that someone could want me and then…change his mind… That was a formative life lesson.

I'll never do something like offer to follow a guy when I know now that love doesn't mean forever.

"And what about you? Are you different than you were ten years ago?" There's an edge to my voice, and he catches it, flinching at the implication that he was not a great guy back then. The jury's still out on now.

He doesn't answer right away. I start to wonder if he didn't hear the question, but then he lets out a long exhale.

"I want to be." He stares off into the distance. "I want to incorporate more into my life, which is why I started work on this house. To test a theory." I want to know why he came to this particular town and bought this particular winery, but I try to keep my mind from wandering and focus on the conversation at hand.

"What's the theory?"

"That I can have balance in my life if I work hard at it. It's never been a priority before."

"Oh. Well, I'm the opposite. Master at multitasking, here." I point to my chest with both thumbs. "My whole life is balancing like a hundred plates at once."

His jaw falls open and cocks his head at me. "I don't mean juggling. I mean balance."

"What's the difference?" I literally don't know what he means. It's practically a school requirement to be able to look at a phone and do something else at the same time. It's all about multitasking in this day and age, and I proudly wear my crown as queen.

His laugh is so abrupt it startles me. "I'm talking about life balance. Things outside of work. Though I'm not one to talk, at least not yet. All I do is play hockey."

"Yeah. I recall." I whisper the words quietly, but the past hurt comes rolling back in my tone. I guess I'm not completely over the way he said he loved me and made me promise I was his forever before abruptly breaking my heart and moving to Canada. Alone.

"Is this...do you want to talk about that?" He leans slightly forward like he might step closer, but then he puts his hands in his pockets and stays rooted in place, his expression wary.

We're standing in an empty bedroom with dust bunnies around the baseboards, peeling paint, and broken windowpanes. In his presence, I feel like this room—battered and worse for the wear—and that's a side I won't let anyone see. Especially this man.

"No. I don't."

The problem is that I don't know what I want. Now that we're alone here, it's awkward and confusing. A part of me wants to be mad at him or hate him, but another bigger part of me wants to take the high road and show him that all he's really good for at this point in my life is a good time. One and done.

"Let's see the rest of the house."

He studies me for a moment as if he's gauging whether I mean it. Finally, he nods. "Okay. Wait until you see the upstairs bathroom. It's purple and black. Definite bordello vibes."

"Well, who wouldn't want that?" I quip, following him up the creaky wooden staircase.

As it turns out, I want a bordello bathroom and more. I love this house. And despite myself, I feel a jittery, schoolgirlish pull toward Ren's broad-shouldered, chiseled form.

There's also something else. The Ren touring me through his house is more reserved and pensive than the hotshot hockey star I knew when he was twenty-two. Now, he has an indefinable air about him—more mature, quieter, deeper. I don't want to like it, but I do.

Once the house tour is done, as promised, Ren brings us right back to where we were an hour ago. Only now, he ups the ante, trailing a finger from my shoulder down to my wrist. He's been doing this for the past hour, leaning in so I can feel his breath caress my cheek. And I've been doing my best not to shudder. Or downright tremble. To be clear, I've been unsuccessful.

The man is hotness in human form. Even as our relationship fell apart, we still had chemistry, and that was part of the problem—it distracted me from understanding what was really happening between us. The tearing apart of first love. I assumed that if I ever saw him again, the past hurt would prevent me from feeling anything.

I was incorrect.

I mean… I don't want him, per se, but I want what I know he can provide. My body wants his body. Badly.

"So," he says, eyes moving over me so slowly that I feel the burn over every inch of my skin. "Would you like to see the casita? It has actual furniture, couches. We could…sit someplace." He can barely hide his cheeky grin.

A blaze of heat races through my veins. I know his bedroom is in the casita.

I'm not worried about him breaking my heart again. That's impossible now. My heart is well-sealed and protected, not vulnerable to his charms. And yet, despite myself, I still want him. Maybe it'll give me some sort of closure to have sex with him. Regardless, I'm curious enough to see how this all plays out.

Laughing like I'm immune to the implications of seeing his room, I take a step backward. Then another. I try my hardest to keep my cool and not let my lady boner make life more complicated than it already is. "Are you renovating that too? If so, sure." My breath comes out ragged, betraying me and cracking on the last word.

A peal of laughter rumbles from his throat. "Like I said, you've changed a bit in ten years."

My exhilaration over the idea of a hot, satisfying quickie turns to annoyance. "Not really. Even back then, I think I could hold a conversation without needing to jump you."

His eyebrows bounce. "Not how I remember it."

I'm about to pepper him with retorts about needing to get over himself when he closes the distance between us in two long strides. Grabbing my hand, he floods my body with that damn electricity that scrambles all thoughts except one—I need him. Now.

"Whatever," I grumble, following where he leads me around the back of the house. I can't help craning my neck to take in tiny details in the eaves and evidence of the original trim colors in places where the sun hasn't bleached it. "You're delusional. It's embarrassing, really."

But I'm the one picking up the pace.

"Not at all embarrassed," he says, leading me down a smaller walkway than the one in front of the main house. This one is quaint, lined with potted plants that look well-watered. They alternate between wandering rosemary and perky lavender, somehow still in bloom in early August.

"So, you found yourself a gardener," I observe as we reach the front door, flanked with two larger pots, each containing a lemon tree laden with fruit and smaller green plants at the base. And daisies, lots of daisies.

They're my favorite flower. There was a house down the block from where Ren lived in college that had a whole hillside of daisies, and Ren would often pluck one stem and tuck it into my ponytail, flower on top of the band. That simple, sweet gesture was what made it so hard for me to accept how easily he seemed to walk away from me at the end—I couldn't believe a man with that kind of heart could turn so cold.

Surely it's a coincidence that daisies are growing here now, but it makes me happy to see them.

Ren stops in his tracks so fast that I run smack into his back. I barely have time to put up a hand to brace myself, and now it's crushed between us, the hard muscles of Ren's back under my palm. He spins around, freeing my hand, and I feel an urge to reach out and touch him again somewhere. The heat of his body is magnetic, and I'm no match against it.

"Nope. Just me. You like the plants?"

"I, um, yes…"

He unlocks the front door and pulls me through it. I barely have time to take in my surroundings, which are quaint and well-kept—tidy white kitchen to the right, stainless steel appliances, small, unfurnished living room to the left—before Ren leads me down a hall and pushes open the door to his bedroom.

I don't know what I'm expecting. A college dorm room? Milk crates for furniture? Posters of hockey heroes taped to the walls?

All of my memories of Ren and his living style are rooted in ten years ago, when he rarely made his bed and left pads and jerseys strewn everywhere. This room is large and immaculate, with a king-sized bed in the center and matching rustic wood bedside tables. Each of them has a small stack of books on it next to a lamp.

"You're a reader?"

"Yes." He smiles. "You want me to read you a story?"

"I, um…" Before I can come up with a logical response to a question that's probably laced with innuendo, Ren presses a quick kiss to my palm. Eyes never leaving my face, he squeezes my hand and leads me to the edge of the bed.

He holds up a finger. "Sit, please. I'll be right back." Then he disappears down the hall. Truman, who has been sitting at the foot of the bed, obediently trails after Ren, his nails skittering against the wood floors.

I feel like I'm not supposed to follow him, so I stay put and think about what I'm considering. Sex with Ren is a bad idea, no matter how tempting. Then again, maybe it will get him out of my system once and for all. The breakup sex we never had.

When I hear him rustling around in the kitchen, opening and closing cupboards and rattling dishes, I push down my ambivalence and scoot myself back on the bed to check out his books. On one side of the bed, I find a stack of performance-related sports books. No surprise. Ren has always been obsessive about understanding different kinds of training and the effects on fitness and performance.

On the other bedside table, however, I find three books of poetry—Emily Dickinson, Pablo Neruda, and E.E. Cummings. I flip open the Dickinson tome and find that several of the poems are earmarked. Interesting.

When I hear Ren's footsteps approaching, I close the book and stash it back where it was. He catches me scooting back to the foot of the bed where he left me. Eyeing me with a quizzical look, he says nothing. Instead, he closes the door behind him and puts a tray down on the bed next to me.

"You still haven't eaten much, and I don't want you passing out on me from starvation. And maybe this will help your nerves." He gestures to a corked bottle of wine and two glasses on the tray. Next to that sits a platter with crackers, three kinds of sliced cheeses, a bowl of pitted green olives, and a dish of dried fruit.

"I'm not nervous," I lie.

"Right, okay." He points to the strand of hair I'm twirling, and I immediately drop it. I hate that I have a "tell" and I hate more that he remembers it.

My stomach rumbles its approval as I take in the snacks. I push away the warm glow that rises in my chest at the sweetness of his gesture. He couldn't know it, but the snack display is exactly the kind of thing I often eat for dinner when I'm alone at home and don't feel like cooking. But I don't tell him because this is a fling, and he doesn't need to know me better than he does.

Putting a slice of cheese on a cracker, I nod. "Thank you."

He watches me bite into the cracker, and I'm aware of the indelicate way a piece falls to my lap. He pops an olive into his mouth and hands me a glass of wine. We nibble and sip in silence for a few minutes, and I feel a pleasant numbness from the wine. I also feel a pang of regret. This is crazy. I should not be at my ex-boyfriend's house for sex. Or…this is exactly where I should be. I can't decide.

"If we do this…"

"Yes…" I'd smack the cocky grin right off his face if it weren't so damn cute.

"It's just a spur-of-the-moment thing. It doesn't mean we're friends again. It doesn't mean we're anything. Just one and done. We clear?"

He nods slowly. "Whatever you say."

"That's what I say. We're not friends."

He smirks again. "Fine."

When I've finished my glass of wine, a bit of my caution slips away, though I still feel a little nervous and tense. Putting my glass on the tray, I meet Ren's eyes. They're just as molten brown and bottomless as I remember loving as a college sophomore when all I knew was that I wanted to stare at those eyes forever.

Now, I feel the heat and pull of him, but none of the emotions or promise of something more. I only feel the need for his body and what it can do to mine. There's no question I want that.

Ren brings me to standing before putting the tray onto the floor. He returns to sit on the bed and guides me closer until I'm straddling his lap. I have all the power in this position, and it allows me to trust him, trust his intentions.

He wraps his hands into my ponytail and moves my face to angle our lips more perfectly. Our faces only inches apart, I meet Ren's eyes, which are soft, molten brown. He cups the back of my head and inhales a long breath before shaking his head slowly and exhaling. "More beautiful than ever."

I feel a flutter in my chest, and my thighs tighten around his. Ren's lips barely brush against mine, but it feels like he's lit a fuse. Urging my face closer with his hand, Ren deepens the kiss slowly, like honey dripping onto my tongue. My mouth reacts to him like it's found a safe haven after years of useless wandering. It's explosive, passionate, heated. So. Damn. Necessary.

Ren's hands move to cup my ass as I grind against his erection.

Our bodies have taken over completely, and I gratefully give my overworked brain a break. I just want to feel him.

Ren rolls me onto my back and hovers over me on his forearms. I'm still a little nervous, so I make a dumb joke. "Last chance to back out…"

"Not. Taking. It." The low, sexy rasp of his voice sends a chill down my spine right before his lips lower to mine. They're soft, insistent as he kisses me again like we have ten years to make up for. No hesitation, no light brush against my lips this time. He kisses like he owns me, and I both love it and hate it, so I bite down on his bottom lip.

His head jerks back and he meets my gaze, the recognition of a challenge in his eyes. He kisses me harder this time, not an apology for the past but an acknowledgment that this is passion without an ounce of love.

"Admit you like me," he growls against my mouth.

"I like this," I pant, cupping his erection and refusing to give him more.

My legs lock around his hips, and our mouths meld in a furious intensity we never used to have. Our tongues tangle and fuse as I shamelessly grind my hips against him, feeling his hard length right where I need the friction.

He rolls us so I'm on top of him and smacks me hard on the ass. Even through the fabric of my pants, I know it will leave a mark. A brand.

"Ouch." I can't wipe the smile from my face.

The wild, feral way we are with each other feels like a match of wills. A white-hot battle of passion that could easily eat us alive. More delicious than I've ever experienced.

"You like me," he goads.

"Barely."

My nails dig into his neck as he kisses me again, his tongue parting my lips and delving inside with a new fervor. We're like a tornado of tongues and hands and skin as I shove his black Henley up so I can touch the hot skin over his hard abs. His tongue trails down my neck, and he lifts my shirt over my head before returning to the sensitive skin of my neck.

He kisses his way to my ear. I fling off my bra and roll us so I'm straddling him, moving against his erection exactly where I want the friction. Nothing coy about what I need from him.

His hands roam up my torso and cup my breasts, thumbs massaging my nipples until they're achy and stiff. That takes all of about a second. It's not at all the way we used to be as love-struck, innocent college kids. I feel claimed by Ren in a different way, appreciated as a grown woman. And I want him for what his body can give me. Only that.

Ren's chest is broader, muscles more developed, abs more rippled and taut. His lats bulge as I run my hands up from his waist and marvel at how many pounds of muscle he's put on since college. Every inch of him is taut and warm beneath my hands, and I can't stop touching him as we continue kissing.

Ren kisses with more confidence, more authority. And when his tongue feathers over one breast and he exhales over the sensitive skin, my nipples respond in a way they never did back then. He's just bigger, harder…more.

More muscular, more commanding. More of everything I want. I start nodding to myself because this is good, so very good. Exactly what I need to get me out of my head and make me stop thinking so much. But not just yet. Right now, I'm so in my head that I don't realize I'm talking to myself. "Yes. So much better than yoga."

Ren stops kissing me, holds my face a few inches away, and laughs. "Better than yoga?"

"Did I say that out loud?"

"Um, yeah. You did." He shakes his head, chuckling.

"You do know that laughing in a person's face isn't a super-hot turn-on, right?"

"I could say the same when you're all stiff and tense and comparing me to a workout class. Would you relax? Are you capable of that?"

"This *is* me relaxed," I grit out.

"Wow. I'd hate to see what you're like when you're stressed."

"Will you please just kiss me like you did a second ago? I promise you I'm relaxed."

He flips me again onto my back and kisses me. Harder. Deeper. His lips taste like delicious, impulsive decisions, and I let out a long exhale and just *feel*. Ren's mouth slides over my chin and down my throat. His fingers roll over my shoulders, my throat, my breasts, all begging for his touch. Then he pinches one nipple hard between his fingers before soothing the ache with his tongue. I feel myself melt into his body.

Our chemistry was good back in college, but it's nothing compared to now. I'm panting, begging for more. And when he slides down my body and peels off my pants, every part of me begins to hum beneath his strong hands.

And his mouth.

I stiffen up again, ready to explain that it's been a long time since someone's gone down on me, but the words die in my throat as his tongue strokes slowly up my center, and I forget all about warning him that I might not be able to come this way. I stop thinking about anything at all except for how good this feels.

And that's all it takes. A momentary separation between me and my brain. Now, all I feel is Ren touching me in places that I was pretty sure had gone dormant from lack of use. It takes me less than a minute for every pleasure center in my body to erupt at once.

For the first time in years, I relax.

CHAPTER *Six*

REN

What she couldn't possibly know is that for all her feisty banter, the hottest thing about Beatrix is that she's given me a goal. A mountain to climb. Something formidable to conquer.

I'm an athlete down to my bones, and nothing gets me going like a challenge.

Getting her to the finish line and scoring an O becomes my only reason for being. And I'm gonna enjoy the fuck out of it.

"You okay there?" I ask as she lies heaving on her back with an arm over her eyes, motionless. "You are alive, yes?"

Beatrix nods, still not removing her arm. "So alive. So very, very alive."

I chuckle at her lack of filter. It's the only time she resembles the girl I knew in college. I like this version. A lot.

The other one…well, I'll just focus on the one murmuring unintelligible things about how good I am in bed. At least, I think that's what she's saying.

Beatrix rolls onto her side and drops her arm. Her eyes are glass, jaw slack. Still in an orgasmic haze. So pretty this way. "Ren, you do not disappoint. I think I experienced nirvana there for a second."

She pushes up to sitting and starts to bundle her hair into the rubber band around her wrist. I shake my head. "Oh no, you're not done yet."

"What? Why?"

"For starters, I didn't give you what you came for." I work my pants down my legs and watch her watching me. She stares as I give my cock a few strokes, and her lips part.

She turns a gorgeous shade of scarlet and re-tucks her hair behind her ears even though there's nothing to tuck. Then she pulls the rubber band out and gathers her hair into a fist, twisting it until it's tighter than her personality, and loops the band around it. I'm dying to reach over and pull the rubber band away entirely. And…fuck it. I scoot closer and reach my hand for her, watching her eyes widen with surprise as I outline her lips with my finger. I guide her chin so her eyes fix on mine and go utterly glassy.

Grazing her cheek, my hand continues its journey, slipping into her hair. I grab the ponytail in a fist and tug it so her mouth lines up perfectly with mine. She sucks in a breath, and I kiss her hard, letting her know that I'm nowhere close to done with her.

I pull the rubber band from her hair, which spills over her shoulders. It's kinked in places from the rubber band, messy. "Better."

"You're not being helpful." Her voice is lazy and unconvincing.

"Kinda seems like this is exactly the help you need."

She sighs and relents, putting a hand on my arm and squeezing. "We always had good chemistry." She can barely get the words out.

I curl a finger and beckon her closer as I move to recline against the pillows. She crawls toward me, and I pull her on top of me, taking her full weight before flipping us over again. "We have fucking great chemistry," I say, eyes boring into hers. She nods.

Pushing my hand into her hair, I sink against her mouth. No more banter, no hesitation. Just want answering want, need battling against need. I can't touch her in enough places to satisfy my urges, but I'm going to damned well try.

She responds to each touch and caress like I'm pulling shackles from her body, and I'm high on the power—sure, I crave a measure of control, but getting her to fucking relax feels like more of a victory than anything else.

When she looks up at me with fire in those pale blue eyes, I know she's done pretending to give two shits about fabric or my renovation.

Good. It's exactly the way I want it. "You're mine, Trix. You've always been mine."

She bites my jaw—hard. "Except, you left. Jerk. And I belong to no one." The sting of her words is blunted by the smirk on her face. A firm reminder that this is one and done. I'm not getting her back. That's not what this is. I'm providing a service, and I'm not forgiven for anything. I hate it because I already want so much more from her, and I already know I'd give her my heart if she asked.

"It was a mistake. I've regretted it for years." I kiss her neck, tasting her sweet skin and licking along her jaw until she sighs.

"Good. Tell me again."

"Worst mistake of my goddamn life," I growl, knowing she's playing with me, taunting me. But as I say the words, I know I'm speaking the absolute fucking truth.

Her eyes go glassy as she nods. "I know. It was."

I sink a finger inside the warm flesh between her legs, swirling against her clit until I hear her gasp. "You good?" I ask.

"Yes," she pants.

I laugh and work my way up her body, pressing my lips against hers. The kiss turns hot in an instant, and I can't hold off any longer without being inside her. Turning to my bedside table, I fumble through for a condom, realizing there's no chance of finding one. I haven't been with anyone in this house—

haven't been with anyone in a long time. My eyes narrow and I panic.

As if reading my thoughts, Trix rolls to the edge of the bed and grabs her purse. "I think I have one, but it's like a hundred years old. Do they go bad?" she asks, producing a little gold package.

"I don't see how." I'm not about to debate the aging properties of latex right now, but I give it a cursory once-over. The package looks fine, so I tear it open, never losing contact with those luscious fucking lips.

"Great. Stop talking."

I do as I'm told. No more talking. I'm wholly focused on her, the way her eyes drift shut when I move against her clit. The way she moans quietly when I circle against her. The way she sighs when I thrust inside to fill her.

I've fantasized about how it would feel to be inside her again, but reality leaves my dreams in the dust. No one compares to the feel of her. We just fit. The sight of her. The scent of her. The tight, wet heat of her. I'm lost to the sensation that envelops every part of me.

"Fuck, Trix."

"I know," she gasps.

Maybe it's because she's waited so long. Maybe she's been banking her libido or something. Because this is not the woman I remember from college. This one knows what she wants and is determined to get it. Makes me hell-bent on giving it to her.

I thrust harder, chasing the feeling that has my senses on fire. I'm aware of her every movement and inhalation. And those sweet sighs and moans.

My hips piston and I drive into her—harder, softer, all at her pace. My hands can't get enough of her body. I trail them over every inch of her skin, fueled by her soft sounds of approval. My mouth on hers, sharing her breath. Impossible to get enough of her.

It's been a while for me too, so I don't have a lot of hope of lasting like she might want me to. When I feel her start to come apart beneath me, I give in, coming hard on a curse and a desperate grunt.

Her name on my lips—it's like coming home.

It feels so goddamn good, and I let my brain empty of thoughts. It feels nice to be in the moment and take a break from worrying about anything else.

Beatrix lets out a long, contented exhale. "This afternoon certainly took a turn for the better."

"Happy to help anytime."

Her eyes snap open and promptly narrow at me. "Just today, thanks. This is a 'one-and-done' situation, remember?"

I'm unconcerned about how she wants to characterize it. I just like that I can get her out of her head for five minutes so she can enjoy herself. But I'm smart enough to know she'll bolt like a deer in the headlights if I say it out loud.

"Yeah, I recall."

She claps a hand over her eyes. "Honestly, I can't believe I just followed my old flame to his house for sex. Not on-brand for me, just so you know."

"Well, just so *you* know, it isn't for me either." I don't know why it feels important that she knows it. I'm not expecting a disbelieving cackle. I boop her on the nose. "Hey, what's that about? You think I'm some kind of man slut?"She shrugs. "If social media is to be believed, um, yeah."

It's not lost on me that she cares enough to follow social media gossip posts about me. "Stalking me on social media, are you?"

"Ha. You wish. If I could open my feed without seeing some dumb picture of you with one of your puck bunnies, it would be a miracle."

Uh-huh. My smirk widens to a full-on smile. "Interesting." I hate that she saw those types of pictures, solidifying her wrong opinion of me. But I'm a little gratified that she's looked me up because maybe all isn't lost. I feel a kernel of hope.

"No, very not interesting."

"Matter of opinion. Clearly, you've trained the algorithm."

"What?"

"You know. These apps have sophisticated computer programs behind them to learn what you like and show you more of it. Lemme guess. In addition to hockey players, you also get a lot of cat videos?"

"Why, because I'm a single woman? I must be a cat lady?"

I shrug. "Fine. Dog videos?"

"If you must know…penguins."

"Penguins? Any particular reason?"

"They're cute." She rolls to the side to retrieve her phone, and I take in the smooth skin of her back, where it tapers to a narrow waist… I'm about to take a bite from her ass cheek when she rolls back with her phone, fingers typing and swiping. She hands it to me. "Look at them. The way they walk…"

I lean over her shoulder to watch the video, taking the opportunity to inhale the scent of her skin. I don't like the idea of being one and done with her. The feisty, confident, straight-talking woman she's become is even sexier to me than the woman I used to know. I want to give her confidence to let me in, to let me see beneath the polished exterior like she just did. Only I want it for more than one afternoon. But balancing love and hockey is not something I've learned how to do.

So it may be one and done for her, but I'm not giving up. I'll just play the long game.

I run a hand down the curve of her waist and let it settle on the swell of her hip, rubbing my thumb back and forth on her soft skin. She's damn near perfect, even more stunning than she was ten years earlier, and I'd been transfixed by her then.

This feels good. Too good. When I signed with the Otters, I hoped it might lead to an eventual reconnection with Beatrix, but I never imagined having her in my bed after a chance meeting. I don't want to blow this opportunity with her, but I'm not even sure it's an opportunity

As I roll to the side and stroke Beatrix's long hair splayed out on my pillow, I replay the unsatisfying versions of relationships

I've had over the years. I never wanted the women I dated to linger in my bed, and I always made it clear that I was committed to one love—hockey.

For the past ten years, when the clock strikes six in the morning, I'm back in training, completely focused. I've never let a woman get in the way of that. I came too close to tanking my entire future over love, and I've been scared straight ever since. That was ten years ago.

Same woman, new circumstances.

I have no idea if I can do better by her without endangering everything I've worked for on the ice, but spending a mere few hours with her has me interested in the possibility. Not that she's offering.

Beatrix rolls off the bed and pads to my bathroom, grabbing her clothes from the floor on the way. Clearly, she hasn't changed her mind—she doesn't plan to linger here.

A few minutes later, I hear the toilet flush and Beatrix emerges, fully dressed. I'm covered in bedsheets from the waist down, sitting up against a few pillows, hands behind my head. I'm not about to ruin the sweet memory of the past hour by dissecting it.

Truman starts scratching at the door, and she glances toward the sound. "Should I let him in?"

"Please."

She opens the door, and my dog comes bounding into the room and jumps on the bed.

"I can see why you didn't invite him in earlier," she says.

"Yeah, not as much fun as a threesome."

She nods, subdued, maybe even…relaxed?

"This was good," she says.

"Glad you got what you needed." On one hand, I'm relieved that even after ten years, we can fall back into familiarity. On the other, it feels like we're just two ships that happened to pass in Oxbow Market, and she seems content for us to sail along in opposite directions. Why wouldn't she be?

"Okay, well, don't get up. I can show myself out."

She starts for the door, but I call her back. She turns, and I beckon her closer with a finger. Looking over her shoulder like I might be indicating someone other than her, she creeps closer to me.

"I had a really nice time, Trix. Thanks for trusting me enough to relax."

Her face contorts into a grimace before settling into a grudging half smile. "Thanks for helping me…relax."

I roll out of bed and pull on a pair of sweatpants. "Here. Lemme walk you out." Truman trails after us, but when I place my hand on Beatrix's lower back to guide her toward the door, she takes an extra step away, so I lose contact. Guess we're back to reality.

"Trix, I know it's been years, and we didn't exactly part on good terms, but I'm glad we can be friends."

"Friends?" Her forehead creases and she seems genuinely confused.

"Yes. It's what happens when two people don't hate each other and can say a few nice words when they run into each other around town."

"That's what you think is happening here? We're gonna be friends?" She shakes her head. "I don't think so."

I feel the blood drain from my face at her words. It's not like I thought we'd be spending every day together from now on, but to act like we're estranged feels like a blade in my chest. I don't think she's as cold as she's trying to lead me to believe, but I'll tread lightly because it's all so new.

"Why not?

Opening the front door, I notice the dim light of evening and the sky turning a dusky blue. It's my favorite time of day, the time that reminds me the most of Vermont. A light breeze rustles through the trees at the end of my driveway The soothing balm to the relentless schedule during hockey season.

"Let's just call it what it was. A good time."

I'm not at all willing to dismiss it that easily, but for now, I let her think she can have the final word.

Truman, sensing the possibility of a walk, barrels past us onto the porch and promptly sits in front of Beatrix. He stares up at her with his large eyes and extends a paw as if to shake her hand. She smiles and reaches down to accept his paw. "Such a good boy. Yes you are." None of her sass for him.

"He likes you," I tell her, somehow feeling proud, as though I had anything to do with it. On the contrary, I think she likes Tru in spite of me, not because of me.

"It's mutual." She drops down onto my porch and sits cross-legged. Truman promptly curls up in her lap, and she pets his head. "Even though it was a little touch and go there earlier when I lost my coffee."

"You hear that, Tru? Never come between a sleepy woman and her coffee." I wag a finger at him, but he ignores me.

"He always misbehaves a little before I leave town."

"Shh!" she admonishes. "Don't say it in front of him. They understand everything, even if they don't know the words." She scratches him behind the ears, and Truman promptly rolls onto his back for a belly rub. He looks ridiculous, practically overwhelming the space in her lap, but they both look so content I'm not about to pull him away. Just then, the mail carrier turns onto my drive and all hell breaks loose.

Truman scrambles to flip back onto his feet so he can chase the truck, toppling Beatrix onto her back in the process. He's oblivious, barking and trailing behind the truck, so I lean over to give her a hand up.

"And we've come full circle," I say.

"Yup."

This time, she doesn't resist when I pull her to her feet. Feels like progress.

"So he knows you're leaving?"

"Yeah. I made the mistake of taking a suitcase out, so the jig is up. Quick trip to see my mom while I still have downtime before the preseason. Tru'll be at the doggie spa in case you get lonely and want to visit."

She looks at Truman, loping along as the mail carrier exits her truck and sets down two packages near the box, waving to me and pointing. I wave back. "Thank you!" She gives Truman a pat on the head and gets back in her truck while he sulks back toward us, the moment of fun behind him.

"Is it really a spa? Or is it one of those kennels where they sit in a cage all day and do one loop around the yard?"

"It's actually my house in Berkeley. My acupuncturist loves him and housesits whenever I'm on the road, but he gets into trouble when I leave town, chews furniture, rips up plants. So he has to stay in a crate when she goes to work all day. I don't love that part."

"You should leave him with me." She looks as surprised saying the words as I am hearing them. Her eyes go wide, and she claps a hand over her mouth.

"Was that your inside voice?" I ask. "You already having dog sitter's regret?"

She nods. "Yes, but no. I do like that little guy. I could watch him while you're gone. He'd have my yard to hang in all day, and I could take him on hikes up Buttercup Hill behind the winery. Plus, my niece would love him to pieces."

She's making it sound like paradise, and I find myself a little jealous of my dog. The invitation to join Trix on hikes doesn't seem to extend to me.

"You sure you don't mind watching him?" I'm grateful because I don't have to concoct another reason to see her again, and I definitely want to see her again.

"Yep, it's fine." She looks me over from head to toe, much like she did when she first recognized me in the parking lot, and nods. "Sex and a dog. Feels like a win-win for Trixie."

I can't help but laugh at the nickname that most certainly doesn't fit her type A personality. But she's right about the win-win part, only I feel like the one who's winning.

CHAPTER
Seven

BEATRIX

I don't know what I was thinking. The last thing I need in my already-packed schedule is a dog. Or rather, the last thing I need is to be entangled with Dominick Renaldi. Why couldn't I let one and done be *done*?

Sex with him did cure me of the testy attitude I'd been sporting for weeks. Julie was right, which is why she's the best assistant I'll ever have and also why I'll pay her bonuses on top of bonuses to keep her. I've been much more focused in the week since our afternoon of orgasms—much more able to put in the hours needed to finalize construction on the lobby of the inn. If all goes perfectly, we'll be open right on time before PJ's wedding.

But now I have Ren's dopey dog to deal with, and I just may be falling in love with the furry little beast. Each morning, he slathers my face with kisses to wake me up. He's been sleeping on the floor right beside my bed, which is where I put the fluffy new dog bed I bought after he'd been with me for only a day. I didn't like the way he looked splayed flat on the hardwood floor. Yes, I know he has fur on his belly, but my house gets cold at night, and I thought he could do better.

Ren keeps texting, thanking me and asking how Tru's doing. I keep my responses brief and all-business.

Me: He's fine

Ren: Just fine?

Me: He's great

Ren: Hope he's not causing trouble

Me: No, you're the one causing trouble by texting me eighty times a day

Ren: Just being a doting dog dad

Me: Well, dog dad, you may need to up your game because he loves it at Trixie's dog spa

Truman seems to be enjoying his new dog bed, so I send Ren photo proof. I send him a picture of Truman sleeping soundly on his bed and a second one of him racing through the vineyards with my niece, Fiona, who's already asked her dad if they could get a puppy. Jax, my middle brother, was none too happy about that, but Fiona has him wrapped around her little finger. I wouldn't be surprised if a new dog shows up at their house before Truman goes home. Jax's fiancée Ruby is a dog lover, so it's practically a done deal.

I text Ren a video of Fiona chasing Truman in a circle on the grass in her yard until she falls to the ground, exhausted and laughing. Then another video of him loping with her through the vineyards at sunset. A third of him sleeping on the rug at my feet while I watch an episode of *Top Chef*.

What am I doing?

I barely have time to meet with the contractors at the inn and approve the fall menus and event calendar at Butter and Rosemary. I'm rescheduling meetings in order to hike with the dog of my former boyfriend who I don't even like. I should have my head examined for even considering dog sitting. Especially for Ren.

And yet, here I sit in my office at the restaurant, flipping through a binder of paint samples and thinking about what I'd do with the main house on Ren's property. I'm mad at myself for letting him disrupt my thoughts at work. I'm even more mad at myself for doing him a favor after our history.

But I'm not doing it for Ren, I rationalize. It's for Truman, because I can't stand the thought of him in a crate.

Ren: Nice. Pretty sweet setup

Me: Yup

Ren: I'm a little jealous he got to see your bedroom before me

Me: Get over it because you're never seeing my bedroom

In case he somehow didn't get the memo, we are not going to have a repeat of last week. After he comes to get Truman, I doubt I'll see him again. No future awkwardness, no questions about what things mean, no repeat performances. Even if we're sharing custody of his dog while he's with his mom.

Ren: You say that now, but a man can dream, no?

Me: A man should know better

Ren: He doesn't

Honestly, I don't know what to make of him. The flirtatious texts feel like the guy I used to know, but that was before he broke my heart. He has no right to flirt with me now. And I need to focus on my job.

I need to decide which company to hire to install wet steam rooms and dry saunas, but today those tasks feel like a burden.

What is happening to you? You used to nerd out on details like that.

I'm probably just suffering from burnout. I shouldn't have told my family I could handle renovating the inn along with running both restaurants. I like a challenge, but I have to admit it's more work than I want to be doing. I can't remember when I've slept more than five hours a night, and it's starting to take a toll on my energy level during the day.

"Did you eat?" My sister, PJ, sends a plate of scones down the big plank table in the employee kitchen down toward where I'm daydreaming. I catch the sliding plate before it careens off the edge of the table and pluck a scone from the pile. I don't have much of an appetite, but we don't have scones on the menu at Sweet Butter, which means our youngest brother, Dash, baked them himself. He's two years younger than me, but miles ahead as a chef, so I have no doubt he found the recipe on some fancy blog and made it even better.

I look up and see Dash eyeing me, waiting for me to take a bite. I break off a corner and let the pastry dissolve on my tongue. Oh my God, it's like a dreamy slice of heaven. I realize I actually am hungry and take another, larger bite before giving him a thumbs-up.

He grins and gulps down some coffee.

I debate texting Ren a response, but I don't want to encourage his flirting. And I hate to admit that a tiny part of me likes it a little bit. It's the most interesting my social life has been in years, even if I don't plan to see him after he picks up his dog.

"This is your meeting." My oldest brother, Archer, looks down at the screen of my phone, which I shut off before he can read the texts. Then I look up at his usual grouchy face to ascertain whether he saw anything. His expression only tells that he's as impatient as always. He's worn a permanent scowl ever since he took over running Buttercup Hill after our father's Alzheimer's disease advanced to a point where he was declared legally unable to run the company.

Unlike my siblings, I don't blame Archer for the scowl or his irritable moods. He inherited the most stressful job, one he never asked for, and we've been digging out from one financial disaster after another since we each took on bigger roles last year.

Looking around, I see all my siblings present, even if busy dawdling over the coffee machine and nibbling on Dash's baked goods. "Right. I'm ready. Should we start?"

Archer nods and pulls a chair out. Its scraping noise against the raw cement floor draws everyone's attention, so I start circulating the design boards I've put together in the days since I picked up the fabrics last week. "These are the color schemes for the inn. The lobby is here, all designed to complement the rustic chic vibe of the old brown barn and the tasting rooms, but it's being updated with vintage lighting fixtures and an oversized hearth." I point out these details on one board before moving to the next one.

"Rooms will all have natural woods, earth tones mixed with bright accents, modern and clean design mixed with antique finds that will give each room an individual charm," I explain.

PJ points to the board with the new fabric swatches. "All the rooms will be identical, right?"

"Not exactly. We want them all to have a similar look, but the rooms aren't all the same shape and size." I walk over and tip the board against the back of a chair. "The suites will have a living room area with these fabrics. This on the couch, these on the pillows." I point to a peach and white paisley print and a brighter accent pattern with stripes and a third in contrasting floral.

Dash and PJ nod and make sounds of approval. Jax is busy staring at his phone, which only means he's going to go with whatever I recommend. He handles finances and has had his feet to the fire because we've been bleeding money, so we sort of have a tacit agreement that I won't mess with his area of the business, and he'll stay out of mine.

Archer and I have no such agreement, and I ready myself for pushback as soon as I finish presenting all of the design changes.

"I'm not seeing it, Trix. Sorry." Archer crosses his arms and looks from the design boards to me. I don't take offense at his tone or his questioning. It's his job to run the winery, which is a multi-million-dollar business, so he'd be remiss if he didn't sweat the details. And I sure don't want his job.

"What aren't you seeing?"

He flicks a hand at the boards. "You're just changing fabrics? We're rebranding the inn as an unrivaled wine country experience. This just looks like any other room at any other hotel, no offense."

I love when people say "no offense" right after they've said something offensive. Archer knows this is only a part of what's different at the inn because I've told him as much. My other siblings know too. "None taken. This is just the design piece. The visual. The point is that there's a calm aesthetic from the moment a guest enters the lobby of the inn right on through the last look at a room before going to sleep. Relaxing music will play in the common areas and in each room when a guest enters. We're adding a gym, a spa, and pickleball courts, which will be available exclusively to guests and a short list of local residents who need to apply for the privilege. The point is to create scarcity and exclusivity."

Archer nods. I'm using buzzwords that resonate with him. "Sounding better. So we're marketing the inn facilities to a hand-picked few. I like that." Just like I knew he would.

Dash pipes up, raising his hand like he's in school. "This is looking great. I just recruited a concierge who I think you'll love. Lured him away from Meadow Hill, and he was the reason that place has the reputation it does."

Meadow Hill produces small-batch wines priced so high none of us believed they'd sell a single bottle. Instead, their vintages sold out in the first hour and inspired half the wineries in the area to come out with their own exclusive editions. "That's a good get, Dash. Can't wait to meet him."

I'll never admit it out loud, but he's my favorite sibling. We've always had each other's backs, even though he's two years younger than me and we didn't interact much as kids. His friends were boys and might as well have been a decade younger for how interested my friends were in having him around. Once we got older, I came to really appreciate the steady, sweet guy he turned out to be.

"I know Ruby would love to work on an exclusive wine list for the inn," Jax says.

"Thanks." Ruby, Jax's fiancée and our newest sommelier at Butter and Rosemary, is the best at her job. I'm grateful Jax is jumping on board with the concept. That just leaves Archer to sign off officially.

He looks around the room but says nothing. Pushes his chair back and goes over to inspect the design boards at close range. Then he nods, sits back at the table, and shakes his head. "I talked to the Fire Investigator yesterday, and they have no leads."

I'd worried that would be the case. We've been waiting a month since a fire burned through our half brother's vineyards one night out of the blue. We later found out from the fire department that the fire was started on a corner of Buttercup Hill, but the winds blew it away from our land and ignited Graham's vineyards next door. Thankfully, the winds died down enough while the firefighters were battling the blaze that he didn't lose too much of his crop, but the bigger issue is why someone set a fire in the first place.

My family's relationship with Graham is precarious and new, so we've all kept it under wraps. There's no way to know if whoever set the fire was trying to burn our property or Graham's as well. Either way, though, we now have an uneasy bond against a common threat.

And so far, all the investigations have turned up nothing.

"I don't get how that's possible," Jax says. "It's their job to investigate arson. That's what they do." He spreads his hands out like it should be obvious.

Archer rubs a hand over the stubble on his chin, which I've noticed has the first hints of a graying beard if he were to let it grow into a full beard. It makes him look more seasoned, and also exhausted. Like the rest of us.

"Don't know what to tell you. They haven't found anything that leads anywhere substantial. It was literally a Duraflame log tossed from the road onto our property. No cameras picked it up. Could've been anyone."

"We should get more cameras," Jax says. "I'll meet with the security company and go over our system."

Archer nods. "So here's where we stand with production." He passes a sheet to each of us. It's covered in columns of numbers I don't bother to read because I know he'll explain everything anyway. "In order to meet our quarterly growth targets and keep shareholders off our backs, we need to buy grapes from Graham. Autumn Lake will sell to us as soon as their vines are established and producing fruit, but that's a couple years off. Even after the fire, he's producing enough to get us where we need to be, but it means we're in business with a guy I'd just as soon forget exists. Anyone have a problem with that?"

The question is met with silence as we all accept that we're between a rock and a hard place.

My phone pings. Ren has sent me a gif of a disco dancer moving across the floor with moves like John Travolta in *Saturday Night Fever*. The guy in the image looks a lot like Ren, so much so that I expand it a little. It's not him, and I roll my eyes at myself for believing it could be.

Me: Seems like you have a little too much time on your hands

Ren: Nah, Coach is working us to the boner

Me: ??

Ren: The BONE. Damn autocorrect. My phone is not my friend

Me: Or maybe it knows you too well

Ren: Come again?

Me: (eye-roll emoji)

Ren: I'll take that as a yes

I don't realize that I'm grinning at my phone until PJ nudges me. "What are you smiling at?" I feel my cheeks heat as I stash my phone under a pile of papers on the table. "Nothing. Just Julie."

PJ gives me a skeptical nod, and I redirect my attention back to the meeting. I need to focus on how to speed up the renovation so our winery can start putting money into the coffers instead of spending it. Once my siblings see that we can sustain the higher prices we're charging for rooms, everyone will calm down. I know they will.

I should not be thinking about a hot guy who brought me orgasms on a silver platter of hard pecs and abs. I don't trust him, and I don't like him.

And after he picks up Truman, I won't see him again.

CHAPTER *Eight*

REN

My plane back from Vermont lands late, so Beatrix agrees to keep Truman for one more night. I crash hard when I get home, wake up amped for hockey, and go straight to practice.

Our team's chemistry on the ice is nonexistent.

It's a big problem. We're still a couple months away from the start of the season, so there's wiggle room, but in ten years of playing, I've never seen a team with this much talent look as unprepared as we currently do.

And our coach is staring at me.

Coach Barrington doesn't suffer fools. When he bestowed the captain title on me, it was with high expectations that I would make his job easier, not harder. He knows the job is tough, but that doesn't make him any more willing to cut me any slack.

Barrington is an interesting combination of a Yoda-like master of quiet wisdom, his sharp blue eyes piercing any bullshit in the room, and a drill sergeant. When he gets riled up, he yells and curses like a thunderstorm, rattling the ice and anyone in range.

His temper gets tested when we aren't meeting our potential individually or as a team. Right now, we're failing on both counts.

I've yet to gain control of all the egos driving this team, and our shoddy performance during training is starting to affect team morale. It's also messing with my confidence as a captain.

I take the disasters on the ice personally because if I can't get us to play better, my teammates stop respecting me. If they stop respecting me, they stop listening. When that happens, I lose any chance I had at motivating them, to say nothing of our potential to win games when the season starts.

It doesn't help that I'm having trouble focusing since thoughts of Trix naked on my bed keep pushing out more productive team strategies. It helps even less that I've been in communication with her daily about Truman, which is entirely my fault because I can't resist texting and flirting with her. While I was with my mom in Vermont, she turned dog-sitting into a three-day vacation for my dog, complete with a video diary of each day.

I could never see much of her in the videos—generally shoes or her shadow on the ground—but that just added to my fixation on trying to see more. The only slight insight into her life was a pair of Oscar the Grouch slippers.

I'd hoped to run into her once I moved to the area, but after one afternoon with her, I'm haunted by feelings I've tried my best to bury. I know our night together was a one-time way to get her out of a no-sex rut, so I shouldn't have any grand ideas about it happening again. But if it happened again…yeah, I'm getting ahead of myself.

It means that even though I'm focused on the team's problems and how we can get our mojo back, a part of my brain is preoccupied thinking about seeing Beatrix again. Thinking about how it felt to have her naked body wrapped around mine, specifically. It's unhelpful when I need my full focus on the team. This is why I don't get involved with women in general. But this isn't just any woman, and my brain knows it.

So basically, I'm fucked.

Relationships and hockey have not mixed well for me, which is why I avoid them. I'm a one-trick pony, and in order to stay focused on the sport, I can't have any outside distractions.

The idea that I could actually renovate the Napa place during the off-season is laughable, now that I've gotten started thinking about it. And adding Beatrix Corbett into the mix brings back memories of how I almost jeopardized my chance at a pro career because I was so besotted with her. I can't focus on more than one thing at a time, at least not well. It's something I've known since I was a kid, instilled in me by my mom back when I was a wild child with too much energy to burn—I need to stay focused.

She was a single mom doing the best she could to work and raise me. And I was a handful, distracted and energetic—Hurricane Renaldi, she called me, right up until I found my way to a junior hockey league and spent hours every day practicing and expending all the energy I didn't know what to do with.

Hockey was my refuge, and I was good. I kept my focus on the ice and said no to anything that could derail my future as an athlete. By senior year of college, with pro offers all but guaranteed, I let myself slip a little bit. Let myself fall for a certain blue-eyed woman and lost myself in her. She was nearly my downfall, and a part of me would have sacrificed my future Stanley Cup wins to have her. That's how dangerous she was for me.

So maybe it's a good thing now that Beatrix made it abundantly clear that her interest in me is one and done. She's a temptation I'm not sure I could leave for a second time.

Case in point, I can't stop thinking about her and sending flirty texts. I know I should stay away from her, but my heart seems to be steering the ship. For the first time in my life, I want to see where it leads me.

"Renaldi, you with us?" The deep rasp of Coach Barrington's voice shocks me out of my reverie, and I refocus on the drill we're in the middle of. The puck sits at my feet, and I've been daydreaming and not doing my job. Shit. This is why I don't get into things with women. Any distraction is kryptonite to my performance out here, and the team needs all my focus.

"Yup. Sorry. Just missed a beat there."

I tap the puck with my stick and take it out on the ice, passing easily to Ludovic Bruner, who passes it back to me before I take a shot on goal. It misses by inches, and my teammates whoop and give me shit for my lousy aim. I take the beating because they're right and because it's a rarity for me to shoot left of goal, especially when there's no one on defense. This is the most basic drill there is, a warmup we do every single day. And five minutes into practice, my attention is drifting to Beatrix. Again.

I shake my head and feel the rattle of my helmet. Gotta knock some sense back into myself. No daydreaming. There's way too much at stake for me to spend a single extra second thinking about Trix and how explosive we are together, even if I've spent the past ten years thinking about her constantly.

One and done.

The next time the puck lands at my feet, I go harder, hustling up the ice so fast that Ludo can barely keep up. He slaps the puck back to me, and I aim for the corner of the goal. Our goalie's hands go down, but he's too late. The puck hits the back of the net. The way it should be. The way it needs to be every time.

The rest of the afternoon training goes well, and I keep myself laser focused on the team and the drills we need to hammer over and over again. The more shots we take on goal, the better. It's muscle memory, even when the circumstances are different in each game—different defender in a different spot, different puck speed, different arena with slicker ice or sticky spots. We need to roll with all of those tiny changes, so the areas of consistency become even more important.

The feeling of my stick slapping the puck into a corner of the goal will always be better than any other feeling. I know my teammates agree, and as captain, I need to capitalize on the slightly better mood I can feel coming off the guys as we head to the locker rooms.

A couple hours later, the team sits at a long table in the training center, and the mood is light. There's a buzz of relief that we trained well today, at least in terms of fitness. Team unity and morale will come. I make a little speech about how each opportunity on the ice is a new beginning, and all the work we do in training is money in the bank for future games. But we need to work as a team and that means swallowing down our superstar egos sometimes.

"I'm as guilty of it as anyone, and I fully admit I need to do better. I want our team to succeed more than I want even a minute of glory on the ice." There are some whistles and nods of agreement. "Everyone looked good today. All fuel for what we do tomorrow."

Coach Barrington nods at me before taking over with a strategy talk and game tape. I've earned back his trust after my daydreaming moments earlier. Hopefully, I'll build some camaraderie little by little, and we'll all hit our groove well before the start of the season. That will take some heat off of me, and judging from the sheen of sweat on the back of my neck, I need it.

By the end of practice, I'm drained. The last thing I feel like doing is driving over an hour to Napa, but Beatrix has already had Truman for four days, and I don't want to push my luck.

More than that, I want to see her.

The drive flies by, and I wait outside the door, wondering if we got our wires crossed because I've knocked twice and there's no answer.

I'm about to knock for the third time when the door flies open and Beatrix appears, hair wet and twisted into a knot. She's not wearing a stitch of makeup, which makes her pale eyes stand out even more against her pale skin and dark hair. Her raspberry ice cream lips curve into a smile when she sees me. It nearly knocks me on my ass to see her light up like that. And if I'd thought I could stop thinking about her, I can see that's not going to be an option. No fucking way.

"Sorry. We were in the shower." She shakes out a towel that was curled up in her hand. I catch a whiff of the jasmine scent of her shampoo.

My heart flutters for a moment before dropping to my stomach. I shouldn't feel the prick of jealousy at the idea that she was showering with some other "one-and-done" guy who had the good fortune of soaping up her gorgeous body. I don't need complications in my life. I just don't want to see the guy traipsing up behind her in a towel. The glimmer of excitement I felt to see her evaporates on the stale breeze that shuffles past in the dry heat. Without intending to, I ball my hands into fists.

Then I see Truman. He crashes through the entryway, flies around the side of Beatrix, and rams into my shins. His fur is scraggly and wet, and his body looks about half the size it normally is. And I'm confused. She showered with some guy *and* my dog?

"So…he's wet…"

"And clean." She bends down and tries to dry him with the towel, but he scoots out of her grasp and tries to hide behind my legs. "Liked the shower but does *not* like the towel." She shrugs and tosses the towel onto a wood bench by the front door. My hands unclench and my shoulders relax.

"So you and he…" It's making my way through my thick skull that the second member of the "we" she referred to may be my dog, and I feel a little foolish for assuming she was with a guy. But the quick shot of jealousy has me on notice. I shouldn't be feeling anything about her being with another guy. I have no right.

"Went for a mud hike this afternoon." Smiling, she points off into the distance at some muddy place I can't see. "There's a waterfall nestled in the hills back there and it stays wet most of the spring and into summer. And this year, with all the rains…"

She stops talking and stares at me. Because I'm staring at her. "Everything okay?" she asks. "How was practice?"

"Oh. It was fine. Team needs some mojo, but I'm working on it." I slap a hand against the back of my neck, where I feel the prick of perspiration at the amount of work I have to do.

"You okay?"

"Yeah. Just feeling the pressure of leading a team of dummies with big skills and bigger egos."

"Present company not excepted, I imagine." She deadpans with the hint of a smile, a sight so pretty it soothes my aggravation, even if she's razzing me at the same time.

"You know it," I admit, feeling a smile pull at my lips. She still has an effect on me that no one else does.

"Do you want to come in? Have a drink or something?" Her brow furrows and she crosses her arms. I sense that she's just being polite, but Truman has no such manners. He comes out from behind me and darts into the house.

"That's a yes from Tru, but I should take this guy off your hands."

"Okay, whatever you want." She drops her arms, and her forehead relaxes. I've made the right call. If sports have taught me anything, it's that it's better to quit when I'm ahead, so I nod and produce a small stuffed penguin I saw in a gift shop. I feel a little silly handing it over.

"It's not much. Just a little thanks for watching Tru."

Trix hesitates before reaching for the plush toy. Almost like she can't resist, she tilts her head to the side and presses her lips together, offering the penguin a small smile. Her smile grows when her eyes meet mine. "Aw. Thank you. You're sweet."

"Glad you like it." We stay like that, eyes locked, speaking the language of a fragile connection, one I don't want to shatter. "Anyhow, Tru and I should head home."

"Okay," she says, eyes dancing. "Let's see if we can get this boy to carry his dog bowl to the car." She holds it out to him, and he cocks his head, uncertain what she wants him to do. "Come on, Truman," she calls. He races back to her, and she tries to coax my dopey dog with a smile that would work on me ten times over.

I inhale a deep breath of fresh air mixed with oak leaves, lavender, and sunbaked grass. This is why I bought my place out here. Deep down, I know that I need something in my life besides hockey, and I know who that is, not what. But the fear is always riding me that I'll lose focus entirely, lose my way, and have everything taken from me.

But a more substantial part of me wants more than time on the ice and a big paycheck. I can't help believing that I'll find what I'm looking for here. Looking at Beatrix, hair loose and untamed, dog treats in hand as she tries to get Truman to do something he's never going to do, I feel a bit of the dark cloud lift. First time I've felt that way all day. It's partly because I'm happy to see my dog, of course, but it's also because I'm happy to see her.

She's the best thing I've laid eyes on in a long time.

CHAPTER *Nine*

BEATRIX

It's been a week since Ren came to pick up Truman, and I've had the blues ever since. I really miss him.

Truman. I miss Truman, not Ren.

Sure, seeing Ren standing on my porch did make my heart flutter a tiny bit, but it was more out of awkwardness about our hookup in his bedroom than an urge to do it again. Mostly.

He did look awfully good, freshly-showered after practice, with his hair slicked back. Tight gray shirt that left no ripple of his abs to the imagination. Low-slung jeans with a rip in the thigh that urged me to ask how he got it.

But I didn't.

I didn't do any of the things that briefly flitted through my mind because he's still the guy who broke my heart. I hate that a part of me still likes him a little bit. So I just let him leave with his dog, and I haven't seen or spoken to him since. Probably won't.

Standing in my kitchen, I glance at all the personal touches that make my home feel like a haven—the collection of chicken-shaped pitchers from designers I love, the mismatched collection of coffee mugs on an open shelf, my pantry staples in mason jars on another shelf, the jug of fresh flowers on the window sill. Even when I'm working myself to the bone, I manage to cut some blooms from the garden here at Buttercup Hill.

I glance through the doorway to the fluffy area rug in my living room. It looks bare without Truman's furry shape snoozing there in the morning sunlight. Would it be crazy to invite him back?

As if on cue, my phone pings with a text.

Ren: Hey. Is it against the rules of "one and done" to say hi?

I almost laugh at the karma of it all. And his incessant need to flirt. That hasn't changed. He was always a gruff asshole on the ice, but with me, all flirting, all the time.

Me: Nope. Hi

Ren: Truman misses you. His ears are droopy

Me: Aren't they always droopy?

Ren: You caught me. Yup, they are

Me: It's okay. I miss him too

Ren: Wanna see him?

I need to think before answering because the real question is whether I want to see Ren. I hate that a part of me wants to see him again, but another part reminds me that what happened ten years ago is ancient history.

Me: Sure. When?

Ren: Next Wednesday night?

Me: (thumbs-up emoji)

I'm pretty sure he's doing the same thing, using Truman as an excuse to see me, and I'm not sure I mind. I'm an adult. I have a full life. I'm in control. He can come over with his dog next week and it will be fine.

I work hard to convince myself of this as I make coffee. I normally don't brew a pot when I'm home because I can grab a cup easily enough at Sweet Butter café, conveniently located between my house and my office at Buttercup Hill. But this morning, I'm exhausted, so Julie is coming here for our morning meeting. It's only a stone's throw from my office on the other end of the vineyard property, but meeting here means I can stay in sweatpants and take things a bit slower, which I need today.

I feel nauseated, probably from the stress of my contractor pushing back the installation dates of the new flooring in all the guest rooms. It's not just PJ's wedding at stake here. Each day that we delay means thousands of dollars in missed revenue, so the pressure is on. We're booked up for the first six months after we reopen, but if we delay even by one weekend, we'll need to apologize to guests whose reservations we've canceled. We need to offer them free dinners at Butter and Rosemary or a free night at the inn if we push back their reservations.

Ka-ching, ka-ching. Dollars racing down the drain. It makes me even more nauseous thinking about it. So much so that...*oh crap.* A wave of nausea hits me so hard that I drop my cup on the counter and run for the bathroom. I make it in time to lose the entire contents of my stomach, all of it coffee. I feel slightly better, but not great. Weird.

Julie knocks at my door, ready with spreadsheets from Jax that detail exactly how much he thinks we can charge for each room type at the inn. A second sheet details how much we need to net each month for the inn to be a profit center for Buttercup Hill. "He told me to tell you the inn can't be a loss leader, so don't even think it," she says, holding out a cup of coffee from Sweet Butter.

I wave it away. "Thanks, but I had coffee here. And it didn't go so well. I guess I'm really nervous about pulling this off." I point to the pages in her hands. The inn has always been a minor part of our business, the bulk of it being selling wine. But we've had some setbacks recently. First, our dad pulled a half a billion dollars from the company coffers and gave it to Graham, our half brother we never knew about until a few months ago. Then we lost some key employees to that same half brother's winery, so we're scrambling to find good people. Plus, we need some of his grapes to fill our international orders, so we're forced to go into business with him if we want to stay afloat.

There's no way to ask our dad if that was his intention all along because his Alzheimer's has advanced in recent months, and he gets so confused when we visit him that his nurse has limited the time we spend so he can focus on his health. It's hard to watch his decline.

I didn't see him often when I was a kid because he was often working, and our care was dispensed to a parade of nannies, but as I got older, my dad weighed in on my life decisions—he was especially supportive of me staying in college and establishing a career, rather than following a "hockey boyfriend." It's strange how life progresses. Crazy that my hockey boyfriend is here now.

I wish I could talk to my dad about the stresses at work and let him be a sounding board, but it seems to set him back when we talk with him about the winery. He just pounds a fist and wags a finger as though we know what we're supposed to do. But we don't. We're all just treading water in jobs most of us never intended to have. Doing the best we can. Trying to keep our finances in line. All of this puts more pressure on the inn when it reopens. It needs to happen sooner rather than later, and everything is behind schedule. Not by days but by weeks. It's falling on me to pick up the pace and shave days off the schedule, so we don't lose even more money.

No wonder I'm stressed enough to puke.

"You don't look so good," Julie says, walking to my sink and wetting a paper towel. She hands it to me, and I look at her blankly.

"What's this for?"

"You're pale and you're sweating. Wipe your face."

It's not until she says it that I realize my skin is clammy. And I feel another wave of nausea hit me, so I race again to the bathroom.

When I emerge a couple minutes later, I feel pretty good, but only because I'm convinced now that there's nothing left in my stomach. And when I looked at my face in the mirror, the color has returned. "Better. Okay, where were we? The numbers from Jax?"

Julie shakes her head. "Hang on. What just happened? Do you have food poisoning?"

I shrug. "I dunno. Maybe. It hit me hard this morning, but I skipped dinner, so I don't know what could've poisoned me. It's probably just stress."

"That, or morning sickness. Any chance your little romp with hockey boy got you knocked up?"

"Please don't make me regret telling you things. And no, there's no chance. We used protection."

I refuse to indulge her ridiculous idea. It's not what I need or want in my life, so I will just will it away.

She laughs. "So said the last person who got pregnant using protection." She takes out her phone and scrolls. "Did you get your period? It should have been in the last couple days, today at the latest."

Another smaller wave of nausea hits me, but this one is super-sized, fueled by the idea that Julie could possibly be correct. I sit in one of the yellow swivel chairs around my kitchen table. It feels better to be off my feet, but the smell of the coffee Julie brought isn't making me feel so good. "Would you put that in the fridge? I'll drink it later."

Julie takes the cup away and then gets in my face. "Not on your period?"

"No, and how do you know my cycle?" It's so *not* the most

important question when the real issue is *how the heck could this have happened?*

She tilts her head as though it's obvious. "Because I'm a kick-ass assistant, and I can do my job better when I know what's up with you." She smiles. "Plus, our cycles sort of synchronized when I started spending fourteen hours in a day with you."

"You do not work fourteen hours in a day." Again, unimportant.

"Don't change the subject. Are you preggers?"

My head spins, my gut churns. I want to tell her she's crazy, but…is she? "We had sex one time! And we used a condom!"

"Okay, good for you. That's how half the girls I knew got pregnant in high school."

"I'm not pregnant," I insist, mainly because I really don't want to be pregnant. It's the very last thing I have time for, not to mention I don't want any entanglements with Ren. Plus, it really doesn't seem possible. *Right?*

"Great. Let's get you a test kit to be sure, and then we can move on to other reasons you're currently green."

"I'm not green."

"Agree to disagree. Come on, let's go." Julie picks up her purse and keys and points toward my front door. I feel like a child being told to put my toys away and go on a field trip to a cemetery.

"Now? I have a lot to get done today. Surely this ridiculous errand can wait. If I am pregnant, there's nothing I can do about it between now and the time it takes to figure out how to get the inn opened sooner."

She stops and stares at me. "Seriously? Don't you want to know?"

"Not particularly. Like I said, knowing isn't gonna help me get the inn open."

She walks to my front door and opens it, calling back to me as she returns to her car. "Bring the pile of stuff from Jax. We can go over it in the car. Let's get you some answers."

"Is it ready?" I ask from under a pillow I've placed over my face. We're back at my house, exactly twenty-seven minutes after we left here to buy the test.

"It's been thirteen seconds, so…no."

My stomach folds on itself with anxiety. I hiccup as my body decides whether to cry or laugh hysterically. "There's no way. I can't be pregnant."

I sneak a look at Julie, who sits resolutely with her lips pressed together. I pull the pillow away and examine the oatmeal-colored boucle, looking at it from all sides. "This is really well made. Maybe we should add couches with this fabric at the foot of the beds in the suites."

Julie rolls her eyes. "I'm starting to worry that your brain is short-circuiting. Are we talking about fabric now?"

"It's better than me bugging you every thirteen seconds about how much time has elapsed, isn't it?" I wait another two seconds before asking, "Is it ready yet?"

Julie sits next to me on the couch and shows me her phone, which has a timer running a countdown. "No. I promise I'm not holding out on you. Do you really think I'd let you sit here and stew if it was ready?"

"I don't know anything about anything anymore," I mope, standing up and going to my kitchen to see if I can find one single thing that appeals to me in my refrigerator. "Oh my God, everything either smells like blue cheese or it actually is blue cheese. How is that possible?"

I'm in the process of making gagging noises and throwing out half the contents of my refrigerator when Julie taps me on the shoulder. "Okay, time's up. Let's go look."

She follows me into the bathroom, where the little pink stick sits on the counter. It looks so innocent from a distance, just a disposable piece of plastic with the power to tell me if my life is about to change. Forever.

"Okay, here we go." I pick it up, prepared to examine it in case the result isn't clear, but there's nothing obscure about the pink plus sign that stares back at me in the little window. No room for misinterpretation.

Oh my god!

My stomach clenches again, and I fling open the toilet lid and heave, but my stomach is empty. I sit back down, a layer of sweat on my brow. I feel overwhelmed with fear, panic, sorrow. A well of tears builds behind my eyes.

Julie watches me and I nod, putting my head in my hands and slumping over because it's easier to breathe that way. She comes over and peeks at the stick over my shoulder.

"One time!" I yell. "With a condom. How is this even possible?" I whisper.

Julie says nothing, so I tilt my head at her and glare.

"Oh," she says, snapping to attention. "I figured it was a rhetorical question. You see, when a man and a woman have fond feelings for each other, they rub their bodies together, and…"

"Oh my God! Are you really reciting the text of some children's book about how people make babies?"

"You seemed unclear on the concept."

"I'm clear. I'm very, very clear."

Julie nods and chews on her lip. "Okay, then."

I stand up from the toilet and toss the test into the trash. I'm tempted to take a second test because maybe this one is wrong, but I decide that for the good of my working relationship with Julie, I shouldn't let her in on the depth of my crazy. Bracing my hands against the sink, I fight off an urge to throw up that has nothing to do with pregnancy-related nausea.

"I'm supposed to see him in a few days. What do I tell him?" Before she can answer, I shake my head. "No, I can't think about that now. I think I need to push through. I need to go to the meeting and convince my siblings that there's no reason to worry about the inn opening on time. And later, I'll think about this. Just not right now." I'm talking at double speed, but Julie nods along as though she's following. "Yeah. I need to stay busy, stay distracted, because if I don't, I'll start thinking about Ren and a baby and my life, and I'll just freak the hell ouuuuut." My voice goes up an octave at the end.

Julie steps forward and hugs me. It doesn't matter that she works for me and I'm often driven and prickly and we've never hugged before. She's the best person in the world, and she knows what I need right now. I cling to her like a lifeline for more than a minute, until I feel my pulse slow and can breathe again.

Julie motions for me to follow her, so I do. We end up back in the kitchen, where she pours a glass of water and hands it to me. I take a small sip, then a larger one because suddenly, ingesting giant amounts of water is the order of the day. I'm parched like the Sahara Desert, and I have no idea why.

Julie goes into my pantry and comes out with a bag of Ruffles potato chips, ripping them open and sniffing the contents. "I used to crave these when I was pregnant. Good memories. Give 'em a try. See if they appeal."

I'm about to tell her that all food on the planet apparently smells like blue cheese, but then she brings the chip back toward my nose and I get a large, heady whiff of fried potato goodness. My hand digs through the bag and comes out with a shockingly large handful. I pop one, then two into my mouth and chew.

"Yessss. These hit the spot. How did you know?"

She shrugs. "Salt and fat are a pregnant lady aphrodisiac."

"And how…how is all of this happening at once? Yesterday, I was fine. Today, I'm scarfing potato chips and puking up my coffee? It makes no sense."

"The miracle of life does stuff to your body," she sings.

"Yeah, okay," I say, ripping the chips from her hand and stomping out of my kitchen. "Remember that thing I said about not talking about pregnancy or dealing with it at all today? That starts right now. Where are we on meetings with the land-scapers?"

Julie consults her folder and hands me a paper. "Here's their bid."

I take it in, seeing numbers that will make Jax crap his pants because they're twice our budget, and for the first time all day, I feel a wave of calm wash over me. "Okay. This bid sucks. This company has a lot of explaining to do, and I need to twist these numbers inside out and sideways by the end of the day and finish sixteen more tasks," I say. "That, I can handle. Can you swing over to Meadow Hill while I'm at the meeting and take some photos of their landscaping? I want to do something similar but different enough that it doesn't look like we're copying it. And for less money."

Piece of cake, I tell myself. *It's all going to be okay.*

"It's all going to be okay," I chirp brightly as every face in the room turns toward me. "I'm getting new bids on the landscaping and pushing the contractor to find a new floor guy if this one can't get the job done. And we'll change the dishes at Butter and Rosemary, as planned, and work up some new menus. I've got it handled." I'd say more, but I'm out of breath. I'm also doing everything in my power to stay focused on what I need to communicate in this meeting, so my mind doesn't wander anywhere else. I cannot think about pregnancy right now. Can. Not.

"Okay, if you really think you can handle all that," Archer says, raising a skeptical eyebrow.

"Why wouldn't I? I'm a great multitasker. Just put it on my list and I'll get it done." I try to dial down my voice, which sounds just shy of hysteria. More slowly and quietly, I explain, "I really feel comfortable with what's on my plate." Smoothing a plaid fabric runner on the table with both hands, I focus on my hands and avoid looking at anyone.

There's an uncomfortable silence in the room, and when I

glance up, I see Jax looking at a pad of numbers and PJ staring at me with creases in her forehead. I offer her a wan smile and urge myself not to throw up again.

"I'm still waiting on the claims department at the insurance company to come by, but if all goes according to plan, we should have money for the new floors and the other damage," Jax says.

"Great," I tell him, closing the notebook in front of me to indicate that I have nothing else to report.

I just need to get through this meeting. Then, I can deal with the rest of my day. And the rest of my life.

CHAPTER
Ten

BEATRIX

I've spent the past few days thinking. And thinking. I always planned to have kids, but sometime in the distant future. But when? I had no rule book or planner with the date marked in pen. But turning thirty-two a few months ago flipped a switch, so suddenly, my biological clock feels very real. I know I have time, but…with the way I work, is it ever going to feel like the right time?

So I do something I haven't done in years—I take a personal day and leave Julie in charge. I give myself a single day to visit the doctor and figure out what the heck I'm going to do about all of this because something Ren said has been bouncing around in my brain.

"I don't mean juggling. I mean balance."

I'd never given it much thought because being a productive achiever felt good. It felt like enough. But now, I don't have a lot of balance. I do want a life outside of work, and maybe motherhood is fate's way of urging me down the path to that life.

But with Ren, of all people? The guy who didn't want to be

with me ten years ago isn't going to want this entanglement now. I've accepted that, but I do have to tell him.

Me: Hey! How's it going?!

I never use exclamation points in my texts, but I'm nervous about what to tell Ren, and it manifests itself in my punctuation. I might as well be shouting at him in all caps, "EVERYTHING'S NOT FINE." Hopefully, he doesn't know me well enough to sense that I'm freaking out.

Ren: Hi! Nice to hear from you! Tru's been asking about you all day

Note to self: Dominick Renaldi has no issue with using exclamation points in texts.

Me: I'm so sorry, but can we reschedule our plans? Work got crazy

Ren treats me to a string of gifs showing sad dogs with droopy ears, dogs crying fake illustrated tears, dogs whining and whimpering.

Ren: Of course. Get your work done and lemme know what's good

Me: Will do. Thanks for understanding

I'm only three weeks past the time I was supposed to get my period—which means I'm somehow already six weeks pregnant, according to my doctor, who I saw this morning. I have a master's degree in design and yet I do not understand pregnancy math. Two weeks ago, I didn't have a clue I was carrying a baby, so I don't see how that could possibly add up to six weeks of anything, but I didn't want to argue with my doctor. Not when she had an ultrasound wand inside me.

On the positive side, the doctor says my cells are multiplying appropriately, and my hormone levels suggest that everything looks good. It's too early to see a heartbeat, which is just as well because not seeing it allows me to live in my state of semi-denial for a little longer.

It only made sense to hold off saying anything to Ren until after my doctor's appointment, which is why I postponed our plans.

I've heard stories about pregnancy tests giving false results, so I wanted to hear it from the doctor herself. "You're six weeks along," Doctor Salinger said, moving the ultrasound wand into uncomfortable positions and looking at the screen. I couldn't make heads or tails of what she was seeing, so I trusted her wonky math, even though a part of me still thinks it's impossible that I'm pregnant.

I wander through Sunshine Foods, willing myself to have an appetite for something on one of the shelves. At first, potato salad sounds good, so I pop that into my basket and make my way to the aisle of chips. I grab some Ruffles and a bag of extra spicy Doritos. Spicy sounds appealing, so I wind through the shop until I find the hot sauce aisle. I load up on a couple different types. Then I decide the idea of potato salad feels sickening, so I return it to where I found it.

That happens twice more with lemonade that no longer sounds appealing after carrying it down two aisles and corn flakes which barely make it into my basket before I change my mind. I walk down the last aisle and spot a jar of green olives and a pickle display. I grab three kinds of pickles, feeling every bit the pregnancy cliché. *I will not eat them with ice cream,* I vow.

I'm not in the mood to talk to anyone, so once I finish my shopping, I stroll down a side street. The fresh air feels good, and for the first time since seeing that pink plus sign, I feel like I can clear my head enough to think about it. I inhale. I exhale.

My brain finally quiets down enough that I can think. The first idea that enters my head seems a little impulsive. It doesn't make any sense, and I am neither impulsive nor nonsensical in my actions.

Um, I think you've proven otherwise…

Point taken. I pull out my phone and dial.

I feel guilty.

"Is this a bad time?" I ask, gesturing around to the small swing set and patchy grass that looks like it hasn't been watered for the past year. Dash surveys the same half-dead grass and play equipment and shakes his head, but he continues to regard me with the same skeptical look he's had since he hopped out of his truck and found me staring at the small, random park.

"It's fine. Weird, but fine." He tilts his head to the side, eyes narrowed. He has a point. In the years we've worked together at Buttercup Hill, I've never summoned him in the middle of the day to look at a dilapidated park. "Is this some kind of design recon for the inn? You planning to install a swing set from the last century and kill all the plants?"

"Not exactly."

I offer him a half-hearted smile because I haven't got much else. No plan, no big reveal that will make sense of why we're here. His easygoing nature is so polar opposite of mine, but he reminds me of how I was once. Sometimes, I regret that I can't find my way back there.

Dash walks over to the abandoned tire swings, which do look like they're left over from another era. They hang from rusty chain links on a fat wooden beam. I kind of like the old-school feel. Dash gives the swing a tug to make sure the bolts overhead will hold and drops onto the round tire. I do the same on the tire next to him.

We glide back and forth like a couple of kids. Dash indulges the activity for a minute before dragging his feet to stop his motion and twisting the swing so he can look at me. "What's up, Trix?"

"Can I ask you something?" I kick at the sand beneath my feet and marvel at this place, completely empty in the middle of the day. Completely unknown to me, who never takes breaks to find the unexpected. In his dark jeans, work boots, and a plaid shirt, Dash looks more at home here than I probably do, still wearing the cashmere sweater I had on for a meeting with the contractor earlier.

Dash nods. "'Course. Anything."

"When was the last time you were on a tire swing?"

He laughs. "You brought me here to ask that?"

"No, but I'm warming up to the real stuff. Let's talk about this first." I feel at ease with Dash, even though he doesn't have kids, and we've never talked about our plans for being parents. But I know he'll follow me through the conversational tunnel and won't judge when I get to my destination.

"Is this about Dad?" The vein in his temple starts thumping, and I realize I'm freaking him out.

"No. It's about me."

His brow creases. "Talk more about that. What's wrong?"

"I'll get to it, I promise. Small talk first, please."

"Okay, fine. The last time I was on a tire swing had to be when I was a kid. I think the preschool had one. Why?"

I shrug, feeling contemplative. My hair, pulled into its usual tidy bun feels too tight, so I loosen the rubber band. It takes me back to the day Ren did the same. All roads seem to lead to that day. And now, maybe, all roads forward will spring from that day. I'd find some calm in the symmetry of that if I wasn't still freaked out. "I was just thinking it's been ages for me too, and it's too bad because this feels nice, sitting here, doing nothing."

"It does. I don't do a lot of nothing these days. Always so many recipes I want to try, stacks of paperwork, places to go. Not a lot of time for sitting idly on a swing."

Putting my head in my hands, I picture my life changing. Many more days like this, only it will be me pushing a baby on the swing. "Dash, I'm pregnant." My heart lurches into my throat as I await his reaction.

He starts to laugh, pushing his tire swing into motion again. "Yeah. Good one."

Okay, I wasn't expecting that.

"No, Dash. I'm serious."

"Sure. Okay, yeah." He keeps swinging, still chuckling to himself.

"Dash." I get up from my swing and stand in front of him, forcing him to stop swinging so he won't hit me. The smile drops from his face, but only for a second. When it returns, it's accompanied by his open arms. I fall into them, and we give each other that awkward brother-sister hug where we don't touch much of our bodies together. Just ringing each other's shoulders.

"You're serious," he says, disbelief flooding his face. His eyes look like round blue pools. I nod. "Hot damn. That's awesome! Who's the dad?"

"I don't know if I should tell you before I tell him."

"You should definitely tell me." He flashes me a cheeky smile.

"Dash…"

"It's why you called me. Tell me."

"The truth is he's an old boyfriend from years ago, and we hooked up, so here I am."

If I thought his smile was impish a second ago, he's the Cheshire Cat now. "Wait, Dominick Renaldi? Mal and I ran into him on a hiking trail a couple months back. I told her you two used to date." It figures he and his fiancée Mallory knew Ren was here before I did.

"Ugh. This is what's wrong with living in a small town. Everyone knows everything. Yes, it's him."

"O-kay…well, I need to ask the obvious question. Are you going to keep it?"

The question lands like a stone at my feet. Not because I don't realize there are options but because I've spent so much time thinking them through. And even though I haven't admitted it even in my mind, I know the answer to his question. "Yeah. I am. I want to do this, be a mom. This feels like an…opportunity, and I'm not sure when it might present itself again. So, yeah. It feels right."

Dash looks like he's trying to suppress a grin, but he fails miserably. "Well, then I'm psyched. And damn excited to be your baby's uncle."

I hold up a hand. "Please don't say anything to the family. I'll tell them soon, but I need to find the right time."

He makes a motion of zipping his lips and locking them, throwing the key over his shoulder. It reminds me of the games we played when we were kids. "It's in the vault. Now, how can I help?"

I blink back inconvenient tears and steady my voice. "I need a guy perspective. If it were you and an ex-girlfriend dropped this baby dad news on you, how would you feel? Would you think she was trying to trap you to get you back."

His eyes go wide and his brow crinkles. "Is that what goes on in that smart brain of yours? No, I wouldn't think she was trying to trap me. And I'd be really happy if she was the right person."

"He's not gonna feel like that. He's the same guy, a flirt who's very into being a pro hockey star, trust me."

Dash shrugs. "You should give yourself more credit. The guy was nuts about you."

"Right up until he dumped me."

"Stop it." He shoves my tire swing, sending me into the air. When I return, I drag my feet to stop.

"You won't know until you talk to him, but from a guy perspective, I gotta say you're a catch, and I'd feel like I was the lucky one."

"You're biased because you like me."

"I do. Now, how else can I help?" Dash launches his swing.

"I want to go shopping."

"You…what?"

"You heard me."

"I did, and I'm pretty sure you know that you picked the wrong sibling if you want fashion advice."

"I picked the right sibling. You don't have to give me advice. Just stand there and distract me while I distract myself with a little retail therapy. Please. Dash, I called you because I knew you'd be supportive without telling me what to do. This is all kind of overwhelming. I didn't have a plan for this."

He pats me on the cheek. "You're in heavy denial, Ms. Type A Planner. This all must scare the living shit out of you. Okay, you can count on me for whatever, and I know you'll be a great mom."

"Thanks." I feel the pinpricks of tears at the corners of my eyes and push them down.

"So, I'm off the hook for the shopping, then?"

I shake my head. "Come on, Dash. Help me calm my nerves with some nice, impractical designer jeans that will no longer fit me in six months. It's the only thing I can think of that's more out of character for me than getting knocked up, so I want to do it."

He nods, smile never dimming. "I have a better idea."

"I don't know about those." Mallory tries to keep a straight face and then fails. What begins as a giggle turns into a full-fledged laugh.

"You're laughing at a pregnant lady?" I ask, my eyes going wide as I describe myself that way.

At first, I didn't love the idea of sharing my news with his fiancée and letting yet another person in on it, but then Dash made the excellent point that Mallory has the best fashion sense of anyone we know, and she just might have some good "lady advice" too about how to tell Ren I'm pregnant. So here we are.

Standing in front of a full-length mirror in a bespoke denim shop, I model a pair of beige leather pants. Yes, this is what my pregnant brain decided makes the most sense for me, even though I normally wear either pantsuits or jeans. The leather is tight, and I've accented the pants with a wide belt complete with a heavy buckle shaped like a star.

"Oh, you'd better believe I'm laughing at you." She holds up a black maxi dress in front of me and tilts her head, considering it.

"You don't like the pants?"

She pushes the dress into my hands. "I love the pants, but they're only going to fit you for about another month. Then what?"

She's right, but I'm in denial. I don't want to believe the cute pants will no longer fit me in a few short weeks or months. I feel like doubling down on the most outrageous, tight outfit I can find that looks like a million bucks on me. Then I'll dare my disobedient body to grow so big that I can't wear it.

"I know I'm being ridiculous," I say, accepting the boring black dress. "I don't even need to try this to know how it will look. I have three like it at home."

"So why are we here?"

She looks at Dash, who has been quietly hovering in a corner of the store and saying nothing. He motions to another rack, encouraging us on.

"Because I'm a bundle of nerves. And if I can find something cute to wear today, maybe I can convince myself I'll be able to juggle my current workload and the job of being a parent. I know it makes no sense, but that's who you're dealing with."

"I kinda like her," Mallory says, swiping a pair of dark jeans from a rack and checking the size.

"Seriously, how am I going to do it all?" I hate the way I'm emotional and whiny at the same time.

Dash's voice booms from the corner. "…Asked every working mom since the beginning of time. You're an excellent multitasker. You'll kill it."

"What he said," Mallory seconds.

I wander to a display of cowboy boots and choose the tallest pair, running my fingers over the three-inch stacked heel. When I look at Mallory for approval, she shakes her head.

"Your feet are going to swell, and your center of gravity is going to knock you right off those heels and onto your face."

"You're making this all sound so very appealing."

She joins me at the boot display and takes the high-heeled pair out of my hands, replacing it with a pair with a lower heel. "These are cute. And it's going to be fine. You're just resisting because it's scary."

"But I want to be able to wear these pants," I whine, looking at them in the mirror. Then again, I don't love the color. And they're tighter than any of the pants I normally wear. "I know they're impractical, but they fit me right now, and I kind of want to stay in the now."

"You can. You should. And if you want the pants, get the pants. Just realize you'll need to put them away for a while when they don't fit."

From out of nowhere, a sales clerk swoops in, holding two pairs of jeans on hangers. "Do you ladies need anything? A different size?" She hangs up the jeans and surveys me in the leather.

"Ladies?" Dash growls from the corner. "I'm here too."

"He's here too." I point and smile at him gratefully.

"I love the pants," the sales clerk says, surveying me. "Do you want to try them with a lightweight sweater?" She gestures to a rack of pale-colored sweaters that all look a little short.

"Are these crop tops?" I ask.

"Yes, that's the style now. It'll look so cute on you to show a little skin." She points to my midriff, and my eyes flit to Mallory, who is stifling another laugh.

"We'll think about it. Thanks," she says, shooing away the unhelpful helper.

"Okay, just holler if you need anything." She straightens some jeans on a rack and goes behind the register.

Mallory takes the midriff-bearing sweater and shoves it back on the rack. She signals to Dash, who approaches from his corner. "If you want to get these pants, get the pants, but let's talk about what's really going on here. You're nervous about telling the father, and you're about to commit a fashion crime to deal with it."

I slump against a rack, suddenly light-headed. She's right—I'm overwhelmed, scared, emotional, and I hate feeling out of control. This isn't how I planned on becoming a mother. I know we don't always get to choose how things happen, but I like a plan. I like being prepared, and I feel betrayed by my own body for making this decision without me. A part of me wants to tell Ren right this instant, and an equal part wants to run away and enter the witness protection program.

"I'm a planner," I whisper. "This wasn't my plan." Tears spring forth of their own accord.

"I know, sweetie. I know."

She and Dash escort me out of the store, and Dash goes down the block for ice cream while Mallory sits with me on a bench. I feel torn, unsure I really want to talk to her about Ren. The shopping was one thing, but this is personal. She's not the likeliest friend in this scenario, but we did grow up together. Plus, Dash really loves her, and soon she'll be family.

Mallory must sense my hesitation. "Listen. Do you remember on my fake wedding day when I was freaking out because I was in love with Dash, and I didn't know what to do about it?"

I nod, grateful to her for putting another image in my brain besides the thought of myself waddling through an unfinished inn with a five-months-pregnant belly.

"You really came through for me by talking me through what I was feeling. I'll always be grateful for that. So if I can help, please let me..."

It's like a floodgate opens, right there on First Street, with its Mexican food place and a trendy hotel tourists love.

"What do I tell him? *How* do I tell him?" I ask, hating the uncertainty in my voice. This isn't me. I'm self-sufficient and capable, but I don't seem to be able to deal with this. "I should tell him, right?"

She nods. "Yes. You have to tell him. But first, you need a plan for how you'll handle it if he doesn't want to be involved and what you'll do if he does. It will make it easier if you're prepared."

There are those people in our lives who we form opinions of and never dig beneath the surface, and Mallory has been that type of person for years. I only saw the snooty façade she wanted people to see and never bothered to dig deeper. I credit my brother for giving her a chance because right now, I can't imagine anyone giving me more perfect advice.

"I want to do this, and I'm prepared to do it alone. He can be involved, but there's no obligation. The last thing I want to do is trap him into something he doesn't want. I know I'll do everything in my power to give this little human a good life. Whether he's a part of it or not, that won't change."

"So maybe," she prods tentatively, "it will be great either way? And whatever he has to say will only make it better and clearer for you going forward. That's a good thing for a planner."

I huff a laugh at that. "Yeah, some planner. I had some vague idea of having kids sometime in the distant future, but maybe this is the universe telling me to wake up and smell the coffee. And then puke."

She laughs. "Morning sickness?"

"It's no joke. Plus, it's crazy, but my body is way past my brain in terms of accepting all of this. My boobs hurt, and they feel bigger. It's like they're already getting ready to be little milk trucks, and I didn't tell them to do anything."

"Maybe it's nature's way of saying you don't need to control everything. Some stuff just takes care of itself."

"Okay, Zen master Mallory."

She holds up her hands in protest. "Hey, I don't pretend I know everything. I just go forth with confidence."

"That makes one of us," I say because I'm so used to pushing the idea away. Then I reconsider. "Actually, no. I have confidence in myself. I just don't have a lot of faith in Ren."

"Tell him what you just told me. Tell him the truth and give him time to process everything. Go from there."

The thought of that makes me queasy, just as Dash returns with three ice cream cones. He hands me the middle one, a chocolate soft serve with sprinkles, my favorite. I get all ready for my stomach to lurch and reject one more of my favorite things, but it doesn't.

Reaching for the cone, I nod my thanks to Dash and take a tentative lick. The cool chocolate lights up my taste buds, and for the first time in days, I feel like everything's going to be all right.

"You two," I say, watching my brother and his fiancée trade licks of their cones. "Thank you."

CHAPTER Eleven

REN

Trix: Hey. Are you around today?

Me: For you, I am. Anyone else, meh

Trix: How do you do that?

Me: What?

Trix: Make everything sound like you're flirting?

Me: It's one of my superpowers

Trix: What are the others?

Me: The rest of them only work in person. Wanna come by?

Trix: Yeah. Sure

All is right with the world. A little banter with Trix turns my wayward thoughts about team bonding into fantasies about how to win her over.

When I started renovating the Napa house, I didn't have a solid plan for how to reconnect with Trix, so I'm grateful to the textile gods for doing me a solid. I'd planned on getting to the paint store first thing in the morning, but then I'd been up most of the night and slept in, landing me in the parking lot of Oxbow Market just as Trix was leaving.

I can't help thinking that running into her was fate's way of giving me a second chance to make things right. To prove to Trix that I'm a better man now than I was a decade ago. To show her just how sorry I am for ever letting her go. If hockey has taught me anything, it's that I have to set up the shot if I want any chance at scoring. From the moment I saw her in that parking lot, I was gone for her all over again. All of my thoughts since then have focused on how to get a second chance with her.

I try to push those concerns from my head as I stand at my sink washing coffee cups from the past three days. Not that I think Trix will judge me for leaving a few cups in the sink, but I have some nervous energy to burn. I'm not sure what she wants to have happen between us. Is this just a friendly visit, or has she been thinking about our one afternoon together nonstop like I have?

I can't get her out of my fucking mind.

Preseason games start soon, and I'm feeling pulled in a million directions. The team is still playing like a disconnected bunch, and if I can't help turn it around, my days as captain are numbered.

Popping the last cup in the dishwasher, I see Trix unfold her long, tanned legs from the car like a bird getting ready to fly. The vision of her knocks the air from my lungs. She's the oxygen I want to inhale instead, and I stand frozen for a moment as my heart swells in my chest. I have it bad for this woman, and I don't intend to fight it.

In white shorts, a loose-fitting, pink flowered top, and a straw hat in her hand, she looks like she'd be right at home on a lounge chair by the pool. It gives me an idea.

"Hey," I say, opening my front door and pointing her to a path that runs alongside the small bungalow where I live. I drop two glasses and a cold bottle of sparkling lemonade in a tote bag on my shoulder. Truman runs out in front of me to nuzzle Trix's legs, making it impossible for her to take another step closer. Dogs have it good. They can let their emotions fly and lick the soft skin of a woman's legs if they feel like it, and no one thinks twice. If I ran up to Trix and did the same, she'd probably slug me.

"Down, boy," I tell him to no avail. I shrug at her. "Sorry."

"Aw, it's okay. I missed this guy," she says. Again, I have a pang of jealousy of my dog. She misses him, but she doesn't seem to miss me, not even making eye contact when Truman settles down by her feet. She indicates the path I pointed to earlier. "Are we going somewhere?"

"Yeah. Come this way."

It's a warm fall day, and I'm in workout shorts and an old worn tee even though I already worked out earlier and showered. It's the best part of living on a vineyard—no one's around to see what I'm wearing or what I'm doing. I'm not a celebrity by any stretch, but people do recognize me when I walk in my neighborhood or shop on Solano Avenue in Berkeley. And now that expectations are so high for the team, I'm more aware of how much people like to share their opinions of our chances at the Stanley Cup before the season's even started and their ideas for what we ought to be doing better.

Here at the vineyard, I can walk for a half hour and not run into anyone. I can loop around the property or follow one of the footpaths through the vineyards and only hear the voices of birds. And then I can have the privilege of seeing the best-looking woman I know walk alongside me. No reason to leave this place unless it's to go to work.

"I didn't bring shoes for a super long walk." Trix points to a pair of Birkenstocks, which look like they've taken her on more than a few walks. The suede is loose, and the soles are curved from use.

"We're not going far. Just to the main house. There's a pool. I thought we could sit." I cast her a side-eye to gauge her reaction, but she keeps her eyes cast toward the ground. It's unlike her. She seems distracted. Even though I've only seen her a couple of times recently, I've come to expect the fierce blue of her eyes, which flash with the passion of her words. It makes me a little sad not to see it now, but maybe once we're settled in a shady spot, she'll relax.

I sneak another glance her way and notice how perfectly put together she looks. Lashes long, a healthy pink in her cheeks, light gloss on her lips. She's swept her hair into a high ponytail, and gold hoops dangle from her ears. She carries the hat in one hand and intermittently pets Truman with the other as we walk.

When we reach the pool house, Truman finds a shady area of grass and settles down for a nap.

I escort Trix around the back, expecting her to perk up at the idea of renovations there. I know this is her happy place. But she barely gives the house a glance and instead focuses on the yard, where two lounge chairs sit with an umbrella between them. The pool area is unkempt, with overgrown grass around the deck and chipped tile in the pool. I've hired a pool man, so at least the water is clear blue and clean, but the rest of my yard is a bit of a wreck. I immediately rethink the idea of bringing her back here. "I thought it might be nice to sit in the shade, but maybe we should just go back to my house."

She dismisses my concern with a wave of her hand. "It's fine," she says, barely looking around. It throws me off to see her this disinterested in her environment, but she follows me to where I keep fresh towels in a storage bench and waits while I drape them over the chairs.

When she sits, she makes eye contact with me for the first time, and I note the fatigue in her eyes. Maybe she's just been working too hard.

I take the cups from the tote and pour each of us a glass of lemonade, then gesture for her to kick her legs up. I do the same. "Make yourself comfortable."

"Thanks," she says, taking the glass from me. She sniffs it as though it might contain poison or something, then puts the glass aside on a table. Self-consciously, I notice the layer of dust on the glass, so I grab another towel, lift the glass, and wipe away the dirt.

Taking the chair next to her, I stretch out. The weather is perfect, the bright sun blocked by the striped green umbrella and a light breeze carrying the scent of lavender and rosemary from the surrounding hedges. But nothing about our interaction so far is comfortable or relaxing.

"Trix." I wait until she turns to look at me.

"Yeah?"

"Are you okay?"

She looks up, then to the side, then back at me. Pressing her lips together, she nods. Then she squeezes her eyes shut and blurts, "I'm pregnant."

What?

Oh. *Oh.*

Okay.

I feel like we're in a rom-com. It's exactly the right time in the story for her to throw a wrench into what I thought was a sweet little second-chance romance. It's weird that my mind goes there instead of staying in reality, but lately, nothing about reality makes any sense, including our hockey season.

Meanwhile, the woman sitting next to me is looking at me expectantly. She deserves my focus—this woman who I've been hung up on for years, so damn beautiful and sweet. But what, exactly, is she telling me?

We had sex exactly one time, and we used protection. My stomach roils at the idea that she's carrying someone else's baby, tempered by heartbreak.

No.

Even if I'm just getting to know Trix again, I know her. The baby is mine. My eyes drift to her stomach and back to her tear-filled gaze. It knocks me sideways, this feeling of disbelief, nervousness, and a measure of joy. My mouth opens and closes again without a word as I absorb what she's just told me.

"We're pregnant?" I ask.

I notice her face relax into a small smile before a wave of dizziness overtakes me. I put a hand out to steady myself, but it's no use.

I fall off my chair.

CHAPTER
Twelve

REN

"Ren! Are you okay?" Trix stands over me, fanning my face with her hat. "Did you faint? Oh my God."

"Um…"

I didn't faint. My head started to spin a little when I heard a set of words that sent the blood whooshing to my ears, such that it blocked out the rest of the world. Maybe I wobbled a little bit, and maybe these lounge chairs are old and a little rickety. So…I tipped over.

I did *not* fucking faint.

Okay, maybe I fainted.

Trix continues fanning me until I push myself up with one arm and flop back onto the lounge chair. Then I raise a hand to indicate I'm fine. She waits for a moment, maybe making sure I'm steady, before going back to her chair.

I have thoughts, lots of thoughts—all overlapping and spinning around in my head. Then the thoughts disappear, and I'm left with only words. Or, well, syllables. Specifically, *Wha…um, how…are you…I…*

Then, I produce a blank stare.

Trix meets my stare with her own, forehead creased with concern. I can do nothing to alleviate it for her because I only have more nonsensical syllables, if that. "I just…what…?" For the first time, I see a glimmer of the woman I've been obsessing over for the past several weeks. Her pale blue eyes flash with amusement, and her lips edge up into a smile. Then she starts laughing, quietly at first, with her hand covering her mouth. The only indication I have that it's laughter is that her body starts trembling.

She removes her hand and begins laughing more in earnest.

"Are you…is this a joke? You're kidding?" I clear my throat and try to get on board with her weird humor, but my heart's still pounding from what she said moments earlier.

"No." She shakes her head, the laughter receding. "I'm sorry. I'm not joking, and I shouldn't be laughing. It happens when I get stressed, and this has been…let's just say it's been kinda stressful finding out about this, let alone thinking about telling you."

"But we used a condom."

"I know, but I told you it was old, if you recall." I do recall. Mostly, I recall the sweet taste of her skin and how good it felt to slide inside her. To hell with a condom that may not have been up to the challenge. And now I want to kick myself for giving reason a recess.

"How old?"

"What?" She looks bewildered even though she's the one who said it.

"The condom. How old?"

She grimaces. "Um, I dunno. A few years, maybe?"

"A few *years*?! So you're…this is…" I still can't form full sentences.

"I am. This is. It's true, and you're the dad." Thank God she can understand my gibberish because I'm not sure I'll ever be able to do better with the English language.

"Do you…have morning sickness? Are you eating enough? Getting some rest? Can I…hug you?"

She nods. "You can hug me. I won't break."

Gingerly, I reach for her as I slide onto the lounge beside her. When I envelop her in my arms, she folds into me, and I realize how hard this must have been for her to carry around.

"Okay, so…" I spread my hands wide to indicate just how clueless I am about how to proceed.

"So that's all the information I have," she says, nodding from side to side. "For the most part."

I have no idea what she means by that, and I don't have the verbal faculties to ask. My only hope is that she'll continue talking, and some of it will make sense to my brain.

"What happens now?" I ask.

"Um, well…I've thought about it a lot and…look, I'm thirty-two with no relationship on the horizon, and that's fine. I don't need to be in a relationship. Right now, it's the last thing I need complicating my life. But I do know that I want to do this. I want to have this baby. I want to be a mom." She flinches when she says the word *mom*, and it's the first moment that I feel the air I've been holding in my lungs start to seep away.

This tiny sign of her own unease with the situation softens the impact of everything she's just told me. Now, it feels like we're in this—whatever this turns out to be—together.

Her forehead creases as she watches me sit here wordless with confusion and indecision. Seeing the tiny cracks in her forward-charging demeanor charms me, this softer side of her personality that isn't wholly comfortable with the unknown. "Okay, good that you know that," I manage. "You'll be a great mom." Just watching her light up with my dog shows me how much love she has to give. She gives me a small smile.

"Thank you. And you can be as involved as you want, but there's no obligation at all. I just want you to know that. No pressure. I don't want you to feel weird about this."

Now, it's my turn to laugh. "Oh, well, good. Because if you wanted me to feel weird, you'd have to lead with something much more shocking than, 'Hi, Ren. You're about to become a dad.'" Once I start laughing, it's a tiny acorn with the will to reach the sky as a full-on oak. I can't fucking stop.

Trix does the only thing she can—she watches me lose my ever-loving mind and waits for me to finish. But I can't. I tip my head back as my laughter roars out of me, and I welcome it because it actually feels good. For once, I feel grateful for life's sense of humor because I couldn't have dreamed this one up if I'd tried. *What the fucking hell?* More laughter wracks my body until I'm short of breath.

Finally, I draw in a huge lungful of air and start to calm down. I'm sweating, so I take a long swig of lemonade, feeling the burn of the bubbles on my throat, and turn to Trix. Now I understand why she couldn't meet my eye earlier.

"Are *you* okay?"

"Am I? I dunno. It's insane, really. The year I finally make team captain and stand at the helm of the worst hockey mess of my career, I'm about to become the baby dad for a woman who likes my dog more than she likes me."

"Yeah, not the best timing over here, either. But…" She shrugs. "Here we are."

I reach for her hand and interlace our fingers. "So we are."

We sit like that for a while, each of us letting our thoughts percolate individually. After a while, Trix squeezes my hand and lets it go, swiveling around to sit up and face me. "Look, I know you didn't want to be with me, so you obviously never pictured me as the mom of your future child. I have no expectations of you. No pressure. I just wanted to give you all the information."

Her words send a surge of bile into my throat. She has no idea how hard it was for me to leave her. Of course she doesn't. I never gave her a glimpse. And now she has no expectations of me.

"When did you find out?" It's not the right question or even the right response to what she's just told me, but I'm having trouble putting my thoughts in any kind of order.

"About ten days ago. I went to the doctor on Monday." I calculate the days since our hookup and start counting. She completes my thought. "I'm almost seven weeks along."

"Seven *weeks*?"

She shakes her head. "Well, six and a half. It's weird pregnancy math. It starts at the date of ovulation, so when the baby is conceived, I'd already be two weeks pregnant, which is how it all adds up to forty weeks, which is really ten months, not nine." She waves a hand. "It's a whole thing. Bottom line is I haven't even seen a heartbeat. It's too soon. So I'm going back in next week."

"Can I go with you?" The words leave my mouth so quickly that I react with surprise, like I'm hearing them for the first time. Then I double down. "If it's not too weird for you, I'd like to be there when you hear the heartbeat."

Trix looks startled, eyebrows rising as her mouth drops open. Then she nods. "Yes, sure. If you want."

"I do. I mean, I think I do. Yes. Yes, I do."

I don't know much about anything else, but this I know for sure—if she's going to the doctor to hear the heartbeat of a baby that's mine, I want to be there. I want to hear it too.

"Okay, then. I'll try to reschedule it for this week."

"That would be great. I have training every day, but I'll work something out to leave early." I have no idea if that's a possibility. In the ten years I've played professional hockey, I've never asked a coach to let me miss practice or leave early.

But now, I can see the urges creeping in. I want to spend more time with Trix. I've wanted that from the minute she left my house. I feel all the old fears creeping in, the way my feelings for her in college spurred some impulsive decisions, missing practices to spend time with her, and almost losing my offer because I was distracted by thoughts of her when I was on the ice. My talent pulled me through, but what if it's not enough now when the team needs my attention?

I close my eyes for a moment to block out the bright, insistent sun that makes me feel like I'm in a spotlight. One thought rises to the surface amid the chaos—I came here hoping to reconnect with Trix.

If I'm going to get her to see me as anything more than an unreliable heartbreaker, I need to clear the air. The timing's all wrong—I'd hoped to get to know her better and prove to her that I'm a different guy now—but I don't have the luxury of choosing my timing.

"Trix…I want to explain why I did what I did back then."

"We don't need to…" She puts up a hand as if to stop me, but it drops into her lap. "Yeah, okay. I guess I'd like to know, especially if it's stuff besides you just not wanting to be with me. Maybe it will help me get over this edgy feeling I have when I'm around you."

As if to prove it, she shifts a few inches farther away from me. I hate that she feels that way, but I need to own the actions that led us here.

Nodding, I stand up and start pacing. Every nervous habit comes out at once—shoving my hand through my hair, tapping my thigh, stroking my non-existent beard.

"It was never about not wanting to be with you. If anything, it was the opposite. I wanted you too much, and that was going to be a problem when I went pro. I was…very distracted by you and willing to let that derail me. I was heading down a road where I thought I'd sabotage my shot at a pro career, and I didn't even fucking care. I needed a clean break, or I was never going to manage. I'm sorry I didn't explain it back then, but I didn't have the right words, and it was easier just to bail. Doesn't make it right, but that's what it was."

She frowns. "I would've understood. I could've helped you stay on track. You didn't even give me a chance."

"I know you would have. But that was part of the problem, too." I choose my words carefully because I don't want to hurt her even more, but she needs to understand what I saw. "You were willing to give up way too much of yourself for me."

Blinking hard, she shakes her head. "I loved you. That's what people do."

I nod. "That's just it. You were willing to give up everything for me and my future. What about your future?"

Her mouth drops open, and I see the readiness to blurt a response, but then she swallows hard. "I thought you were my future." Her voice is quiet, vulnerable. Her features soften, and I see the twenty-year-old woman who was far less sure of herself than the one sitting next to me now.

"And look at you now."

"Trix, I'm so sorry I hurt you, but I couldn't let you give up your life for mine, especially when I knew it would take one hundred percent of my focus, and I didn't know what I'd have left for you in return."

"Why didn't you just tell me that? I always thought it was me, that I wasn't enough."

"Because I was bad with emotions and worse with words. So I just looked forward. I convinced myself I was doing right by you in letting you go, so you could find your potential and crush it." Her jaw slackens again, and I can't tell if she's fully understanding me, so I clarify. "And you did. I'm…in awe, frankly."

I watch her face for signs she accepts my explanation. Trix stares at me, blinking softly. Finally, she nods.

"I never saw it that way, but I guess…maybe I was willing to sacrifice too much." Her words are halting, and she grimaces.

"Hey." I put a hand on her knee, grateful that she doesn't flinch or pull away. "I loved you for all of it. And for what it's worth, a part of me always hoped to find my way back to you."

CHAPTER
Thirteen

BEATRIX

Ten Years Earlier

I've run out of things to throw, which is a good thing. Throwing Ren's sweatshirt on the floor and knocking his backpack and baseball cap off my bed made me feel better in the moment, but as I look at his belongings on my floor, I feel foolish.

Maybe I want to feel foolish about throwing his stuff because it distracts me from what I really feel—like a naïve girl who actually considered dropping out of college to follow a guy to Canada and cheer for him at center ice. Five minutes ago, I was that girl. My face, heated with embarrassment, continues to betray me even as I backpedal.

"You…don't want me to go with you?" I try to keep my voice steady, but it breaks on the last word as the tears come in earnest.

"I—of course I would want you with me, but I think you'll be miserable. I'll be training around the clock and traveling…it's not the makings of a good relationship. You deserve better."

"I don't want better. I want what we have." I don't want to beg him to change his mind, but I can't believe he's ending things this way. Right now. Without warning.

"Trix..." Ren takes a careful step toward me from where he'd stood leaning against my desk while I took my feeling of betrayal out on his clothes and bag. His face, beautiful with those chiseled cheekbones and soft lips that have done amazing things to my entire body, sags in a mixture of pity and regret. Not regret that he just broke my heart, but regret that I'm not handling it well.

"Don't." I hold up a hand, trying to keep him from coming closer because if he comes closer...I won't be able to stop before folding myself into him, letting him be the cushion for the pain, even if it's pain he's causing.

He advances anyway and wraps me in his arms. I let him because it allows me to bury my face against his chest and avoid looking at him. I don't want to see his warm, deep brown eyes that seem to shine only for me. I can't look at his soft lips that have kissed me senseless so many times and never will again. And I don't want to see the expression on his face, telling me what I somehow didn't understand—that he always planned to leave. Without me.

"I can't have distractions. It's going to take all my focus to get in shape and earn my place on the team," he explains, hands out like he's making a deal with me.

"In shape? You're in phenomenal shape," I say, still finding fault with his reasoning, even though I can't change his mind.

"Pro hockey is different. I need to put on muscle. The schedule's relentless, games every other day—"

"I just—I thought we were forever." I sound naïve, but I'm too sad and hurt to care if I'm exposing my vulnerability to him. I feel gobsmacked, my entire vision for my future evaporating in an instant, and the worst part is that I don't have the vaguest clue what I'll do without him in my life tomorrow. And the next day. And the next year.

"I'm sorry. I know you passed up that design internship with that fancy hotel group. Maybe you can still get it?"

My face, streaked with tears, heats with embarrassment. I gave up an impossible-to-get opportunity for him, not that he asked me to do it. But I thought he was worth it. "It was the Four Seasons, not just some hotel group. And no, I can't get it back."

"Shit. I'm so sorry, Trix. This isn't how I wanted things to end. I just thought—I don't know—I guess I didn't understand how real everything would get when I went pro. Like I said, you deserve better in so many ways." His forehead is creased, shoulders slumped. I see the agony in him. He doesn't want to break my heart. But that's not stopping him from doing it anyway. It's not stopping him from leaving for Canada before graduation and not looking back.

There are probably things I should say. I could be mature and tell him I understand. Wish him luck. But I'm too gutted by the idea that Ren is moving on, and he doesn't even seem that bummed about it. He's just...getting on a plane and going. Moving forward, moving on to the career he's dreamed of, and I'm the one being left behind. "You should leave. I'm sure you have photo ops or pro hockey things to do."

I sound petty and hurt, but I can't help lashing out. And the worst part is that I'm more upset with myself than I am with him. I feel lost at the idea of not being Dominick Renaldi's girlfriend, and it's embarrassing. Somewhere over the past year of dating him, I lost myself in him and forgot about myself.

Who is Beatrix Corbett and who does she want to be?

Ren leans in and kisses my forehead as his arms wrap around my limp body. I sort of hug him back. We stay that way for a long time, but eventually, his embrace loosens.

Looking at the floor, I barely notice when he opens the door and slips outside. I'm too busy thinking about my future. I have two more years of college to come up with a plan. And when I do, there won't be anything—or any man—that can stop me from achieving it.

CHAPTER
Fourteen

BEATRIX

Present Day

I guess I was too shocked and hurt back then to hear what Ren was trying to tell me.

"We were so young…" I say, thinking back to my naïve self at twenty, willing to leave college to follow a guy. Maybe Ren did set me free to grow up and find my purpose. Not that I want to thank him for dumping me, but his explanation makes me feel a little less wounded over how we ended. And I love my career, and it satisfies a creative hunger I didn't know I had ten years ago.

"We were," he says, plopping onto the lounge beside me. "And now…look at us. About to have a kid? Guess that means I'm not a kid myself."

I offer him a small smile. "Says the guy who plays sports for a living. Ren, you will always be a kid at heart, even when you're a dad on the outside."

He draws a shaky breath. "I'm just…not sure I know how to

be one. I didn't exactly have a great role model." His body folds over in defeat, and it hurts my heart.

I can remember Ren talking about his dad only once. "My mom said he wasn't a bad person; he just did bad things," I recall him saying. Specifically, he drank too much and didn't think twice about getting into a car when he could barely see well enough to put the key in the ignition. Ren's mother tried for years to get him to seek treatment, but when Ren was only six years old, his dad drove off the side of a mountain road and died. The saving grace was that he didn't involve anyone else in the accident.

"I'm sorry," I say, pretty certain I had the same response back then. I wish I knew now how to say something more helpful.

Ren covers my hand with his. The tiny reassuring gesture reminds me that he still knows me after all this time. "I know alcoholism is an illness, and it wasn't his fault that he had the disease, but I still hold him accountable for not treating it like one. Then again, I barely knew him. I've spent a lot of years in therapy talking about my resentment, and it made me want to double down and be the best father I could. Someday."

"Just not today." I can't help but clarify. I know this wasn't his choice, and I want him to understand that I get it.

He shrugs. "It wasn't the plan, but maybe now it is?" He squints like he's uncertain of what he sees in the distance.

"Maybe. Or not. You should take your time thinking about it." I know it's the right thing to give him space, even if a part of me really wants to know right now what he'll decide.

Ren nods and inhales deeply. "Okay…sure." He sounds like he's agreeing to get takeout instead of cooking. He twists, stretching his neck and back. I feel bad for dropping this bomb on him, but what choice did I have? "Honestly, it's all I can do on most days to get Truman fed and walked." He doesn't say what we both know—his travel schedule doesn't lend itself to much of a stable home life. "It's why I always put parenthood far down the road. But…plans go awry." A boyish grin pulls at his lips.

That, combined with his explanation for why he broke things

off, cracks my heart open a smidge, and I can't deny a glimmer of old feelings. I tell myself it's dangerous to feel anything for him, but my heart disagrees.

Gingerly, he reaches for my hand. It feels right to let him, though I can't articulate why. "I think..." He lets out a long, slow breath, and I get ready for a big pronouncement. "Maybe we should get some food."

I can't help but laugh. "Maybe we should."

It's six in the evening, and I haven't eaten all day. This is what happens when I wake up nauseous and spend several hours worrying about how Ren will react to my news.

The sun disappears behind the hills, but the sky still has that hopeful afternoon light that makes me believe in endless summers. It's still warm enough for shorts, though Ren offers to swing by my house if I want to change. "I'm good. Let's go someplace casual."

We drive south on Silverado Trail, passing one winery after another. Tru naps in the backseat, and I watch the wind from the open window ruffle his wavy fur. I still feel leftover nerves, which translates into me yammering about the local history. "The owner of that one and his wife split, and she opened her own winery right across the road," I say, pointing to the dueling signs that have similar fonts and similar names. "He took her to court, saying she ripped off his name and design, but he lost. Now, people assume they're connected because they look so similar. When they visit his, they visit hers. So even though she's brand new, she gets a ton of business." I'm talking too fast.

We drive past another one and point to a wooded area where the road disappears. "That's Meadow Hill. It's kind of the gold standard for expensive, small-batch wines. We're watching what they're doing very carefully. Everyone is."

"Interesting," he says, finally, when I let him get a word in.

"It is, isn't it? If you live here long enough, you know everything about everyone."

"So that means people will know about this in a minute," he says, pointing at my belly.

"Oh." I inhale a shaky breath at the idea. "I hadn't really thought of that, but yeah. I guess they will."

We continue driving, but my who's who of the Buttercup Hill area has lost some steam. "That one's been around for three generations. The kids all live out of town, so it's not clear if there's an heir to take it over," I say, pointing vaguely to the left.

Ren puts a hand on top of mine. "I appreciate the greatest hits tour. But I can tell you're working really hard not to talk about the elephant in the room."

Another glimmer of warmth unleashes in my heart at how well he knows me. Even after all this time. It makes me a tiny bit excited about the prospect of raising a child with him, but that's putting the cart way in front of the horse. This horse hasn't even decided if he's steady on his legs yet.

"I guess I don't want to freak you out."

"I'm not freaked out," he says, keeping his eyes on the road.

"Okay, well, maybe you should be. It's freaking me out that you're so calm."

He lets out a long breath. "I'm just...I don't know...I guess I'm trying to take it one step at a time. First step seems like getting some food in you."

I can't help but chuckle. "That's how we got into this trouble in the first place. You insisting on replacing my muffin."

"Your muffin, indeed." Ren smirks and I feel my face heat. His eyebrows bounce as we pull into the parking lot of a taco place. "Tacos okay?"

I nod, worried I'll spew more innuendo if I speak.

At the little stand just outside of town, we order beef and chicken tacos and take them to a picnic table under a tree. The air between us feels heavy as we sneak looks and awkward smiles at each other and chew through the food. Maybe this is a new normal for us—uncomfortable silences.

Wordlessly, Ren answers my concern by coming around to my

side of the table and sitting on the bench next to me. He puts his hand on the small of my back and rubs soothing circles. I never said my back was aching from the muscles stretching as my insides make way for a baby, but he knows.

Tentatively, I tip my head against his shoulder and sigh at the warmth of his body. His hand comes up to smooth my hair, and we stay like that, each lost in our own thoughts and maybe bound by a similar one—whatever this is, we're in it together.

One hour later, we arrive back at Ren's casita, and I stand in his driveway, expecting him to hug me and say goodbye. After all, I've given him a lot to think about, and I can see the fatigue etched on his face. Truman exits the car and takes off into the vineyards.

"Do you…want to come in?"

The obvious answer is that I need to go home. He's just being polite, and I'm worn out from the anxiety of anticipating telling him my news and the emotions of rehashing our breakup.

"Sure. That'd be great." Apparently, I have no control over my mouth.

Truman greets us happily, circling around our legs and getting his share of belly rubs before disappearing to his doggy bed.

"Can I get you anything?" Ren asks, turning to face me at the base of the stairs. I shake my head, still unsure why I stayed, but knowing I want to be here.

Ren meets my uncertain gaze and reaches for my hand. Interlacing our fingers, he brings them to his lips and softly kisses my knuckles. "I don't know what this is." His voice is a quiet rumble that sends a flood of sparks through my body.

Taking a step closer to him, I let out a slow breath. "Me neither. But I think I like it."

"Last time you were here, you said you didn't like me. Is that still true?"

Slowly, I shake my head. It seems impossible to dislike him now. "In some ways, this feels like us—the old us. But I know we're different now."

He takes a step closer. "Maybe not so different."

I freeze, intensely aware of the heat of his chest, which is only a couple of inches from mine. I swear, if I lit a match, the electricity between us would send the room up in flames. I'm uncertain what he's feeling, yet a part of me responds to him with a deep understanding.

There's vulnerability in his eyes, along with something more intense. Smoldering.

I feel a closeness that comes from finally understanding why he did what he did all those years ago. And from our current situation, however it pans out in the future.

"I, um, you should know that my pregnancy hormones are making me…feel some things."

Ren barks out a laugh. "That your way of telling me you're horny?"

I nod.

He smirks, running a finger from my temple to my cheek and over my shoulder. His hand continues down my arm until our fingers intertwine. "Well, I'm here for you. Whatever you need."

I nod again, leaning closer to him until we're breathing the same air. My forehead rests against his chest.

"*Anything* you need." The heat in his growl makes my stomach flip and my core burn hot.

Ren leads me up the stairs, and I don't question it. When we reach the hallway outside his room, he spins me so my back is against the wall and leans a forearm against the wall over my head. His eyes are molten as he lowers his lips to mine with such slow, intentional precision that it feels like he's moving in slow motion. By the time his hand slides into my hair and his lips make contact, I'm a shaking, writhing bundle of need, desperate for the taste of him.

He takes his time with this kiss, overwhelming me with the

heat and sensation of his mouth on mine. It's a kiss I never want to end, a kiss I'd betray my country for.

It's the polar opposite of the last time we were together. There's no sparring or salty retorts. I could question the wisdom of letting my guard down with the man who broke my heart, but I'm too addicted to the feel of him to bother.

As we move into the room, Ren strips off each piece of my clothing so deftly that I don't even realize it's happening until the backs of my knees hit the bed and I realize I'm naked.

"How the heck did you do that so efficiently?" I sigh, hating that I need to break our kiss to ask, but needing to know.

He smiles against my mouth. "I know efficiency is your love language. I'm adapting."

"Right when I didn't think you could turn me on any more…" I giggle.

I can't get Ren's clothes off fast enough. Belt—ripped through the belt loops. Shirt—unbuttoned and on the floor in under ten seconds. I have none of the grace or finesse of what Ren managed to do, but I'm suddenly so fired up for him that I don't care. I lean back on the bed and pull him toward me until his body is flush with mine. His groan of pleasure matches my own.

"There's something so hot about knowing you have my baby in here," Ren breathes against my belly. His hands leave goose bumps in their wake as he runs them along the skin of my hip and waist.

Maybe the pregnancy hormones are on overdrive because I've never felt so turned on in my life. Then again, it might just be him. I have no way of deciphering the origin of my feelings, and I have no interest in trying. Not when Ren holds himself over me on his forearms and my hands trail over his hard pecs and abs. I just want one more night with him where my body can feel only pleasure and my brain can take a break from worrying about what the future will hold. His mouth is hot and commanding as he works his way from my stomach to my breasts and closes his mouth over one nipple. "Oh, God!" I cry out so loudly that he stops his gentle assault on every one of my senses and looks at me.

"Did I hurt you?"

Shaking my head, I try to explain, even though I don't really understand it. "Just sensitive." My breasts are already a big erogenous zone for me, but now that they've been called to action by pregnancy hormones, they're like a beacon on a dark night, begging to be seen. And touched. "Keep going, please."

Ren comes to my rescue with guns blazing. "Don't have to ask me twice."

His tongue runs light circles around each nipple, sending ripples of heat through my body. I'm dying for him to suck and bite and kiss me. It's a new sensation of pleasure mixed with an ache that makes me yearn for more. I'm both marveling at how my body has changed in a matter of weeks and telling my brain to shut up for a few minutes so I can enjoy this.

I hum my approval as Ren flips me over and I straddle him, staring down at his hard chest and his beautiful cheekbones. I inhale deeply, and his manly scent of pine and soap is the first smell that makes me feel calm instead of nauseous. He's the balm to my hormonal spikes.

With a strong hand gripping each hip, Ren moves me up his chest until I'm sitting on his face.

Reaching to the side, I grab a throw pillow and prop it under his head. "Here. That's more comfortable.

He smiles. "Are you seriously worried about my comfort when I'm getting ready to devour you? I'm like a king at a banquet."

I shrug. "I can't help it. I'm a host down to my bones."

"You," he rasps against my skin, guiding my hips so they're locked around his head. Each word vibrates through my center, followed by a surge of pleasure. "Are the perfect host. You are the appetizer…" His kisses burn my skin. "The cocktail, the main course…but I never could wait to get to my dessert. You're the most alluring goddamn banquet."

His hands sear my skin in every place he touches, and I sigh as he ravishes me with his tongue. My brain takes a back seat to the ribbons of heat coursing through my veins. I'm fully present and also losing my mind.

I may not be good at feeding myself at regular intervals, but I am very good at knowing what my body really wants. It's the man who looks like a Greek god and kisses like a saint. The rest of life is negotiable.

CHAPTER
Fifteen

REN

I wake up feeling fucking happy. For the first time, a new day hits me without the emptiness that comes from my heart's missing piece. I'm no longer pining for a woman who seemed lost to me forever because she's right here. Today, I feel free.

I'm pretty sure it's early morning, but I really have no clue. I don't dare move for fear of waking Trix, who's starfished on her stomach with one leg draped over my hip and an arm across my chest. Her hair is untidy and free, splayed out on the pillow, and her long lashes fan out over the tops of her cheeks. I could stare at her naked body forever, and there's just enough light seeping through the blinds to bathe her in a pale glow.

Gazing at her, I feel a familiar sense that everything is right with the world—familiar, even though it was ten years earlier that I last felt this way. That feeling lulled me to sleep, despite the bombshell shoving its way back into my consciousness. *One more minute to enjoy this please,* I beg my own brain.

The last thing I remember is how good it felt when she curled her body into mine and drifted to sleep while I smoothed her hair.

The birds are awake, sitting in whatever types of trees flank my house, chirping their little hearts out about the dawn. Otherwise, the room is quiet and still, which allows me to think.

Preseason games begin in a few days, and we have an afternoon training session later. I need whatever mental energy I can muster to come up with a new form of pep talk that will inspire the guys to stop fucking around. We need to start playing like a team instead of a roster of superstars trying to hog the spotlight. I've said it a hundred times. Maybe it's time to start saying something else.

Once my mind gets going, there's no chance I'll fall back asleep. Now that I'm awake and alone with my thoughts, there's no escaping the truth. I'm going to be a dad.

I could think of it as pure biology. My genetic material will be part of a new baby, and Trix made it clear she doesn't expect anything from me. I could go on my merry way, play my home and away games like usual, and pop in occasionally to visit like the mysterious, fun uncle. I could be an absentee dad and let her raise the kid with her big, involved family. They'll barely know I'm missing.

But as the child raised without a dad, that's the last fucking thing I want for any kid, let alone my own.

My own kid.

The words still ring hollow in my mind because they're so new, so unfamiliar, so unplanned.

That's the beauty of life, though, right? Not everything goes according to plan.

I can see Trix struggling with that idea. The woman I'm getting to know has plans and organizers and lists. Seeing her try to surrender to something outside her control makes me want to wrap her up and take on the world so she doesn't have to. Or do it with her.

Isn't that why I came back to town, to try to rekindle something?

Yeah, but not like this.

"Trix," I whisper, running a hand lightly down the smooth skin of her back.

She stirs and murmurs, "Mm-hmm."

"Good morning."

She turns her face toward the sound of my voice, eyes still closed. "First rule of parenting: never wake a sleeping baby." Her voice is soft, but the small smile is teasing.

"Yeah. About that…"

Her eyes blink open, and she rolls to the side. Leaning her cheek on her hand, she looks instantly awake, ready for business. I'm still getting used to this woman who's so much more goal-oriented than the one I knew in college. I kick myself for waking her out of the sleepy, soft state she was in a moment ago when she was pliant, draped across me, and unconcerned about anything.

"We don't have to get into that—" she stammers and shakes her head.

"No, I want to." I run a finger across her lips, silencing her as my hand continues to trace the delicate features of her face. "I'm in, Trix. I want to do this with you. Share custody or whatever they call it."

Her smile grows. "Co-parenting. It's called co-parenting."

"Yeah, okay. Call it what you want, but I'm here for it. I want to be a dad."

"Yeah?"

"Yeah." Saying the words out loud makes my heart race a little bit because I've just made it real. I've made a commitment, and there's no going back on being a part of a person's life. It means I'm tying myself to Trix in some way too, and I can't tell if it thrills me or terrifies me. What if I fuck it up again?

She presses her lips together until she can't stop the smile from taking over. "Okay. So…okay."

I think it's okay, but our blazing chemistry scrambles everything in my brain. "But what about this?" I gesture between us.

She mimics my motion, and it looks like she's swatting bugs. "This?"

"Clearly, I'm just as hot for you as I was in college, but I don't want to complicate things even more."

She nods. "Ah. That."

I push myself up to sit, noticing her eyes glide the length of my torso, snagging on my pecs and abs. Her gaze goes hazy, and she tilts her head like she's admiring a piece of art. I'll never get tired of her looking at me like that.

"Trix, it feels good, being with you. Easy. Ten years didn't change a thing."

She hauls herself to a sitting position and faces me, legs crossed. "Well, some things have changed. We both have demanding careers, we're both adulting. But yeah, it kind of feels like no time has passed."

Reaching over, I run a hand over her hair and smooth the crease in her brow with my finger. "I feel like there's a 'but' coming. What are you worried about?"

"I'm worried this will be too much." She gestures between our naked bodies. "It feels so good to be with you, but I don't want to be reckless. There's a child involved, so maybe we set up some ground rules."

"Sounds like you've given this some thought." I don't like that she's walking things back when it feels so good to be with her again.

She shrugs. "Just thinking out loud. I like us like this, but I'm worried about blurring the lines. We're co-parents, not a couple."

But we could be.

I don't say it because it's clear she's not on the same page… yet. I've had years to think about being with her again, and she's only here because she was blindsided by an accidental pregnancy. I don't like how it feels, but I don't want to jeopardize our tenuous bond. So I nod.

"And if it gets too complicated, we need to do what's best for the baby."

"Yeah, makes sense. Agreed." I try to keep the disappointment from my voice as a new emptiness replaces the old because she's not really mine.

Her eyes fix on mine as if assessing my honesty. "You're sure about this? It's a lot. I don't expect you to make this decision without giving it a lot of thought. This will change your life, Ren." Her tone is dire, and it occurs to me for the first time that maybe she doesn't want me in this with her, even though she gave me the option.

"I know that. But I guess..." I say, running a hand through my hair and letting it land back on her shoulder. "I've always imagined myself as a dad, knocking a puck around with a feisty kid, being the kind of influence on an impressionable little person that I never had. I do want that. And Trix, you're my OG soul mate—" I hold up a hand when I sense her starting to object. "I know that's in the past, and I'm not trying to push you into anything. I just mean that I know you. And I trust you as a partner in this." I pause. "If you want me as yours."

She nods slowly. "I do, Ren. I trust you too." She swallows hard, her only indication that taking this step forward with me is as scary as it feels to me. But I can't deny that I want this. "You'll be a great dad." She says it so quietly I almost don't hear her.

"Okay, then. We know we're going to do this, whatever that means. We have seven months to figure it out." I like that this tethers us together. I'm not about to tell her that because it's too much, way too soon. But it is what it is.

Trix rolls off the bed with a grin on her face and pulls on her hoodie. "Seven and a half months," she corrects, grabbing her phone. She starts tapping on the screen. "That's four months after PJ's wedding, so the inn will be done. It has to be done. So that leaves plenty of time to get things ready for a baby."

I can't help but smile at her proficiency, moving full bore ahead into task mode. She's a force of nature, this Beatrix Corbett, and I kind of love it.

"Check," I say. "Seven and a half months from now—baby."

She rolls her eyes at me, but it doesn't stop her from tapping whatever lists she's making into her phone. "Laugh now, but you're in this with me, and you'll learn to love my multitasking abilities, I promise you."

I don't bother to tell her that I'm hardly in this for the multitasking. I'm in this because it's *her,* which means I'm here for the foreseeable future.

Longer, if she'll have me.

CHAPTER
Sixteen

BEATRIX

The late afternoon heat hangs like a blanket over Dash's backyard, a flat grassy patch ringed in rosemary hedges. I'm always hot these days, so I'm wearing a tank top and sitting under a patio umbrella on the wooden deck that separates the clapboard house and the yard. A light scent of barbecued chicken wafts from the grill, where Jax chats with PJ's fiancé, Colin, and moves things around with a pair of tongs. The rest of my siblings are huddled around a picnic table on the grass, where PJ is assembling chips, dips, and appetizers.

"Hey, will you try this guacamole?" The back door of Dash's house slams behind him as he exits with a basket of chips in one hand and a bowl of guacamole in the other. He walks it straight over to me for the first taste. "Is it too lemony?"

I feel myself go guacamole-green at the idea of lemons, and fortunately, Mallory is hot on his tail to rescue me. "Lemme try it," she says, swatting him with a dish towel. "Only chocolate ice cream and potato chips, remember? Everything else makes her queasy."

"Ooh, sorry, sis. I wasn't thinking."

"It's fine. And I can eat stuff other than ice cream. Potato chips, mainly."

"Check! They're on the picnic table." Dash points to the table and swivels to give Mallory a taste of his guac. She nods her approval. "Maybe a little more salt." He goes back inside to make adjustments before the rest of our family arrives. We get together every couple of weeks for a barbecue or casual family dinner, but this one has me on edge for obvious reasons. I have no idea how my siblings will react to my baby news, despite Dash's reassurances that it'll be fine.

Dash puts the chips and guac on a picnic table shaded by a tree in his yard. I follow him back to the house, where he grabs a saltshaker and returns to fix the guacamole. "Not sure it really needs salt because the chips are salted, but I guess it couldn't hurt."

"Plus, you love her, so if she wants it salty, you're gonna do it," I say, wondering what that feels like. Wondering if I'll ever have that with Ren. It's absurd to even think about it when we're just getting along, but I can't help entertaining an idle fantasy.

"That too." Dash takes a seat next to Jax, who watches his fiancée Ruby play with his daughter's hair. Fiona is almost eight years old and is more of an adult than some of my siblings. She sits calmly on a chair made from a stump of wood while Ruby winds the strands into a long braid.

"You miss doing her hair?" I ask. Jax was a single dad for years before he met Ruby, and he's the best, most protective dad I've ever met. But the pigtails and braids always tripped him up. I sometimes got a panicked call on the way to school some mornings when he felt outmatched by whatever style Fiona was requesting that day. They'd stop by, and I'd twist her hair into a ballerina bun or french braids while Jax muttered things about how Fiona learned her eye-rolling from me.

"Not a bit. Styling that long hair was going to be my undoing.

If I hadn't met Ruby, Fiona would probably be sporting a pixie cut by now."

I inhale a mock gasp. "You wouldn't."

He shrugs, much less grumpy these days than he used to be, now that Buttercup Hill finally has more black ink than red on its balance sheet. That's mainly thanks to PJ's fiancé, Colin, who pitched in and invested in the vineyard to keep us afloat.

"I wouldn't have really done it because she's adorable, but there were days I was tempted. Do you remember when I pulled up in front of your house, and she had the most hideous knot in the back?"

"Oh, yeah. That was something."

I laugh, thinking back to the agonized expression I could see from ten feet away. I'd just received a panicked text asking me if I was home. Before I had time to respond, Jax tore up my driveway, and I raced outside, worried someone was sick or dying. Jax flung open the door to the back seat, revealing his tiny blond daughter, who couldn't have been more than five years old.

"She wants a messy bun." My brother, normally a strapping, tall man who intimidates other people by merely glaring at them, looked utterly defeated. "Everything I do with her hair is a mess, but not the right kind of mess, apparently."

Fiona sulked, twirling a strand of hair around her finger.

I used some conditioner and unmatted her hair before twirling it into the kind of bun I knew she'd probably seen on a Disney show. She nodded and hugged me when she saw the result in the mirror, and Jax looked almost annoyed that I'd gotten it right when he couldn't. "Thanks," he'd said, grudgingly.

Maybe he's finally over it.

"She and Ruby are thick as thieves, and I couldn't be happier," Jax says, leaning an elbow on the picnic table and sipping from a bottle of beer.

Eventually, the rest of our siblings join us at the table, and Mallory brings out a vegetable platter big enough to feed my family three times over. "What?" she asks when we all look at her with wide eyes. "I'm an only child. I don't know how to feed a group this big, and I don't want to run out."

Dash slides onto the bench, pulls Mallory onto his lap, and looks at me expectantly.

"So, I have some news," I begin.

"If it's about the inn being delayed again, that's the kind of news that can wait until the work week," Archer says. He has zero sense of humor about anything related to Buttercup Hill and its ability to turn a profit.

"No! It can't be delayed. My wedding, remember?" PJ gasps.

"Like any of us could forget," Dash drawls.

I shake my head and pick up a potato chip. The green shade of the guacamole nauseates me, so I turn away and take a bite of the chip.

"It's not about that." I eat the rest of the chip and take a deep breath. *This is your family. They'll support you no matter what.* I just need to get the words out, and then I'll feel much better. So I close my eyes and speak quickly. "I'm going to have a baby. I'm pregnant, ten weeks now, and I wanted you all to know. It wasn't planned, but I'm getting my brain around it now and I want this, so I hope you'll all support me."

Fiona is the first to react. She jumps from her seat and runs around the table to hug me. "I'm really excited. Ooh, I'll babysit! Is it going to be a girl?"

"Um, oh. I don't know yet," I tell her, realizing that people are going to keep asking me that question, and I should have a better answer prepared. "I'm not sure if I'll find out beforehand. I may just let it be a surprise."

Fiona squeals once more and then excuses herself to bake cookies in the house, which she does every time we have a family dinner. I watch her go until she disappears inside, stalling before turning back to my brothers and sister, all of whom look at me with varying degrees of surprise and opinions on their faces.

"That's great," PJ says. Colin, sitting next to her, nods enthusiastically but says nothing.

"Yes, congratulations," Dash adds, offering me a wink.

"Who's the dad?" Jax asks. The air around us goes silent as everyone leans in and waits.

"Um…" I begin feeling my face flush. "That's an interesting story. Do you remember Dominick Renaldi, who I used to date in college?"

"Of course I remember. Wait, your baby's dad is Renaldi, as in the GOAT of the NHL?" Archer says, perking up for the first time.

"Yes." I fill them in on the details, how we ran into each other, how he's going to be involved, how we're not a couple.

They pepper me with questions about how it's all going to work out, but the main message is that they're excited about a new family member, and they're happy if I'm happy.

"But you could be a couple. Right? It's possible after all this. Remember Ross and Rachel in *Friends*?" Archer is more animated than I've seen him in a while, and I can't understand it.

"Arch, you sound kind of personally invested here," I tease. "What's up? You looking for a bromance with him? Or, like, the inside scoop on hockey GOAT life?"

Archer shakes his head, but I notice that he's suddenly turning pink. "No. Nothing like that."

"Archer, do you have a guy crush on Dominick Renaldi?" Jax asks, never able to pass up a chance to rib his older brother.

Archer pushes himself up from the table and crosses his arms. "Hardly. I just like the sport and I respect the players. That's all." He stalks off toward the house and Jax high-fives Dash.

PJ laughs. "Well, if you do decide you want to be a couple, it looks like you may have some competition."

I exhale a sigh of relief, grateful that my family seems to be taking this well.

"Hang on. Is he being a good guy about it? I mean, are you not together because he's being an asshole or because that's what you want?" Jax asks, sweetly protective of me.

"He's not an asshole. Not at all. He wants to be involved, but we're still figuring out how it's all going to work. I'll keep you posted, I promise."

"Okay," Dash says. "Leave her alone. You can jump all over her once you get a plate of food. Get it while it's hot."

I shoot him a grateful glance, and he nods. Then, he slips me an empty bowl from behind his back. "There's chocolate ice cream waiting for you in the freezer."

It's either because he's the best brother ever, or it's the hormones, but I burst into tears. Fortunately, they taste good mixed with the chocolate.

CHAPTER Seventeen

REN

I've had a month to get used to the idea of being a dad, but it still feels surreal every time my teammates pull out photos of their kids, and I realize that at this time next year, I'll be able to do the same. But I haven't shared my news with them yet. I don't want to do anything to distract them from focusing on the team, which has been playing only slightly better ahead of our first preseason game on the road.

I've kept my personal life personal, as it should be, and tried to figure out why this group still isn't gelling the way we need to. I can already see the headlines if we lose: "So much potential, wasted." I can't let that happen.

It's just two days out of town, which is a relief. Trix insists on watching Truman, but I feel guilty leaving her to drag my goofy dog around on a leash when she's also carrying a baby. Even if the baby is the size of a walnut, according to the ultrasound.

A *walnut*.

I need to keep things in perspective. A walnut is tiny. Harmless. I shouldn't get too wound up about a walnut or anything that would fit inside the shell of one.

But I can't help it—I'm wound up. Even though a preseason game doesn't mean much, and it's mainly a chance for us to interact with fans and get footage for the team's social media feed, I can't help feeling like we'll be lucky if we can win just one of the two games. Even if it's due more to our opponent's missteps than any symphony of chemistry on our part, I'll take it.

Right now, I just need to see my woman, even if it's just in the form of a video call. She's a calming balm to all my worries and jangled nerves, and I've been waiting hours to hear her voice.

"Hey, Hockey Star," Trix says by way of greeting when she answers. My ego loves the nickname.

"Hey there."

"Uh oh. What's wrong?" I love even more that she knows I'm not at my best just based on a "hey there."

"I've got the hotel blues. I used to love games on the road. I don't know what happened." It's late in Miami, and I should be getting some sleep before tomorrow's game. Instead, I'm sitting up against the wooden headboard in the hotel, with two pillows behind my back and my phone turned up on my lap so I can see her face on the video call.

She's curled up in one of my tee shirts on her couch downstairs, and I see a cup of tea on the table in front of her, along with a display of design magazines.

"You've been stressed about these games on the road. Maybe that's part of it," she says.

"No, that's not it."

"No? What, then?"

"Something feels wrong. I used to love hotels. The room service, the crisp sheets I didn't need to wash myself, a nicely made bed, and fresh towels in the shower. And I felt important when we arrived with our bags and took a private set of elevators to shuttle us away from the crowds."

"Sounds nice."

I roll my eyes. "I'm telling this to someone who's renovating an inn. You probably couldn't be less interested in hotels."

The soft sound of her laughter feels like warm honey. "Au contraire, my friend. I spend more time thinking about hotels than the average person because I'm into it."

I hold the phone up and give her a tour of my room. "Do you like this one? The bed had all these decorative pillows and a thing at the end that I assume is meant to hold the pillows at night." I show her the small burgundy couch at the foot of the bed, where I've stacked the six decorative pillows, all in various shades of beige. "Closet's over there, along with the bathroom, which has a full-on tub. That's not going to get any use by me, but the shower's decent. Rain head and some sprayers on the sides. Better than average."

"You're not going to show me that?" She smirks at my laziness.

"Nope, because I'm dead tired after training."

"I really hope you still have your ass because it's damn cute."

"You're damn cute," I say. "Let me see that baby."

She obliges, tilting the phone camera down so I can see her stomach, which she pushes out to make it look bigger than it is. She holds the fabric tight against her belly to emphasize the size, but it's pretty flat. "Still just looks like I had a really big dinner."

"Looks perfect. I wish I was there to rub the soreness out of your back and feet."

"Aah, if that's up for grabs, please get on the next flight back here. I've been running around all day looking at chairs and tables to put in the rooms at the inn, and my feet are swollen like little hot dogs."

I shift the phone camera again to show her another part of my hotel room. "You mean desks like this one?"

"Now you're talking." She lays back, and her hand disappears from view as she fake-moans. "Show me more of your hotel desk, Ren. Please. Don't hold back on the little drawers."

I almost think she's serious.

Maybe she is serious.

In the name of fun, I zoom in on the desk and give her a detailed look at the chair, the inputs for various computer cords, and the little cubbies with hotel stationery. "This desk will get no use because I don't have anything to write. Not sitting down to write letters at the hotel, I'll tell you that much."

"Don't discount a good writing space. Maybe you should write a letter." Another moan turns to a peal of laughter.

"I'm not writing a goddamn letter."

"Fine. Save it for your diary. I know you brought it with you. Probably right next to your teddy bear and blankie on the bed."

"Okay, yeah, you got me," I say, turning the camera to the bed so she can see it's just me and my legs clad in sweatpants on the bed. "The only teddy bear I'm interested in sleeping with is you."

"Ren," she says quietly after I bring the camera back to my face. Her expression is suddenly serious.

"Yeah? Is everything okay?"

She nods and presses her lips together. "Are you wearing a shirt?"

She knows I'm not. "No. Why?"

Blinking those soft blue eyes at me, she asks quietly, "Can I see?"

"See what? Me not wearing a shirt?"

She nods.

Oh, my little horny baby mama.

I hold the camera out so she can see me from the waist up and clock the grin that spreads across her face. She says nothing for a while, just stares at me. I'm happy too, gazing at her face. I could do this all night, especially when she gets that hungry sparkle in her eye.

"Thanks. I needed a little pick-me-up. That did it. Hope you don't mind being objectified for a minute."

"Are you kidding? We hockey stars live for that shit. Objectify me, baby."

"Ha. Good."

Even though I'm the one in the later time zone, I can see Trix's eyes get heavy. "You've been working since the crack of dawn, haven't you?" I ask, knowing how determined she is to work against probability to get the inn open in January of the new year.

She nods.

"Time for bed, honey."

She nods again.

We say our good nights, and I look back at the silly desk in the corner of my room. No use for the thing at all. Except that…there is that stack of hotel stationery that I'll bet no one ever uses. Maybe I'll be the first.

I may never send it to anyone, but maybe Trix is right. Sometimes, it's good to get all my thoughts in one place. And right now, all my thoughts are of her.

CHAPTER *Eighteen*

REN

Maybe it wasn't the best idea to ride my mountain bike to Trix's house this morning. Turns out, it's a long fucking way from my place on the Vine Trail when we're having a heat wave. There's always one weekend in October when it feels hotter than any summer day, and it sends forth a kind of optimism that I see in the face of everyone who's out in shorts and a tee shirt one last time before fall takes over again and the days get shorter.

It's supposed to be an off day from training before our first home game, and my coach would have my hide if he knew I was sweating out electrolytes in the bright sun instead of resting my muscles for tomorrow night's matchup against Toronto. Well, what he doesn't know can't hurt him.

I want to be outside. I need the sun on my face. I spend so much time inside an ice-o-plex that I'm probably criminally low on vitamin D. At least, that's my excuse for riding this morning. That, and the fact that we won both games on the road. I woke up this morning energized with a sense of invincibility—everything in my life is right where I want it to be.

Trix and I have plans today, but I told her we're not going anywhere before noon. The woman holds herself to a grueling schedule, even three months pregnant, and I want her to get some sleep. It's Sunday, for crying out loud. Nothing needs to get done today that can't get done on Monday.

Riding feels good. The valley floor is flat, so my legs don't have to work that hard. Half the time, I'm just coasting along, looking at the vineyards sprawling out in all directions, feeling the sun at my back.

I had a strange sense earlier that I couldn't quite identify, and it's taken me over ten miles of riding to put my finger on what it is. Happiness. I know that sounds glib or overly obvious, but the kind of happy I feel right now is different from the adrenaline rush of scoring the winning goal or reaching playoffs with the team. It's not about achieving something. It's about being lucky. It's about chance and fortune and magic.

Falling in love with a woman like Beatrix Corbett once in a lifetime is more than a guy like me could hope for, but getting a second chance makes me feel like I've woken up on Christmas morning, hit the lottery, and won the Stanley Cup all at once.

It's been almost three months since we ran into each other at the Oxbow Market, and I keep coming back to that day—how I meant to get to the paint store earlier, but then I stayed up late getting muddled up in design plans, which I've never done before. Then I slept in, which also never happens. Almost like the renovation gods were conspiring to push us together. If you believe in that sort of thing. I never did.

Maybe I do now.

Maybe I put a little more stock in the idea of fate.

The roads are getting crowded as the day trippers arrive to drive the wine route, so I pedal a little faster down the stretch to Buttercup Hill before it gets crowded. I know that if Trix sees people flocking to the restaurants on the property, her hosting instinct will kick in, and she won't be able to tear herself away.

And she promised me an entire day off to do something fun.

When I ride up the driveway outside Trix's house, she's sitting on a rocking chair on the porch, sipping a cup of tea. The flag on the teabag spins in the breeze, and the sun hits her face. Trix rests a hand on her belly, as if willing it to swell into a bigger baby bump. It's fucking adorable.

"You rode in this heat? Are you nuts?" The smile in her voice washes over me. Or that could be the sweat bath I've brought on by riding.

"Maybe a little." I lean the bike against the side of the house and take the porch steps two at a time. "You ready for our date?"

"We're going on a date? I thought you said we were running errands." She has the nerve to look disappointed.

"I did. We are. Sort of. I knew that if it sounded efficient and useful, you'd have to agree," I tell her.

"Sneaky."

"Yup. I hit you in your little type-A happy place with the idea of errands, but I'm sorry to tell you, honey, we are going on a date."

Pushing herself up from the rocking chair like she's nine months along, she hams it up to remind me that she's doing all the hard work. I'm not about to argue.

Reaching out to give Trix a hand, I rest a hand on her hip and reel her in, the other hand reaching up to cup her cheek. I cradle her face like she's precious—because she is—her big, blue eyes gazing up at me. My thumb sweeps along the apple of her cheek, feeling the soft skin there. "Can you forgive me for the tiny deception?" I ask, leveling her with my biggest smile. She rests her cheek against my chest and nods.

"I suppose. Just don't do it again."

"I won't."

But I will.

It's getting harder to convince myself that I'll be satisfied with something casual with her. *I mean, who the fuck am I kidding?* I don't know whether I'm falling in love with this woman all over again, or if I never stopped loving her. But if I need to trick her to get her to relax for a few hours, I'll do it again and again.

Once I've showered, we set off in my car. "Can I get a hint?" she asks, looking down at a tote bag she's brought along. I know she probably has real errands to run, like a trip to the grocery store or pharmacy, but those are the last places I'd take her on a date.

I shake my head.

"Infuriating." There isn't even a hint of playful frustration in her voice. It's pure fury.

Trix warned me that she doesn't like surprises, but it's not really true. She *hates* surprises. Judging from the grilling she's given me over the past ten minutes, she can barely hold it together without knowing where we're going, for how long, and why.

It just makes me wish we had a longer drive.

"This is good practice for you," I tell her, knowing I'm infuriating her even more. I can't help it. Seeing the color rise in her cheeks as she gets progressively more irate makes me want to wrap her in my arms and watch her calm down progressively as I drop tiny hints for hours. Then I'll keep her forever.

Forever?

I do a little gut check at that thought because I can't confuse my forever status as the father of her child with a forever relationship with Trix. But it's like being in the middle of a hockey game —I need to make the best plays I can without a guarantee of how it will end.

"Good practice for what? Wanting to murder you and not doing it?"

I chuckle at the lack of humor in her voice. "When you're a parent, you won't know what's going to happen from day to day. You might get dressed for work, and that's when the baby decides to spit up all over your shirt. Or you need a good night's sleep, and that's when the baby cuts a tooth and keeps you up all night crying."

She holds up two fingers. "Okay, two things. First, when did you get so knowledgeable about what babies do? And why do you keep saying 'you'? I'm not the only one staying up all night with a teething kid."

I pat her leg in a useless effort to calm her. The muscles under her long skirt are tense and tight as rocks. "Remind me to schedule you a massage when we get back."

"I don't have time for a massage! I barely have time for this date."

"Oh, grasshopper, you have so much to learn," I say, referencing *The Karate Kid,* which we watched together in college. Glancing at her, I catch her smiling at the reference. "I will be there for at least half of the teeth since we're sharing custody, and maybe more if I spend the night. And as for my knowledge, I'm a reader, remember? I bought some books." She gnashes her teeth, but I feel the muscle in her leg relax a tiny bit as each answer to her questions seems to calm the savage beast that seeks order and progress all the time.

"You bought books?" The softness in her voice feels like a well-worn shirt.

"Several." I rub circles on her knee.

I signal and take a left at a fork in the highway, following a skinny gravel road to where it dead ends at a white farmhouse with green trim. The sign in front leaves no mystery as to where we are—Carraway Farm.

"Wait, are you serious?" She swivels in her seat to face me, eyes sparkling with childlike glee. "We're going to the farm. Like, *the* farm?"

After Trix told me about her obsession with the Carraway Farm she'd been following on social media for the past year, I did a little digging. Turns out the place is not just social media catnip. They walk the talk, raising animals and growing all the ingredients to make the desserts they feature in their videos. The only thing more surprising than learning Carraway Farm hosts visitors was that Trix didn't figure it out first.

"Yup."

"Are we allowed to just show up?" She slumps down in the seat a few inches as though she needs to hide. As though she's capable of keeping a low profile with her enthusiasm.

"We're allowed. I called ahead and made an appointment. Come on."

I exit the car and go around to her side, opening the door before she can do it herself. I extend a hand to help her out of the car. Before we reach the front of the farmhouse, the door swings open to reveal a woman our age in a blue overall dress and a straw hat. Long blond braids hang over her shoulders as she waves at us with both hands. "Welcome, you two!"

She comes down the front stairs to greet us. But there's no need. Trix hustles a little faster to shake her hand. "Oh my gosh, it's so nice to meet you. I had no idea we were coming here, and I can barely handle it. I've seen every one of your videos, and I follow your socials religiously."

It's a different side of Trix than I've ever seen. Normally so pulled together, she's fangirling hard, and it charms the fuck out of me.

The woman turns and shakes my hand, introducing herself. "I'm Radish."

I can barely stifle my laugh. *Radish? That has to be made up… right?* I school my expression as Radish envelops Trix in a bear hug. They smile at each other like reunited sisters. I'm almost jealous. That is, until Trix leans over and kisses me hard on the mouth and rings her arms around my shoulders. "Thank you," she whispers in my ear. "If you feel like getting down with a pregnant lady later, I know one who is very fond of you right now."

"You two are cute," Radish says, surveying us like a chef trying to decide how to slice and dice a chicken. For a moment, I worry that I haven't done nearly enough research about this place. If she's as zany as her name suggests, I might need to keep my guard up. But she just smiles at us. "But *cute* doesn't pull carrots out of the ground. I'm putting you both to work."

She signals for us to follow her into the farmhouse, pushing open the heavy front door to reveal a great room with high ceilings and rough-hewn beams. The walls are painted white, and the roof has large rectangular skylights, letting in so much sun there's no need to turn on any lights. The walls are covered in framed photographs of the farm animals Trix was gushing about. Tiny lambs. Flocks of chicks following a chicken in the grass. Brown rabbits, white rabbits.

Radish points to a group of small easels in a corner, each with a hanging sheet of paper covered in a finger-painted mess of color. "We host a preschool here three days a week for some of the local kids. We call them seedlings." She leads us past wooden bird feeders decorated in feathers, sequins, and paint.

Trix inhales a sharp breath, and her eyes shoot to mine. I know what she's thinking, and I nod in agreement—our little one needs to come to school here with Radish and all the other little seedlings. I feel myself drinking the Kool-Aid I didn't even know Radish was serving.

We stop in front of a door with a hanging plaque that reads *The Chick Inn*. Radish waits for us to smile at the pun. Trix squeezes my arm. I just gape at the total transformation of a tightly-wound woman into her own brand of seedling—wide-eyed and excited by the natural world. All thoughts of deadlines, renovations, menus, and agendas seem to have faded into a pleasant blur of animal photos and paint.

"I was just about to feed the chicks, but there are a lot of them, so it'll go faster if we divide and conquer." Radish opens the door to The Chick Inn, which is a chicken coop worthy of the Queen Mother Hen.

Looking down at her long, flowy skirt, Trix hesitates. "Am I dressed okay?"

I look down and notice the floor of the coop covered in sawdust and what is probably chicken shit. I should have thought of that earlier and told Trix to wear some old sweats. "I have some practice gear in the trunk. I can run back and get you something to change into," I offer.

"No need. You're perfect. As long as you don't mind brushing off some wood shavings when we're done," Radish says.

"I don't mind at all."

Radish leads us into the coop, which is tall enough for us to enter without bending down. Once inside, I take in the size of the place—easily as big as my spare bedroom with shelves along one wall and a window that leads to the next room. It's all made of raw wood with its own skylight in the roof.

"Aw!" Trix gasps. I look down and see a swarm of yellow chicks surrounding her ankles. They're bigger than newborn chicks, about twice that size, but they still fit in the palm of my hand when Radish bends down and hands one to me.

Trix plops herself down in the sawdust and gathers four baby chickens into her lap. She hugs them close and pets their tiny heads. I've never seen anything more adorable in my life. And I've never seen her look happier.

"Oh my God, Ren. This is my happy place."

"Yeah? Even more fun than checking shit off your to-do list?" The joy in her laugh answers my question.

Radish crouches down with a pail and hands us each a little pile of dried worms. They stink. But the chicks love them, so I play along, sitting next to Trix and hand-feeding a worm to each chick in the place. Soon, they've all figured out that we are the keepers of the worms, so we're swarmed with squawking chicks.

"How many can they have? I don't want to overfeed them," Trix says.

"A couple more each, and then we have to get them into the other room so they can roost."

I have no idea what that means, but I follow Radish as she scoops up the chickens, lifts them to the window, and pushes them through to some location I can see. I do the same, chicken feet scratching at me as I try to keep them in my grip. Soon, all the chicks have been moved over, and Radish slides the window shut.

We follow her around to the other side, where all the chicks are now in for the night under a large, warm lightbulb. "They need to sleep in here where it's warm," Radish says, moving us along to another area of the barn where the laying hens live. We harvest eggs, pet the hens on the heads, and say hello to a pen of roosters who seem none too happy to be separated from the brood.

"I feel you, guys. I'd want to be with the ladies, too," I say. Trix gives me a playful punch, and I pull her against my side.

"Thank you," she sighs. "For the record, I'll go on a date with you anytime."

I squeeze her closer, fully intending to hold her to that promise.

CHAPTER *Nineteen*

BEATRIX

"I want to drive the tractor." There isn't a hint of teasing in my voice, so I don't understand why Ren starts laughing.

"What?" he asks. Okay, maybe he didn't hear me.

"I want to drive the tractor." I stand up from where I've snapped enough cherry tomatoes from their stems to fill two crates. Radish has me sitting on a cow milking stool, so I don't need to bend over to do the work. I have yet to milk a cow, and I already told Ren we can't leave until we try it.

I mean, I'm at a farm. I'm going to milk a cow.

"You're serious." He cocks his head at me in that golden retriever way like he really doesn't understand the words I've now said twice.

"Of course I am. Radish?" I call out to our host, who is twenty yards away, busily plucking radishes—shocker—from a raised bed full of them. A wicker basket dangles from the crook in her arm as she pops the little red bulbs from the ground with the other. I understand now why she doesn't use machines to do the picking. The whole point of living on her farm is getting her hands dirty. It gives me ideas about a side hustle we can offer visitors in our food garden if they want to be at one with the soil. I imagine what having a small working farm at Buttercup Hill could do for our business when so many people are interested in sustainable agriculture and farm-to-table food. It's a perfect complement to the mission of Sweet Butter, and I know guests will love it.

I haven't told Ren about this new venture because he'll probably throttle me for taking on yet another side hustle when I'm already so busy, but I think it would be a great addition to Buttercup Hill.

"Yes?" Radish calls, looking at me from under the wide brim of her hat. I swear, everything about the woman screams social media post, and she's not even trying. PJ would have a field day here documenting everything and sussing out media opportunities.

"Can I drive the tractor?"

"Do you have any outstanding moving violations on your record?" she shouts, never missing a beat in plucking radishes.

"Nope."

"Good on you." She stands and wipes the dirt on an apron tied over her skirt and fishes in the various pockets until she finds a key attached to a blue crocheted octopus keychain and hands it off. "More than I can say. I keep rolling stop signs and getting nabbed." She shakes her head, and her braids flip back and forth.

I pocket the keys. "Can I drive it wherever, or do you have suggestions?"

Radish spreads her arms wide. "Anywhere you want, hon. Just don't run over the seedlings."

At first, I think she's referring to the preschoolers she mentioned earlier, but when I squint into the distance, I see tiny sprigs of green up and down the rows. I wave Ren over to the tractor. Painted a shiny red, it's clearly been cleaned up for photo ops. There's even a straw basket hanging from one handlebar, and I can imagine it filled with vegetables or flowers.

It's just one more reason why I like it here so much. Everything is functional but also aesthetic, similar to my vision for Buttercup Hill.

"I can see what draws you to this place," Ren says. Warmth swells inside me because he understands. "You could absolutely get this vibe going at Buttercup Hill, with an upscale twist that matches your brand. It begs to be photographed." I think I squeal louder than the piglets and jump in the air, throwing my hands high.

"Yes! Exactly. You get it. This is my vision, only with great wine and stellar food and the best inn in the county. It's just… we're not there yet."

"You will be." Ren nods, spreading his arms wide at the potential. "It's going to be awesome."

I kiss him on the lips and survey the tractor, which looks much bigger closeup. I have to hike my skirt around my knees and put a foot on the step, but the pregnancy has messed with my balance. That, or my center of gravity isn't where I expect it to be.

"Hang on," Ren says. "Let me help." He gives me a boost, and I slide onto the seat. Flexing my biceps, I get ready to ride.

Ren takes a few steps back and gazes at me, a smile forming on his lips. "You look like you were made for this, honey."

My head whips around. "Did you just call me 'honey'? That's the second time today."

Possibly realizing his slip, he takes a step farther away, as if that can somehow erase the offense. I told him I hate that word, and clearly, he remembers. "Sorry. Slipped out."

"No, I liked it."

"Really?"

I nod. "Coming from you, it's sweet. Please always call me that when you feel the urge."

After only a couple hours on a farm, I feel myself starting to shed some of the ropes that keep me tied in place. It feels good, and I love that Ren is a part of it.

Handing Ren my phone, I survey the farm. "Would you snap a

photo or two of me, you know, so I can remember this when I need some inspiration?"

"I'll do you one better."

"What do you mean?"

"Start 'er up." He points to the tractor, and I turn the key. The beast rumbles to life, and I test out the gas and the brake. Moving slowly, I start down one of the rows of corn, and Ren promptly jogs along with me, snapping action photos of me driving the tractor and shooting some video.

After driving to the far end of the property, I slow down the tractor and pull to a stop. Ren catches up in a few paces, more refreshed than winded from running. I slide over on the seat and flutter my lashes. "Wanna come up?"

As soon as I say the words, I feel silly. I mean, Ren has been amazing to indulge my farm fantasy, but I'm acting like we're a couple. And we're not.

Ren confirms my fears as he surveys the rounded seat that's most definitely fit for one and shakes his head. "Don't think I'll fit."

"Right. Of course. Forget about it."

He winks. "Unless you want to sit on my lap." As Ren steps up and slides onto the seat, I stand so he can move underneath me. I stopped the tractor at about the farthest point from the farmhouse, long outside the range of sight of anyone looking. Accident? Nope. Ren pulls me onto his lap, and I shimmy hard against him, just in case my intentions need explaining.

I want to have some farmyard fun. "Are you comfortable with me right here?" I move again, slower this time. Ren's cock doesn't need to be told twice that this is an erotic bicycle built for two.

"You wanna get fucked on a farm?" he asks, his voice a low rumble. Sexy and hot. "Is this a fantasy of yours or more of a spur-of-the-moment thing?"

I laugh and flip my hair over my shoulder. Ren nuzzles my neck and lets his hands roam over my thighs, where he pushes my skirt up around my waist.

"This is why you wanted to ride the tractor?" he rasps into my ear, and my body shivers from his breath on my skin. "I could do this all day long just to hear the way your breath hitches when I run my hand up your leg." He demonstrates, and I gasp on cue. "Scratch that. I'd do it forever. Full stop."

"Really? I'm not saying no, even though my plan was just to be a cowgirl for a few minutes."

He laughs. "You realize that cowgirls ride horses, not tractors, right?"

"Do you really want to mince words when I'm sitting on your hard-on?"

"Oh, honey, I want to do everything with you."

He hikes me a little higher on his lap, but my foot can still reach the pedal. I give the tractor a little gas, and we start moving forward. "I'm taking it slow here, just making sure I can control this thing with your hands where they are."

"Afraid of getting distracted?" he whispers low against my neck, fully distracting and thrilling me. Fortunately, this metal beast seems to top out at five miles an hour. At least, that's how it feels as we roll slowly through a field planted with strawberries in neat lines.

"I don't want to run over any of these berries." My eyes stay glued to the row ahead of us, even as Ren lifts my skirt a little higher so it's bunched on my lap. "Hmm, nice breeze," I murmur, barely able to focus on driving.

The feel of him hard beneath me has me at a loss for words. I'm done talking, fully focused on his finger sliding beneath the elastic of my panties where it meets the top of my thigh. I lean back against Ren, but my challenge is keeping the tractor moving steadily forward. I'm getting off on the multitasking, not gonna lie. One hand stays on the steering wheel, and the other drops to Ren's leg, where my fingers grip him hard.

"Nice quads, Hockey Star."

"I try," he grunts as I shift again on his lap. "Fuck, honey, you're gonna make me come if you keep moving like that."

I laugh and shake my hair out the way he likes. It blows against the side of Ren's neck, and he grips me tighter. I'm overcome with the feeling of wanting him closer, wanting him permanently. The more time I spend with Dominick Renaldi, the more lost I feel to him. It's a cascading waterfall I can't possibly control.

Right now, feeling him hard beneath my thighs, holding one hand against my stomach where our child is growing by the day, I only want this.

"Ren..." My voice sounds brittle as Ren moves his finger past the elastic of my panties and into the hot wetness that makes him groan against my ear. One finger, then two. He moves them slowly in circles against my flesh, paying extra attention to my clit. He knows it makes me go crazy.

One press of his finger on the hot bundle of nerves has me bucking against him, but I'm still driving the tractor steadily forward, down the row of strawberries. Not a single berry is damaged by our shenanigans, and I feel myself starting to come.

"No idea how you can drive straight, hon. I can't keep my eyes focused on anything but you."

"I'm a multitasker, remember?" I pant, my head falling back against Ren's chest.

He keeps moving his hands, and I keep enjoying every stroke that takes me higher, closer, until...*God*. I hit the brakes, and the tractor stops moving. I fall limp against Ren's chest, my head dropping to the side. A light breeze washes over me as I ride out my climax, and Ren keeps pumping his fingers in and out. I feel him rock harder beneath me, grunting as if my release is his own.

As my breathing slows, I blink my eyes open slowly. "You really outdid yourself," I tell Ren, feeling the already-deep blush on my cheeks intensifying.

"I feel like you just gave me a new challenge," he says, smirking.

"Nope. You gave me one."

I slide off Ren's lap, leaving him on the tractor seat, hard and desperate. A cool breeze blows across the fields, sending my hair flitting around my face, so I twist it into a knot.

It's silent out here, save for the quiet trill of a few birds. I catch sight of a bluebird house a few rows down with its tiny hole, which is large enough for the kinds of birds that are important to vines and crops but too small for the types of birds that are predators. But none of that holds my focus like Ren and his hard-on. I reach for his hips and encourage him to turn in the seat to face me.

"Zipper down, cowboy." I nod. "I know, I know. You're on a tractor, not a horse. Just indulge me…and I'll indulge you."

"Not one to argue when my beautiful woman orders me to unzip my pants."

Ren obliges immediately. Pants and boxer briefs down around his ankles, he sits ass-naked on the tractor seat and gazes at me. Eyes greedy and wide, I take in Ren's body. My hands follow, gripping his thighs as I stand closer to the tractor, close enough to lean forward and sweep my tongue over the head of his cock.

Perfect height. They should put that on the tractor ads.

It's a good thing we're far away from humanity here in this field because Ren curses and yells my name, not even trying to stifle his reaction to my hands sliding up and down his shaft. "Fuck, Trix."

I nod and take him fully into my mouth. Ren looks down, his eyes glassy as though mesmerized at the sight of my lips around his rock-hard cock. The expression on his face is worshipful, loving. Just…gone. It's the most satisfying thing I've ever felt to please this man in this way. I loved him when we were younger, but each day I spend with him now makes me realize how much better we are today. The three of us.

Ren comes hard. I close my eyes and swallow every bit of what he gives me. It makes any fears I have about our future slip away for the moment, and I allow myself to stay in the present. That is, except for the tiny part of me that can't help thinking about a future.

CHAPTER
Twenty

REN

My luck at poker on the team jet is worse than our performance on the ice a few hours ago. First league game loss, and already fans are posting mean shit. I can't let it get to me. We have more than eighty games ahead, and one matchup tells us nothing about what's to come.

"I call your bluff, both of you," Coach Barrington says, looking at me over his reading glasses. Then he turns to Ludovic and does the same. Even wearing the rectangular granny glasses that highlight the bits of gray at his temples, the man looks formidable. He calculates his chances of winning and then strikes like a viper. It serves us well on the ice, and it's putting me on notice now in our game of Texas Hold 'em.

If he's calling my bluff, it's because he has a good hand. Either that, or he has the best poker face on the planet.

I don't know which it is because he's never joined one of our games before. Normally, he sits at the front of the jet when we travel and confers with the other coaches. He lets the rest of us take each other's money and rolls his eyes at our foolishness.

"Good thing you guys are well paid because you sure waste a lot of money," he always says.

But tonight, he's playing. He lost quickly in the first game, and he hasn't said much this time, but he keeps throwing chips in the pot and raising a little on each hand. It's clear he's played before, even if he's never played with us. Ludovic tends to stay in until the very end, hoping against hope that the last card will give him a victory. It almost never does.

Ludovic looks at Barrington once more before throwing his cards on the table. "I'm out."

Barrington turns to me. "What about you, Ren?"

"I'm in. Bet's to you."

"Call."

"Raise you twenty bucks." I can't tell anything about his game from the fact that he called. It could mean he has cold feet, or he's just messing with me. In either case, it only costs me a twenty to push him a little and see what he does.

He throws in a red chip without expression. I'm starting to regret my part in coaxing him to play. For all I know, he has four aces, and I'm about to get my clock cleaned.

"One more round of betting?" he asks, picking up another red chip. "I raise another twenty."

I throw my red chip into the pot, which is a tidy mound of blue, yellow, and red –over six hundred bucks in there.

"Call," Barrington says.

I fan out my cards. "Straight flush, nine high."

It's a good hand. Maybe even a great hand. But there are still plenty of ways this could go wrong for me. A nine of spades isn't that hard to beat, especially with three spades in the river.

My eyes stay fixed on our coach because I'm dying to understand what goes on inside his head. Slowly, he starts to nod. Then he tosses his cards on the table, facedown. "You got me. Nice work, Renaldi. Next game, I want to see the exact kind of resolve you just showed me here. You do that, we'll turn our season around."

"Yes, sir." I nod as he gets up from the table. I'm less excited about my winnings than I am about what feels like a second chance from our coach. I need it, and I'll take any sign I can get.

We land an hour later, and I don't even consider going back to my place in Berkeley. I haven't slept there in weeks. Trix insisted on watching Truman during this set of away games, and I need to relieve her of dog duty, but that's not why I'm rushing to Napa.

I can't even pretend it's about my dog.

I always used to be at home on the road. Dressing in a suit to meet fans was another sign I'd made something of myself and reached hockey success. More and more, I feel like home is here in Napa, where I can be with Trix and Tru. They're my happy place.

"Hey," I say when I pull up and find her sitting in the rocker on her porch. She looks exhausted, a tired smile on her face, her eyes lacking their usual vitality. Juggling so many projects and working long hours on her feet are kicking her ass. I want to order her to go lie down, delegate more work to other people, and let me rub her shoulders. But I know my stubborn woman, and she would never listen to orders. Doesn't stop me from worrying over her.

Truman is leaping in circles around me, darting this way and that so fast that I can't even pet him.

"Someone's happy to see you." She laughs but doesn't stand up.

"Someone's happy to see *you,*" I say, shuffling up the stairs like a tired soldier. My legs ache after sitting for hours on the plane and driving for another hour. I kiss her lightly on the lips, and my body immediately wants more of her. "I've been thinking about you all day." I kneel in front of her and plant a kiss on each knee, each thigh. Then I push myself higher and drink in her lips. For every knock I took on the ice, she's the balm. "Daydreaming about your lips. Waiting to do this."

She hums against my lips as I kiss her again, delving a little deeper before standing up with a groan. My legs are cooked.

"I'm happy to see you too."

She picks up a big tumbler of water and sips from a straw. She offers me a half smile but doesn't invite me inside. We still sleep at our respective houses—one more reason I need to reel myself back from feeling too much for her. So I stuff my hands in my pockets and look for my dog. Truman is now running in circles around my car, barking and jumping every few feet.

"I swear I walked him. We even went on two hikes," Trix says.

"I believe you. He has a lot of energy to burn. I can run him for an hour, and he'll still be ready for more after he sloshes down a bowl of water."

She nods and looks away. Something's up, and I have no idea what it is. If I was a more intuitive guy, maybe I could read her better, but since I haven't got a clue, my only choice is to ask.

"You okay?"

Her eyes return to me. "What? Oh, sure. Yeah. I'm good."

"Really? Because it seems like there's something you're not saying."

"Damn." She shakes her head.

"What?"

"Guess a girl can't have a feeling around here without Ren the Detective figuring it out. I guess I was thinking…I dunno." She shrugs. I wait, but she doesn't finish the thought.

I hold up both hands. "I wasn't trying to pry. If you say you're good, you're good." I look back at my dog, who lopes up to me with his tongue hanging out of the side of his mouth and his eyes round and glassy like a lunatic. "Come on, buddy. Let's get you home."

Grabbing his leash from where Trix has it hanging over the pale blue painted banister of her porch, I loop it over his head and rein him in. He sits at my feet and looks up at me as if to say, "Okay, you've got me here. What's next?"

"Thanks again for watching him, Trix. I'll take him back to

my place, get him out of your hair." Turning to go, I feel a twinge of sadness in my chest that I fear will take on a life of its own and grow by the time I get home. This subdued reaction from Trix was not the welcome I was hoping for. Not after spending two nights sleeping alone in a hotel room and thinking about her. The sun's rays lighting up her face. The soft feel of her skin under my hand. The way her eyes dance when she's giving me shit.

But maybe I've been letting my heart misread her cues. Sure, we've been having fun and I feel the spark between us, but maybe it's just me. To her, I'm just the baby dad, a way to turn an accident into something positive. I should rein in my feelings and get my head on straight.

Then I feel a hand on my shoulder. "Wait."

Turning, I realize Trix has followed us to the car, and I was so caught up in my thoughts that I didn't hear her feet on the gravel. "Yeah?"

"Can you stay tonight?"

My shoulders drop, and the tension I didn't know I was carrying falls away. "Sure, I can stay. I didn't want to assume."

"Assume." She turns and starts walking back to the house. It's then I realize why I didn't hear her footsteps. She's barefoot, padding slowly on the rough gravel because it probably hurts her feet.

"Hang on."

She stops and looks over her shoulder, yelping as I scoop her into my arms. "I've got you."

"Ren..." she starts to protest, but I pull her in tighter. She weighs nothing compared to the heavy weights I have to lift in training, and it feels good to be useful.

"Let me do this. Can you try to just let me give you a hand?"

She sighs against my chest, and I take that as a yes. "You're infuriating." I take that as a yes as well.

"I told you I want to be here for you, and I didn't just mean I'd be here to write a check for diapers. I meant I'll be here for *you*."

Until I say the words out loud, I don't realize how much I mean them.

Maybe I surprise Trix, too, because she twists in my arms to look at me as I take the steps of her porch two at a time. "You can put me down now. No more gravel," she says as I turn the knob of her front door and walk us into her house like I own the place.

"I could, but what if I don't want to?"

"Ren, please put me down. I don't like feeling useless."

"You're never useless." I place her on the couch and take a seat next to her. Truman winds himself in two circles before dropping to the floor at her feet. From the outside, we probably look the part of the perfect family tableau—young parents-to-be and an eager dog. Just another night of domestic bliss on the couch while the world has its way with everyone else outside.

Only I know better than to believe we're going to be the kind of family I fantasize about with her. Key rule of sports is to never let the appearance of a team get in your head—never assume you know how they'll play the game until you see it unfold on the ice. I need to do that here, too.

"So why'd you invite me in?" I still don't understand her about-face from seeming put out by my mere presence to asking me to stay. Maybe it's a pregnancy hormone thing.

"Because I missed you. I know it's crazy because I saw you two days ago, but it's true. I missed you."

She looks tentative, gauging my reaction. I grab her hand and interlace our fingers, feeling a flood of endorphins race through me, a high so much better than winning a poker game.

"I missed you too." It's the truth, and it feels good to be honest about my feelings. But I stop there. I want to tell her that my heart feels wrung out and empty when I'm away from her. I want her to know how distracted I am by her all the time. I want to tell her I fucking love her.

But I don't say any of these things. I just pull her in tight and inhale the sweet scent of her skin and feel damn lucky she wants me to stay. It feels like the beginning of something good.

Trix leads me through the entryway to the couch, where she likes to curl up in the evenings with Tru at her feet. Before we've even seated ourselves, Truman circles around twice on the rug and settles in for a nap. I sit on the couch and pull Trix into my lap so she sits sideways with her arm around my neck. For just one moment, I inhale the sweet scent of her damp hair and revel in the feel of her body against mine. There's nothing better than this feeling. With Truman at our feet, it really does feel like home.

"Hey, I was thinking..." I nuzzle her ear and plant a row of kisses along her jaw.

"You're always thinking," she laughs, her hand sweeping over my thigh and squeezing.

"True. I'm thinking you should come to a game. Wanna?" My casual tone belies my nerves. It means a lot to me for her to see me play again. I want her to understand why I've made the sacrifices I have over the course of my career. I want her to witness my love for the sport and what I've made of myself on the ice. Maybe I want her to forgive me for leaving.

I reach down for one of her bare feet and start rubbing slow, massaging circle. She lets out a grateful moan.

"Would I get to watch guys get into fights?"

I laugh. "Almost guaranteed. Yes."

"Cool! I'm in." Her head falls back against my shoulder as I press deeper into the arch of her foot. "Mmm, that feels good. My feet are so tired."

"As a side bonus, you'll also see me play."

She tips her head up to look at me. "Oh, Hockey Star. That's not a side bonus. It's the whole paycheck."

Our lips meet, and the loss on the road starts to fade into the distance. I only want to focus on her. On us. Trix takes my face in both hands, and our kiss deepens. It's not the frantic, playful way we've been in the past. This feels slower, intentional, real. And as Trix wriggles from my lap and leads me by the hand toward her bedroom, I have a singular thought—there's no denying it. I love this woman.

CHAPTER
Twenty-One

BEATRIX

I think I'm more nervous than the day we found out that Butter and Rosemary was getting a Michelin star.

"Why am I all jittery? I'm not the one playing," I tell Archer, who gave me little choice but to bring him as my date.

"It's just what happens. I feel it too."

We're sitting at center ice right behind the plexiglass, which means that I have the best view in the house. I feel the chill coming off the ice, hear the constant roar of the spectators getting restless before the players appear. Nachos and pretzel smells mix with a pervasive hoppy smell of beer. The excitement builds all around us as the clock ticks down toward game time, and music starts blasting through the arena, getting fans amped.

I'm in Ren's game jersey, which is huge on me, despite the new roundness of my early baby bump, and as I look around, I see lots of other fans with Renaldi jerseys. I feel a mixture of pride in Ren's career and nervousness over the impending matchup against Calgary.

It's just as well that it's my grouchy older brother by my side because he views this outing as just another sporting event, albeit one where we have seats near center ice, right on the glass. He wouldn't understand the first date feeling rumbling in my chest, nervous that something will happen tonight and change the course of my life. It's ridiculous because Ren has already changed my entire trajectory. Watching him play is like a dab of icing on top. Barely noticeable.

"Plus, you're about to see your boyfriend in a whole new light. In a sport where everyone's a badass, he's among the select few that will be remembered for it. If you weren't in love with him already, you will be after tonight."

Oh. Okay.

So, watching the game with my brother won't just be a normal sporting event. We're going to do this sibling bonding thing—here at the game, which is about to start in ten minutes. I could feign a bathroom emergency and eat up those ten minutes easily, but if the past few months have taught me anything, it's that I need to lean into uncomfortable situations.

"Those are some lofty pronouncements. You sure you're not a little bit in love with Ren yourself?" I ask.

"More than a little bit," he says in all seriousness. "It's a guy sports thing, a bromance."

"Does it count as a bromance if he doesn't love you back?" I tease.

Archer's forehead creases while he considers the question. "I think he'd love me if he got to know me."

"I'm sure." I'm happy to talk about my brother's hockey crush all day long if it keeps him out of my business, and the change of topic seems to be accomplishing that nicely. I reach for the bottled water in the cupholder and unscrew the cap. The announcer calls out the names of the Calgary players as they skate onto the ice. There's some polite applause and a lot of booing.

"Nice sportsmanship," I mutter.

"You ain't seen nothing yet, sister. It's gonna get brutal."

The fury of the crowd rises in volume as Calgary's star

forward skates onto the ice, followed by the goalie. I can't make out the various catcalls amid the booing, but the arena is vibrating.

Then, the Otters take the ice. At first, I can't tell the players apart with all the padding and loose shirts. I look at the numbers and spot Ren as he skates around the ice like he owns the place. Hot enough to melt the ice right off the floor.

Ren has barely touched the puck, and I can tell my brother is right. There's no way I'll make it through an entire game with him looking like that and not fall a little bit in love. I know just how muscular he is under that jersey, yet he skates with effortless grace and passes the puck back and forth with his teammates as they warm up.

Then they start to play.

Ren is like a bull on the ice, skating fast and slapping the puck so hard, and I react like it's his hand on my ass. I swear, if my brother wasn't sitting next to me—not to mention an arena full of fans—I'd be touching myself right here up against the glass. I blame the pregnancy hormones a tad, but mostly it's Ren.

By the end of the first period, the Otters are up by one. The team seems to have settled into a rhythm, and I have my hands squeezed together in a fist. "Just gotta get through two more periods for a win," I shout at no one.

Archer answers dryly, "Thanks for the recap."

"Quiet, or I won't invite you back."

He leans back in his seat and sips his beer innocently. "So, has it happened yet?" he asks.

"Has what happened?"

"Falling in love." He points to the ice, where Ren starts yelling when a Calgary forward knocks down one of the Otters' defenders. The referee says something to him, and he gets in his face, pointing and gesturing. The fans around us start yelling, too, loving Ren's bravado and cheering even louder. "Your man. He fucking owns the place."

My gaze hasn't left Ren, who skates away and gets back into

the game. Calgary takes a shot, but the Otters goalie deflects it. They try twice more, and my heart starts pounding. "Get 'em out of there!" I yell, feeling the pressure on the goalie and the inevitability of the puck getting past him after that many shots.

Finally, Ren gets the puck and races past the Calgary defense, lines up a shot, and scores a second goal.

With a two-point lead, the fans go nuts. The blare of the air horn fills the arena, and everyone is on their feet, shouting and applauding. Ren's teammates fist-bump him, and he skates in a circle, basking in the glory of a perfect shot. He skates right past the glass where Archer and I sit and hits me with his cocky smile, a little salute, and a wink, like that goal was a little hockey demonstration just for me.

"Hope you don't mind if the entire world knows about you two." Archer nudges me with an elbow.

"Why do you say that?"

He points, and I see my face on the jumbotron for a second before it switches back to where Ren skates back to take his position. It didn't occur to me that the cameras would follow Ren after his goal and zoom in on the person he was saluting. "That little display had *girlfriend* written all over it. If he hasn't said anything to the press already, there are going to be questions."

And that's when I feel it—I'm falling hard for the guy. Archer is right. If it's not love, it's sure headed in that direction. It's not the foolish, reckless dive bomb into love that I experienced at twenty. This is a slow, delicious slide into something deep, unpredictable, and solid. It's love for the same man, but it's somehow deeper and more substantial this time around, and it has nothing to do with us having a baby. I have the overwhelming sense that I do want to be his girlfriend. Or maybe something more permanent. I know it may come back to bite me in the ass, but right now, it's what I want.

"Be interested to see how he answers them," I say.

Archer laughs, a surprising sound coming from a guy who's more tightly wound than me. He's the hardest working sibling in the family, and I often feel bad that the entire burden of running Buttercup Hill has fallen on him. He never asked for it. Never said he wanted to be a winemaker. But when the need arose, he stepped up for our dad and the rest of us.

His grumpy attitude is a lot to deal with, but I have to remind myself that he and I aren't so different. We both put work first and look around at what's left over for ourselves once the obligations are satisfied. Of anyone, I know how hard he has it.

I don't realize I've been staring at him until he raises his brows. "What?"

"Thanks for coming with me here tonight. And not being too annoyed that I don't know squat about hockey."

"How did you date the guy for a year in college and not learn about hockey?"

"I wasn't dating him for the hockey knowledge," I deadpan.

"But you went to games, right?"

"Yeah, but I didn't pay that much attention to the game. I just watched my hot hockey boyfriend and cheered when other people did."

"Well, I guess you can do the same thing here. Thanks for inviting me." He gives me a partial smile, which, from Archer, is like finding a gold nugget in a muddy river. He gestures to the ice with a nod of his head. "You know enough. And whatever you don't know, I bet that guy'd be happy to teach you."

Ren is right when he promised I'd see a fight. I just didn't expect him to be the one in the penalty box after the ref missed a call. The entire arena sees it when the defender trips him and sends him skidding across the ice, right into the stick of a Calgary player. The crowd goes nuts, yelling and booing, and Ren wastes no time skating up to the guy, getting right in his face, and yelling. That's when the defender loses his shit and gives Ren a shove.

I don't blame Ren one bit for getting riled at the guy and

pushing him back. Three other teammates join the scrum, but it's mostly yelling and a little bit of shoving for show. "Why aren't the referees doing anything?" My high-pitched voice sounds as scared as I feel.

"It's part of the sport. They're giving fans what they want." The fight fuels the fans like nothing I've ever seen. For a second, I get a little nervous. It feels like the place is rocking off its foundation. "Fans don't fight with each other, do they?" I ask Archer.

He puts an arm around me and pulls me close. "I've got ya. No one's messing with you *or* my future niece or nephew."

The referees let the melee go on for a few seconds longer before pushing the players apart. They throw Ren and the defender into their respective penalty boxes.

"Your boy just earned the respect of everyone in here for keeping his cool after the ref missed that call. He's gonna have a swollen jaw later on. Be nice to him." Archer has never taken the slightest interest in anyone I've dated, not that there have been many, but still. He's legitimately on Team Ren, and I'm here for it. I vow to take Archer to every home game I can because this is the best time I've ever had with him.

"Got it. Be nice to Ren." I say the words robotically, as if there's any question.

The final buzzer ends the game with a win for the Otters, and the crowd erupts once more in raucous cheers and applause. The players take it all in, and Ren does a lap around the ice, slowing down near the glass in front of us to blow me a kiss. I feel my face turn crimson as the camera following Ren lands on me. I bend down like I've dropped something important. "They're gone. You're safe now," Archer laughs. Finally, the team skates off the ice, and Archer and I head down to the clubhouse, where Ren said to meet him.

He shows up an hour later in a navy suit that fits him like a glove. His broad shoulders pull at the fabric of the coat, which tapers to his slim waist. The top two buttons of his white shirt are unbuttoned, showing off the contour of his pecs and a hint at the smooth skin that lies beneath the fabric. All I can think is that I'd like to tear every stitch of it from his body.

Seriously, hormones, I hear you loud and clear!

Even Archer seems to know how hot I am for Ren because he pets my head like a puppy. "Down, girl. You're panting."

"Am not."

"Right. Guess it was me." He actually looks nervous as the Otters file in one by one and find their people in various corners. They swipe beers off a tray near the door and spend a few minutes more shaking hands with various VIPs in the room—friends of the owner or investors, according to Archer.

"I had no idea you were such a hockey fanboy. When did this happen?"

"I like sports in general, you know that."

"Yeah, but this is next level." I wave to Ren, who's coming our way from across the room.

Archer shrugs. "We all have our things."

"Ha. I'd say you have more than one." I'm thinking of his type A personality and his obsession with running, to name two. But I'm liking this side of my brother. Seeing him relaxed and enjoying the scene gives me a window into what Ren must see when I let my guard down and mess around with him.

Ren kisses me hard and wraps me in his arms. He doesn't seem to care a bit about my brother sitting two feet away or the peering eyes in the room. He hums as he backs away from my lips. "Best part of my day." He keeps me in a tight grip and turns to Archer, who extends his hand to shake.

Ren wraps him in a bear hug, and the tips of my brother's ears go a healthy shade of pink. "Thanks for coming, man."

"Great game. You killed it."

"Ha. Almost got killed, but that's part of the fun." Ren sits on a stool at our table, and I get a good look at him for the first time. He rubs at a spot half-hidden by the stubble on his chin, and I notice how swollen it is.

"You took a good one," Archer says, proudly holding up his beer in a toast.

"Looks painful. Are you okay?" I ask, gently touching the spot. Ren takes my hand and moves it to his lips, kissing it.

I laugh as Archer grimaces. "Get used to it. I'm stuck on this one, so you're stuck with me." He says it so casually, so full of the usual Renaldi charm that I allow myself to believe Ren wants to be with me for the long haul. And the longer I sit here, watching his easy banter with my brother and thinking about him spending time with the rest of my family, the more I realize I want that too.

CHAPTER *Twenty-Two*

BEATRIX

You know those things you swore you'd never do again?

Spending time with Ren's mom is one of those things. The woman didn't like me back in college, and I can't imagine things have changed much. She always worried I was a distraction for Ren, threatening his career. If I'm a distraction, I can't imagine what she'll think about a baby. Guess I'll find out.

Ren's mom is visiting for Thanksgiving weekend, so we're meeting her for lunch in St. Helena. Seems harmless enough. But I've directed the long way around Napa, circling through Calistoga and coming down the other side. It's at least fifteen minutes out of the way.

My excuse is that I want to take some photos of a farmstand produce place in Calistoga, but when we get there, Ren calls my bluff. "This is just a normal fruit stand, like about a hundred other ones. Why'd we need to come here?"

I mumble a fake answer he won't hear as I hop out of the car and make a beeline to the persimmon display. They're the most photogenic thing here, amid onions and blue kale. Still, I keep up appearances and shutterbug my way slowly from one end of the produce stand to the other. When Ren comes up behind me, I pretend to examine a purple onion like it's a rare amethyst stone inside a giant geode. "So pretty, right?" I ask, unable to look Ren in the eye.

I feel a hand on my shoulder, and Ren spins me around like I'm a hockey puck on slippery ice.

"You're stalling. I know you don't need pictures of purple onions." He looks around at the sagging roof and the fading signage haphazardly placed near the wrong boxes of produce. "This place is a dump. Even I have enough of an aesthetic eye to know that."

I let out a frustrated exhale. "I was hoping to find a dog treat for Truman. I'll be sure to tell him you said to stop."

"Something tells me he'll be just fine after Fiona spoils him all afternoon."

"Fine." I stomp back to the car, and he follows.

Safely ensconced in the passenger seat, I'm tempted to lock the doors so he can't get in and drive us the rest of the way to lunch. But I don't, if only because he's holding the car keys in his hand.

When he gets in the car, he picks up my hand and kisses it. I snatch it away and fold my arms.

"Wow, you are really worked up. Is this something that happens whenever you eat a real lunch, or is it just reserved for my mom?"

That earns him a glare. "You're hilarious." I push the window button, but he hasn't turned on the ignition, so nothing happens. "Can you please let some air in here? It's hot as hades."

He obliges, and I roll my window all the way down and stick my head out like a dog on a joyride.

"Why do you think she hates you? Are you just saying that so the reality will be better than what you're expecting?"

"Oh, you poor, misguided soul. No, I'm saying it because the woman hates me. Were you not there on the phone call I just heard?"

Ren grimaces, unable to deny the truth. He made the mistake of answering a call from his mother on speakerphone in the car just now, and she said some very not nice things about me. "I don't like seeing you tied down, is all I'm saying." Those were her parting words to her son. With me sitting right there.

"She says that about any woman she thinks I'm dating. If she opens a *People* magazine at the market and sees me in the same room as a woman, I get a text and a call and a letter from a carrier pigeon telling me not to get trapped. It's not about you."

"Does she really want you to be sad and alone your whole life with only a hockey stick to snuggle with on the bad days?"

"Of course not. But you have to understand—growing up, it was just the two of us. She wants me to succeed and live my dream. Shed worked hard for me to be able to afford everything to pursue hockey. She's just protective."

"No, *my* family is protective. Your mom is a human gargoyle, sitting on the roof, ready to scare off all prospective girlfriends. And I'm the worst of them all because I've trapped you for life with this baby. Wait until she hears about that." I sound breathless, which makes me sound hysterical. The bigger my belly gets, the more the baby pushes on my lungs, and the more out of breath I get doing normal things like walking to the mailbox and now, apparently, talking.

"This is good," Ren says, unable to prevent a smile from taking over, which makes me unable to stop looking at him.

"Why?"

"Get it all out now. Tell me all the ways you expect this to be horrible and get a good image fixed in your head. That way, when you actually meet my mom again, you'll be pleasantly surprised because it can't possibly be as bad as what you're imagining."

"It can," I say in a huff, not liking that he's making light of my distress.

"It won't."

"It will."

"Impossible. No one could hate the woman I love. I promise."

All the breath leaves me in a whoosh that sounds like an impending windstorm. I turn fully in my seat to face Ren. "What did you just say?"

I wait for him to realize his misstep and backtrack. I'm giving him a chance to take it back and tell me he just meant that he likes me an awful lot. But he doesn't. Instead, he levels me with a serious expression, his eyes lock on mine, and he nods. Then, slowly, a smile creeps across his face as though he can't hold it back any longer. He takes my hand and holds it to his heart.

"I love you, Beatrix Corbett. I want to be very clear, so there's no way to misinterpret my words. I. Love. You."

My jaw drops open, but I think I've stopped breathing. The air in the car goes utterly still and silent. Except for the pounding thrush of blood in my ears—that won't go away. He loves me? "You love me?" I say finally, allowing the Tetris blocks to drop into place in my head. Slowly, ever so slowly, so as not to leave gaps or misplace anything.

"I fucking love you."

"Oh my gosh, Ren. I love you too. So much, but...but..." I smack his shoulder. "Why the heck didn't you tell me that sooner?"

In classic Ren fashion, he seems baffled by my insistence on details. "Because it's the most obvious truth there is. So I kinda thought you knew."

The most obvious truth there is...

I keep quiet for the rest of the ride, digesting this new information. It's reassuring, familiar, complicated. Because I have an obvious truth, too—I can no longer protect my heart from Dominick Renaldi. I gave it a valiant effort, but now it's too late. I love him.

For the second time in my life.

CHAPTER
Twenty-Three

REN

"Dominick! Over here!"

The shrill voice cuts through the air in a restaurant with its stone floors and industrial beams for a ceiling. In other words, the place is loud, but my mother is louder.

I follow the source of the voice, my eyes landing on a dyed eggplant shade of hair that I've never seen before. Interlacing Trix's fingers with mine, I guide her through the Cheesecake Factory, noticing enormous salads, full-sized pizzas, and whole broiled chickens on the plates of the people in the room. Of course my mother chose this place. The menu is a fourteen-page book with every imaginable dish, but she plays this game where she can't decide on one thing, so she orders two. Then she realizes she's less hungry than she thought and has the waiter wrap everything up for the next two nights of dinner.

I've called her on it plenty of times and even offered to arrange a dinner delivery service for her because she hates to cook, but she won't hear of it. She has her ways about certain things.

Trix isn't wrong in her assessment of my mom, but she doesn't need to worry. I won't let anyone disparage Trix or make her feel like she's in the wrong, least of all my own mother. But I'm still hoping the meal will go off without any drama.

I wave as we squeeze between two tables for eight to reach my mother's outstretched arms. Trix's grip on my hand borders on painful. My mother has already ordered her typical iced tea mixed with lemonade, but she hasn't touched it, which means she'll be sending it back.

Mom pushes her chair back and stands, absently stroking the top of her hair, which is shoulder length and wavy. The color matches her lipstick, her only bit of makeup, which makes her look more innocent than she is. There's always an agenda, usually getting me to visit more often, even though she knows my schedule is nuts during hockey season.

"Hello, hello," my mother says, reaching for me. I go in for a hug, and my mother pats me on the back and kisses the air next to my cheek. She never used to do that, but she's been watching reruns of *Dynasty,* and now, it's her standard greeting.

"And Beatrix, it's been a long time. How are you doing?"

"I'm doing well. It's so nice to see you, Mrs. Renaldi."

"Please, it's Ellen." My mother smiles at Trix like she hung the sun and the moon. Maybe this will all be fine. My mom takes her seat, and I pull out a chair from Trix. "So, tell me everything. The team needs its chemistry, I can see that, but what else? Fill me in!"

I don't want to bury the lead item for our visit, so I just blurt it out. "Trix and I are having a baby together."

The din of restaurant chatter and silverware against dishes continues, and I'm grateful for the noise because our table has gone silent. Trix looks from me to my mother, who sits with a blank expression like she can't have heard me correctly. She blinks slowly as a smile spreads across her face. Then she turns to Trix and looks from her face to her belly. "Is this true?"

Trix nods. "Yes. I'm just starting my second trimester."

My mother makes jazz hands and stands up, coming around the table to hug me from behind. She does the same to Trix before fanning herself and sitting back down. "This was not what I was expecting. But I'm thrilled! Dominick, why did you keep this from me?"

"We wanted to tell you in person." It's not the entire truth. In part, I was avoiding telling my mom because I knew she'd have opinions. I just had no idea what they'd be.

"Well, glory be. I'm just tickled about your little bundle of joy." My mom stirs her iced tea for longer than she needs to mix in some sugar.

Trix and I exchange glances, each of us letting out a sigh of relief. I guess that's the magic a grandchild can bring. Based on my schedule, my commitment to hockey, and my refusal to date anyone seriously, my mother didn't have high hopes for grandkids any time soon.

I look at Trix as if that's evidence she has nothing to worry about, but the fear still creases her brow.

We take our places at the table, and I look from my mother to Trix and try to imagine what's going through their heads. Curiosity? Competition? Détente?

My mother takes a tiny sip of her drink and pushes it to the edge of the table. "Too sweet," she says, looking around for our waiter, even though she's the one who just added a packet of sugar. She'll now go through the ritual of having the waiter spill some of her drink out and add more iced tea until it reaches the right balance of flavor.

I think I did a good job of convincing Trix that lunch would be okay, but my insides are knotted like a pretzel. Trix isn't wrong about my mother disliking her, but it was always more about my career than about her. My mom saw early on that hockey was my gold ticket to a good life, and she steamrolled anything or anyone that could get in the way. There were so many parties I missed during high school when I had training the next day. Proms I missed because she wouldn't let me go. College graduation I skipped for a signing event in Canada.

Looking back, the sacrifices were worth it because they got me to where I am today. No one can argue with the trajectory of my career, and it's hard to regret missing a high school party all these years later.

I only have one regret—losing Trix. I can't blame my mother entirely, though she encouraged me to break things off. "You need to eliminate distractions, or you won't make it in the pros," she said back then. Trix was my biggest distraction, albeit a welcome one. But I had to let her go—not just for my future, but for hers. It was the right thing to do.

Our waiter brings my mother an entirely new drink, and she seems content. "This is good. Do you kids know what you want?"

"We haven't looked yet." I hand Trix a menu and scoot my chair closer to hers so we can look at it together. We each choose a salad, and my mom orders a pastrami sandwich with mustard and a side of potstickers.

There's a lot of small talk about the team and its prospects, and I try to downplay the stress I'm under as captain. "It'll take work, but we have what we need to win games. We'll get there."

"I hope so. The last game went well, but those earlier ones…" my mom says, looking to Trix for confirmation.

"Eyes on the future," she says as the server brings our food. My mom asks for a to-go box before she even takes a bite.

Pushing her drink away, Mom leans toward Trix, her tone conspiratorial. "Well. I'd just like to propose a toast to you two and my future grandchild." She looks around the table as if three champagne flutes will have appeared from nowhere and settles for raising her iced tea glass. Trix and I each pick up our water glasses.

My stomach lurches because I'm not sure what she's planning to say, and with my mother, it could be almost anything.

"It's sweet that you two found your way back to each other again. Honestly, with the way this one used to talk, I never thought I'd be a grandma. So thank you, dear, for roping him in."

"That's hardly how it went. I feel like I'm the lucky one here,"

I say, putting my arm around Trix and hoping my mom will chill the hell out.

"Of course you do, sweetie. You always see the best in every situation." She turns to Trix before either of us can unpack her statement. "Do you have any cravings? I always wanted ice cream."

Trix smiles. "Me too. I think the baby's going to come out asking for a chocolate sundae."

"Or asking for a hockey stick," my mom adds. "Wouldn't be the worst thing. Sports are so good for children. It taught Dominick about perseverance and commitment, not that I need to tell you that. After all, here we are, and he's doing what's right."

Her subtext has my stomach lurching and my heart thudding like I've spent an hour on the ice. Protectively, my hand shoots to Trix's knee, which I rub reassuringly.

"I'm doing what makes me happy," I clarify, more for Trix than for my mother. Maybe what my mom said didn't strike Trix as badly as it sounded to me. But I feel the way her leg tenses up.

"I do appreciate his commitment." Trix smiles sweetly at my mother and forks a piece of lettuce. "I appreciate all the facets of him, especially how hard he's trying to find balance."

"Balance?" My mother scrunches her face up as though she doesn't recognize the concept.

"Yes." Trix takes a bite of her salad and looks at my mom innocently. It's like a duel between masters, and my vocal cords feel suddenly frozen.

"You mean back in the summer, before the preseason games?" Mom clarifies.

Trix shakes her head. "Even now. We see each other between games. It hasn't been an issue."

I know Trix thinks she's telling my mom what she wants to hear—that I'll be a good, devoted father because my entire life isn't hockey. But I feel my blood drain at my mother's disapproving scowl.

I feel a muscle in my jaw start to tick. I'm about to say something, but Trix grabs my hand under the table, and her eyes dart to mine, letting me know she's got this. We're fine.

"You okay?" she whispers, looking from my mom to me with wide eyes.

I simply nod, trying to think of a way to divert this conversation. My mother will always worry about me. She'll think fatherhood is too much for me to juggle, and she'll fear that I'm sabotaging my livelihood.

"Dominick, are you having this girl drive back and forth to Berkeley several days a week? That's not going to be able to continue in her condition, you know," she scolds.

"No, Mom. I've been spending time in Napa."

My mother visibly flinches. She picks up her iced tea and takes a sip. She doesn't need to say more. The implication is clear—I'm right back where I was ten years ago, a love-struck fool who's jeopardizing his hockey future over a girl.

"I see," my mom says, finally. "But what about the team? You have a big responsibility as captain, and you told me the team needs a lot from you."

"They do, and I'm giving it to them. I'm handling it all." It's not entirely true, and I feel a pang of guilt over the team's lack of focus and Barrington's misplaced faith in me, but I won't lose this woman to hockey a second time. "Have some faith in me, Mom. I'm happy. I intend to be a good dad. And I'm in love with an amazing woman. I'm handling it all, and I'll continue to handle it all. Nothing is falling between the cracks with the team." I sit back in my chair and inhale a slow breath to calm my nerves.

My mom's face is a stern mask, one I know well. She worries about me. But I'm not twenty-two, and I don't need her to sabotage my happiness. I'm about to become a dad. Why can't she just let me have this?

"I understand your worry, Mrs. Renaldi. Ellen," Trix inserts, clearly not wanting me to implode my relationship with my mom. "We both know Ren's a standup guy. He won't let the team down."

Trix shifts in her chair so I can't see her eyes, and she holds up her water glass for a toast.

"What are we toasting to?"

She clears her throat, and her voice comes out strong and unwavering. "To being a standup guy."

"That he is." My mother holds up her iced tea. "Cheers."

Trix puts down her water glass and picks up her fork. I try again to catch her eye, but she stays focused on her meal. My mom doesn't notice anything, but I can tell something's bothering Trix.

"*You* okay?" I whisper when my mom signals for the waiter to bring dessert menus.

She puts her hand on mine under the table and tilts her head to rest it on my shoulder. It's not an answer, but it gets me through the rest of our lunch.

CHAPTER
Twenty-Four

REN

"What *was* that?" Trix asks as soon as my mother is out of earshot.

"I know, I'm sorry. She can be a bit much." I scrub a hand over my face and try to explain why she's so protective of me. "I'm her only son, and it's just been the two of us since I was six years old."

Trix steers us past my car and down the block. I don't ask her why because I assume she just feels like walking while we talk, but the reason becomes clear a second later when we're standing outside an ice cream store.

"Did you two have some sort of pact that you'd never be a father? What did she mean when she said you used to say that?"

"Because I always told her I didn't plan to have kids." I hold up a hand before Trix can freak out. "But that was then. I didn't know what I was talking about. I just knew I had a shitty father, and I didn't want to be like him. Saying that to her was me being a dick, taking out my frustrations. It has nothing to do with our situation."

"Sure, because you're a committed guy. Of course you'll follow through, but that doesn't mean this is what you want."

She pulls open the door to the ice cream place and waits for me to follow her in, but I don't. She lets the door swing shut and rejoins me on the sidewalk. "No ice cream for you?"

"Trix." I grab both of her hands and pull her close enough that our chests are nearly touching, our hands sandwiched between us. Her pale blue eyes hit me like lakes I want to wade into and never leave. "*This.* This is what I want. I'll say it every hour of every day until you believe me. I want this baby with you. I really, really do."

Her eyes soften and go a little glassy. "Me too."

Reaching for my hand, she interlaces our fingers. I take the opportunity to guide her into the ice cream store, where we each order a double cone. She chooses two different types of chocolate, and I opt for mocha fudge. Trix smiles as she takes the first lick. "I swear, when people say pregnant women are eating for two, they've never met me. I think I'm eating for six."

"Maybe you'll give birth to a hockey team."

"Heaven forbid."

I make a mock-offended gasp.

"Look, I love me a hockey player—you know that. There's nothing like you and your muscles, Dominick Renaldi, and I like what goes on in that brain of yours, too. But six babies, you've gotta be kidding."

We leave the ice cream store and walk back toward the Cheesecake Factory parking lot.

"Ren, please tell me about stuff. I want to know you better, and I can't do that if you don't let me in."

She makes it sound so easy. Let her in.

I'm ten years older than I was when I left her behind instead of letting her in. I bought my place in Napa with the idea of finding her again. Planning to let her in. Hoping I could do it without it derailing me.

And now I'm not sure how to do it. One more downside to not having a male role model to teach me to be a man. But maybe it's time to stop blaming my absent father for things I don't know how to do. Maybe it's just time to learn.

"Talk to me, Hockey Star. Tell me what challenges you're worried about handling. We're a team, right? Isn't that what we agreed on?"

She's right. The mere mention of the word *team* knocks the resistance loose. She and I, we're a team, as much as the Otters are. My mind edges open, and I feel the stuck words start to flow.

"I know I said I want balance, but I'm not a multitasker. I do one thing and I do it well. What happens if I'm a shitty dad? Where does that leave you and the baby?"

It's so many thoughts at once that I'm not sure she'll be able to parse through them. I'm not sure I can. But that's the thing about Trix that drew me to her all those years ago. She sees me more clearly than I see myself.

She holds out her hand, palm up, open and ready for me. Her soft skin feels electric and reassuring at the same time. The connection grounds me.

"Okay?"

"Yeah. Better."

"Good. Now, relax. You're going to be an awesome dad."

I shake my head. It's not that simple. "I don't have any idea how to do that."

"You're underestimating yourself. You've taken such good care of me over the past few months. You've taken care of your mom. You may not be able to see that it's in you, but I see it. And remember something. You're not alone in this. That's the beauty. Realize that, and you'll succeed."

I'm not ready to give up the gauntlet on this. There's too much self doubt for me to accept her words.

"Fine, then, maybe that's the one thing I'll be awesome at. I'll focus on that because of course I want to be a good dad. But what if I ignore you or hockey in the process? Where does that leave my career? I've worked my entire life to get where I am, and I'm supposed to just half-ass it now?" We reach my car, and I lean against the door.

Putting a hand on my shoulder, she steps closer to me. Then closer. Then she wraps her arms around my neck, and I pull her in tight.

"You're not going to do that either. You're going to learn to do more than one thing at a time really well. You're already doing it. You're spending time with me, and hockey hasn't suffered. I have full faith in you, Ren."

She says it like it's not even a discussion. But she doesn't understand. The team is suffering. I haven't been able to fix our chemistry, and if I wasn't distracted by Trix and her pregnancy, maybe I'd have turned things around by now.

The worst part is that I want to be with her more than I want to think about the next pep talk or individual meetings with my teammates. Here, with her in my arms, it doesn't feel like a problem. So I allow myself to push off the worries. For now.

CHAPTER
Twenty-Five

BEATRIX

"Knock, knock." The sing-song voice could only belong to one person.

"PJ, since when do you ever knock?" My sister has always been a little pushy, probably a necessary survival skill as the youngest of five kids. And given that my office door is open, her formality is silly.

Julie appears next to her, holding an armful of flowers. "Since she highjacked your afternoon meeting with the landscape architect to talk about wedding flowers."

I start to panic. "What do you mean? What happened to Perry? We had an appointment." Protectively, I pull my desk planner closer.

"Relax. I moved the meeting to Thursday, so you can go home early today," Julie says. "You need to get off your feet so they don't swell. I know you want to fit into those cute booties tomorrow when you meet the couples who are considering the inn for their weddings next year."

"Oh my gosh, that's so smart," I say, turning away because I feel tears spring from my eyes, and I will not weep in front of PJ. Julie's seen my waterworks daily this week—at nearly four months pregnant, my hormones run my life and my bump is starting to show—but my sister still thinks I'm a little bit sane, and I don't want to spoil the image.

PJ doesn't seem to notice, too busy inspecting the flowers in Julie's arms. Different sizes, colors, shapes, and holy hell, the smells. I almost gag at the overly floral medley. "I need help. Do any of these go together?" With her wide eyes, PJ looks like a little lost deer.

Julie lays the blooms on the wooden table and starts separating them by color. "For your bouquet?" I ask.

"Yes. And the décor around the altar. I really like the pinks and oranges."

I'm about to tell her I don't like the pinks and oranges, but Julie elbows me, anticipating my lack of filter. "Sure. We can put something together with these. Do you like the pale green leaves mixed in?" I pull a few more blooms and leaves to show her a sample arrangement. "This could be really pretty with deep gray linens and even some tiny lights on the altar."

She nods and drops to the couch with the flowers in her lap, making me realize they're not the primary reason for her visit. "Peej, what's up?"

"I just wondered… How'd lunch go with Ren's mom?"

"Good." Maybe I answer too quickly because she raises an eyebrow.

"Are we lying?" She blinks at me in the patient way she did when we were kids and she wanted me to choose a board game for us to play.

"No."

Julie huffs a laugh, and I glare at her. She rolls her eyes. "I'm just loving that you think you can fool the people who know you best."

"Okay, you two. Stop ganging up on me. The lunch was fine. She's a piece of work, but I already knew that. It was…fine."

"I'll be out here with the flowers when you're ready to tell me I'm right, and details are welcome," Julie sings, walking out the door and closing it behind her.

I look at my sister, grimly gripping her flowers. "What are you worried about?"

She shrugs. "Meeting the mom is always kind of a thing. I wanted to check on you."

Her concern makes those tears threaten again. I've stopped feeling resentful when my emotions take over because I'm learning that pregnancy—and parenthood, I expect—is about relinquishing some control. Even though it doesn't come easily, I know I can't fight it. "I'm okay, thanks. I'm just in my head a lot, thinking about Ren, where life with him is leading."

PJ plays with one of the leafy branches, arranging the leaves in her lap. "Yeah. I'm sure."

"What's that supposed to mean?" I'm more curious than defensive.

"This is Ren. I just remember how much he hurt you back then," she says.

I start to tell her she doesn't know what she's talking about, but I can't.

"You remember that?" I meet PJ's patient gaze with one that hopefully hides my concerns.

"Yeah."

PJ and I are four years apart, which would have made her sixteen when Ren and I broke up. When I was sixteen, I was at the height of self-centered high school angst. And maybe I stayed that way into college because I barely remember what PJ was doing back then. For me, it was all about moving forward, dating my hunky hockey player boyfriend. And once he dumped me, it was all about the future.

"How?"

She explains. "The younger ones always know what the older ones are doing. I idolized you, Trix. Don't you remember how I used to dress just like you? You couldn't stand it."

As soon as she says it, the memories flood back. I came home for one winter break wearing one of Ren's hockey jerseys over skinny jeans and navy blue Chucks. The next time I came back to Buttercup Hill, PJ had practically transformed her wardrobe into hockey jerseys she bought at a thrift shop, and she made a point of showing me her blue Chucks. Back then, I did not see imitation as flattery and told her to get a life.

She didn't. She copied my miniskirts and vintage riding boots, my puffed-sleeved shirts, and my vintage tees with Sesame Street characters. I finally gave up and would just leave whatever clothes I wore home in her closet before I went back to school.

"I'm sorry I was such a bitch," I tell her. "How do you even still stand being in the same family as me?'

"Seriously? Copying you made me the coolest kid in school. You had style, Trix. It may have annoyed you, but I didn't care. It was like having my own personal stylist."

The thought had never occurred to me. "You mean, you didn't hate me for being so awful to you?"

"You weren't awful to me. You were a normal older sister, and I idolized you despite your crabby moods." She laughs. "And I'm pretty sure I did you one better on moodiness. Just ask Dad."

As soon as she says it, she claps a hand over her mouth. "Oh. Crap."

"I knew what you meant. And I wish we could ask him too."

We sit quietly for a minute, and my mind drifts to what it used to be like when I could ask my dad things. It feels like it's been years, mainly because he was always so consumed with work, even after our mom divorced him and moved away. I hated that they split up, but I was old enough to understand why. And secretly, I hoped that when it was just our dad left and the five of us, he'd feel a greater parental urge. Instead, he doubled down and worked even harder. Rather than becoming a more involved parent, he hired an extra nanny to shuttle us around and do whatever he assumed our mom used to do for us.

Needless to say, it was hardly the same thing.

Now we see our mom about once a year when she's not traveling. Not the kind of mother I'll ever be. I may not know much about motherhood, but I know that.

PJ is quiet also, seemingly lost in thought. I wonder how different her memories of those days are. She was just a kid when our mom left, and of all of us, she was our dad's favorite. He spoiled PJ because she was little and cute. And loud. No one could ignore that kid.

"You probably miss him even more than me because you had more real time with him," I say, thinking about the years when PJ was the last kid in the house.

She shakes her head. "I didn't really have time with him. He was all about work."

I've heard people describe our dad that way for years, and it always seemed like a *him* problem. "Workaholic." "Works so much he doesn't see his kids." "Forgets to live life because he's all about work." People in town were never very quiet about their opinions, and even though I defended our dad when I could, I knew his reputation was well earned.

But now, for the first time, I hear those descriptions as though people are saying them about me.

"Do I seem like him?" I ask.

I don't know what I'm expecting. PJ is my sister, but she has her own life, and I don't imagine she spends a lot of time thinking about my work habits. I guess I think she'll tell me what I want to hear, that we're similar in the important ways but I'm not a workaholic.

"Yeah. In terms of work, yeah."

"Oh."

I feel the air slip out of my lungs like a long, slow balloon deflating into an empty shell.

A rueful smile spreads across her face, and she tries to cover it by taking a sip of wine. "Sorry. I thought you knew."

"I mean, I did, sort of. But I kinda hoped I was wrong. Am I really that bad?"

The smile morphs into a frown and PJ smooths my hair.

"Oh my God, you're smoothing my hair! It's so much worse than I thought! I'm an emotionless workaholic like Dad used to be."

A bark of laughter explodes from her.

"No, I didn't mean it like that. But you have the same drive as him, and look, it led him to do great things. He made Buttercup Hill into a legendary business. When you talk about your vision for the inn and the restaurants, you have the same passion he used to have. That's what I meant. But you know where to draw the line. Especially lately. Since you've been with Ren, I see a difference."

"Yeah? How?" I feel like a groundhog, gingerly creeping out of my hole and hoping to see my shadow.

"You're…a little mellower. It's a nice vibe. I guess that's why I'm worried for you. I like this new you." I nod, touched that she came in here on the pretext of flowers to check on me. "Okay, yeah. Since you asked, I guess I'm a little worried I trapped him into all of this. I mean, he's a good guy. A standup guy. I think he wants to believe he loves me and that this time will be different, but…what if he's confusing his emotions about fatherhood with his feelings for me?"

I perch on my desk, ankles crossed, facing her. Exhaling a long breath, I feel unburdened saying the words out loud. Maybe they'll float away on the breeze and take my worries with them.

"He hurt you. Even if it was ten years ago, it can still sting a little. And you don't want to open yourself up to that again. I get that." She opens her mouth to say more but shakes her head instead. "Maybe that's why it's a little hard for me to trust him now. I know, I'm just being overprotective."

The idea of my little sister protecting me hits me right in the feels, and I feel myself tearing up. I don't want her to think I've come completely unhinged, so I manage to choke back the sob forming in my throat. I look at my lap and instruct the tears to go back from where they came. I swallow over the lump in my throat, inhale a shaky breath, and look at her.

"Thank you. I appreciate you looking out for me. But I think it's different. He wants to be a dad, and at the end of the day, if he doesn't want me, I'm okay with that." But his mother's words continue to ring in my ears—he's a good man who understands commitment. Maybe I'm taking advantage of his goodness and trapping him.

PJ smiles again and gathers the flowers we chose to make a bouquet. "I love these. They're perfect." There's no point in bringing her down by voicing my concerns about whether I've baby-trapped Ren into being with me.

"Okay, good. That's all I need to hear. You're a good judge of character, so if you're happy, I'm happy. And I'll try to be nice to him when I see him."

"I'm not worried."

"But if he hurts you at all, I'll go full-on frosty."

I reach over and hug her. "I appreciate that you'd kick his ass if the need arises."

"It'd better not."

"It won't," I tell her, knowing Ren is committed to being a dad. I just don't know if he's committed to being with me.

CHAPTER *Twenty-Six*

BEATRIX

I've been staring down for the past ten minutes, trying to see my feet. Yes, my feet.

Ren comes into my bathroom and finds me wrapped in a gray flannel bathrobe with a disposable razor in my hand.

The frown on his face matches my own. "Honey, what's wrong? You look like Truman does when he can't find his stuffed hedgehog."

"It's worse. I can't find my feet."

I'm four months along, and somewhere in the past week, my feet disappeared from view. "With the holidays around the corner, guess it's the perfect time to ask Santa for some jumbo pajamas, and I'll just wear them until May." I think back on the leather pants I almost bought. That day feels a world—and a big baby bump—away.

Ren looks down to where, sure enough, my feet are probably right there at the ends of my legs, but that's not the point. Seemingly overnight, I have "popped" and gone from looking like I ate a large lunch to the unmistakable pregnant vibe of carrying a watermelon under my shirt. There's no mistaking that I'm quite pregnant, practically unrecognizable to my former self, the one who wanted to buy leather pants. Mallory's point, well-taken.

I was waiting for this day, envisioning taking a slew of cute baby bump photos that would make me look whimsically fertile and cute, but now that it's here, I feel overwhelmed by reality. This is a real person here inside me, and I'm in love with him. I wasn't prepared for either one, but the latter scares me a lot more.

Because it's Ren.

Stop-my-heart-in-its-tracks Ren, who reminds me of just why I fell for him years ago and makes me equally afraid of history repeating itself.

"You are exceedingly adorable, and I'm sorry you've lost your feet," Ren says, kissing me on top of the head. "They're right here, I promise."

"Great," I huff, not reassured by the fact that he can see something I can't. I sit down on the toilet and try to bend forward, but that's a no-go as well. My belly blocks the way to my lower legs, which was the point before I discovered the missing feet. I'm still holding the disposable razor, so Ren clues in.

"Is it the wrong time to tell you you're gorgeous? Sad and disappointed, but still unmistakably gorgeous." The way he looks adoringly at me nearly erases the injustice of not being able to balance on one foot. And there aren't too many occasions where I need to do that anyway, so it's a net-positive.

"Not the wrong time. Never the wrong time." I tip my chin up and meet Ren's lips gratefully. I've tried to tamp down the feeling that he and I might have a real future, but more and more, it seems possible. Soon, I'll need to give up the fight and lean into the idea that it's different now than it was ten years ago. I want to trust that Ren's here for good.

"Why do you look so discouraged? What's up?" he asks, stroking my hair and tangling his fingers in the strands. I hear Truman padding around in my bedroom before the cover-ruffling sound that indicates he's on the bed. I like that he warms it up for us.

I hold the razor up and wince at my thwarted effort. "I need to shave my legs, but I can't reach them." I demonstrate by trying to bend over and only getting partway there.

"Ah."

"Ah?"

"I see the problem. I've got you," he says.

"You've got me?"

I half expect him to pick me up and take me somewhere, so I don't need to worry about unshaven legs. Instead, he extends his hand, palm upward. "Let me do it."

My insides twist with a combination of nervousness about letting someone else shave my legs and a secret thrill at having Ren take on this personal task. "Really?"

He laughs. "Yes, really. Do you not trust me?" He points to his face, which is currently clean-shaven. He has a point.

"Of course I trust you. It's just…are you sure?"

"I'm more than sure."

He wiggles his fingers, and I hand over the razor, which he places on the counter.

Ren's gaze traces over me from head to toe, and his eyes flash hungrily. I feel a sudden rush of heat to my core and an intense desire to have him touch me. Anywhere.

"Hang on," Ren says, hopping up and opening the medicine cabinet, where he's stashed his toiletries. He pulls out a can of shaving cream and puts that on the counter next to the razor. Then he pulls a pink towel from the stack I keep on a shelf and lays it out on the floor in front of the glass shower door.

I don't expect his strong arms to wrap around my body and lift me into the air, so I grab his shoulders with both hands. "I've got you," he reassures, bringing me down gently to the floor on top of the folded towel. He puts another towel behind me so I can lean comfortably against the shower door. Then he straightens each of my legs so they're extended comfortably in front of me. I exhale a breath and take in this man. I want so much more of this. Of him.

He grabs the supplies from the counter and drops down to sit cross-legged next to me. His biceps flex under the worn fabric of his tee as he squirts a dab of shaving cream into his palm. I inhale his scent, that manly forest smell when he's just shaved. I let out a long breath as he smooths a layer of the cream over my right calf. "Sorry if it's cold."

"It's not. It's perfect," I say, leaning back against the shower door and marveling at how erotic it feels to have him lather my leg. And if I thought that was a turn-on, it's nothing compared to the sight of him leaning down and carefully swiping the razor along one side of my leg. I have to shift my weight on the towel to relieve the sudden rush of need at my core. And he notices.

"You like this?"

"Mm-hmm," I purr, not embarrassed in the slightest that he's reduced me to a sighing puddle with one touch. "Thank you."

"Oh, honey…" he murmurs, leaning closer to make sure he doesn't miss a spot. "You have no idea, do you? I'm the one getting the good end of the deal here."

He pops up and swishes the razor under the running water in the sink, and I'm expecting him to repeat everything on my other leg. So damn hot I can barely stand it.

When Ren drops back down to the floor, he leaves the razor behind. His eyes trace over me again hungrily, and he licks his lower lip. My heart rate ticks up a notch because I know he's planning something. Typical Ren to go off-script and take me somewhere I can't even contemplate at the moment. I'm so fixated on the fact that he just expertly shaved my leg and turned it into sensual art that I don't dare imagine what he'll do next.

With one strong hand, he traces the contour of my newly-smooth calf and continues his journey higher up my leg. Nudging my knee to the side, he opens my legs enough to give his hand room to feather the skin of my inner thigh with his fingertips. My head falls back against the shower door, and I gasp at how good his touch feels. All my senses feel heightened as I breathe in the heady scent of the shaving cream. I close my eyes to focus on the sweet burn of his hands on my skin.

My robe falls open as Ren parts my legs a little more. I open my eyes and see a look of feral hunger on Ren's face. His eyes meet mine for an instant, dark and heavy with need, before he dips his head down and takes a long, slow swipe along my inner thigh with his tongue.

"Hockey Star, you have no idea what you do to me…"

Those are the last words I'm able to string into coherence.

"Ah, hon, this is all for you, but…" He breathes me in, and I feel the air catch in his throat. His hands quiver as they trail over my thighs, and each guttural word he exhales feels like he's at war. "The way I want you feels impossible. Hurts so fucking much I can't see straight."

His words are a growl against my flesh, sending ribbons of electricity burning through me. "You. Wreck. Me…"

I gasp and close my eyes against the intense rush of pleasure as his tongue licks straight through my center. His lips ravish me, and his tongue circles my clit until I cry out at the intensity. I've never felt this turned on, never felt this close to losing control after under a minute.

But it's Ren… He's always had this power over my body, and I want to lose myself in him. I *need* it.

And now it feels like something more. Adding in a baby and a second chance at love overwhelms my senses.

His light exhale against my most intimate parts curls my toes. I fist the towel I'm sitting on and shudder against the sensation of Ren's tongue circling, delving deeper, *wrecking* me right back. And taking a decisive swipe at my heart.

I grab at his shoulders, rolling my hands over the muscled contours and settling around his rounded biceps. His strength, coupled with the intimate, soft movements of his mouth against me, is an intoxicating combination. "Ren, *God…*"

My self-control is shaking, then crumbling into dust as he

slides a finger inside me. Just as erotic as that day on the tractor, only less playful, more intense. He's working me with intentional pressure, taking me to the crest until I can't hold anything back, and I scream out. "Ren..."

"Come for me, hon," he breathes against my clit, circling once more. Twice...and then I'm gone. My vision goes spotty, taken over by pulses of light and so much pure sensation that all I can do is moan my agreement with everything he's doing.

As though he hasn't just decimated me, Ren resumes the task of dabbing shaving cream on my other leg. "Need to be thorough," he explains.

"Oh my God, yes."

I close my eyes again because I'm starting to see Ren differently when I look at him. Instead of the standup guy, I see a man driven by love. And I see us as a couple...with a future. Dangerous thoughts, but I can't stop them any more than I can stop my baby bump from becoming a baby mountain right before my eyes.

CHAPTER *Twenty-Seven*

REN

It's a home game. But I know Trix isn't watching from center ice. She's at work, where there's a special holiday menu at Butter and Rosemary during the month of December, and she's also decorating the place for Christmas. On top of that, she's been working around the clock to get the inn finished in time for the wedding next month. A full house of guests that will stay at Buttercup Hill for the weekend. It's only three weeks away, and the days are flying by.

So is her pregnancy, over four months along. She's still taking long daily walks around the vineyard and going to yoga, but I think she barely notices anything except the ticking clock on the renovation. The floors and walls are finished, and now she's taking huge furniture deliveries every day and pointing to where everything should go.

I find myself racing back to the locker room at the end of training to check my phone for her texts. Each little update and heart emoji brings a secret smile to my face, a stark contrast to the grimace I wear on the ice as our coach works us to the bone.

Our team schedule has been herky-jerky, with an away game followed by an extra travel day and a long day of training. It's been more efficient to stay in Berkeley—not to mention that I need the sleep—so I've barely seen her in almost two weeks. It's been good for my game, good for the team. Good for Truman because he gets more time at Buttercup Hill with Trix and her niece. Less good for my heart, even if my focus has been sharper.

Feels eerily familiar, even though it was ten years ago that my coach and my mother warned me against getting distracted. As soon as I broke things off with Beatrix back then, my focus became laser-sharp, and my career took off. The thrill of success helped bury my own heartbreak, but I refuse to let her go this time.

I don't want that one-dimensional life anymore, yet I also owe my team more than I've been giving. And maybe, at the end of the day, I'm not capable of being in love with hockey *and* a woman. The idea makes my heart sink to a depth I haven't felt since I reconnected with Trix.

I try to banish the thoughts and fears, but they're a drumbeat in the back of my mind, as insistent as the feeling of pure joy I have when the image of her crosses my mind.

I keep my phone turned off during the day, so I miss a lot of her texts. At night, I try to call, but our away game schedule throws things off, so I've missed her a few nights in a row. I hate it, but we're in the thick of the season.

The good news is I've had time for some one-on-one dinners with Sam Skinner and Johnny Grimm, both star players who haven't been finding their groove on the ice. It feels good to feel useful, but I miss seeing Trix.

I push thoughts of her from my head as I charge toward the crease. No room for any thoughts right now except the puck, the goal, and the other guys on the ice.

We've had the lead for the first two periods. We're playing well, even though we still look like a bunch of talented guys doing their own thing out here. Now, halfway through the third, I'm feeling good. Optimistic that we could end with a win.

Then, the cracks start to show. A penalty. A powerplay. And Dallas scores with two minutes left. We're tied.

Nothing wrong with a tie, but Skinner shouldn't have a high-sticking call when we're up with two minutes to go.

Our enforcer is thirty seconds from getting out of the box when the Dallas forward takes a crazy shot from just over the line. And…scores.

I can feel the air drain from the arena. We all can. What should be cheers for a win—or even a fucking tie—turn into boos and an overall feeling of gloom about our prospects. Skating off the ice, I can already hear the interview questions headed my way. "What are you going to do to get out of this slump?" "How'd the team choke with two minutes left?" I don't have answers for any of them, but I'll do my best.

"That was a fuckup," Grimm snipes at Skinner as we head down the tunnel.

"It's a team sport, dude," Skinner retorts, but I can see in the hard set of his jaw that he feels some responsibility for the loss. He missed two key saves, which put unnecessary pressure on our goalie. I've been watching Skinner during practice, and his accuracy is spot-on. For him to miss two defensive opportunities plus the high-sticking is not like him.

"I did my part, in case you're inferring I didn't." Grimm isn't going to let this go. He's like a Doberman with a squeaky toy when it comes to anyone suggesting he's a dumb jock.

"Implying," Skinner corrects quietly. I roll my eyes because the guy just doesn't know when to keep his trap shut.

"Excuse me?" Grimm gets in his face, breathing into his eyes because he has a good six inches on our starting guard, who has to walk faster to keep up.

"Nothing." Skinner reacts like he's looking at a butterfly, not more than two-hundred pounds of muscle and testosterone. It's why he makes a good enforcer. Nothing scares him, and he doesn't mind checking an opponent for even a shred of impropriety.

"Not nothing if you feel the need to correct me. So be a man and tell me to my face."

"'Inferring' means you're taking information from a source. 'Implying' means you're trying to prove a point. Get a dictionary." Skinner's tone is icy. Poking the bear is just plain dumb.

"Enough, Skinner," I tell him, moving past him toward the locker room, intentionally putting some distance between Grimm and him. The last thing we need is a fistfight among guys on our own team, and tempers always run hot after a loss. I hear Skinner let out a low whistle behind me and I ignore it. Not getting into it with him.

Fuck. This is on me. Whatever's going on with Skinner didn't get fixed over one dinner. I need to put in more time with him. Stay one hundred percent focused on the game. I shouldn't have to watch the team rack up losses to learn that lesson.

I slam the door to my locker and debate going to see Trix. She'll make me feel better, but I don't deserve to feel better when I'm not getting these guys where they need to be.

"This isn't working."

I close my eyes and pray that the words don't mean what I think they do.

"What's not working?" I keep my tone light and glance around the locker room as though there's some new detail I'll notice. There's nothing. Same purple painted lockers with our names on them. Same team logo of a fierce-looking otter painted on the back wall. Same benches where we sit and shoot the shit after a great game. My coach tips his head toward the office next door, and I follow him until he closes the door behind us.

"You're not rallying the guys. I'm concerned you're not up to the job."

I know my berth as team captain teeters on the edge of every loss we suffer. This shouldn't come as news. But it stings to hear the words out loud. I've always been a guy who knew how to put the team first.

"It's a chicken-and-egg thing. The worse our bonding gets, the worse we do out there, and the worse we do, the more guys start sniping at each other." I'm telling him things he already knows. It's my job to go above and beyond to fix these things, and nothing I'm doing is working. I need to do better.

But at what cost?

I'm not willing to give up the life I'm building with Trix, but I need to be the captain of this team. Ever since my stunt in front of the glass, my teammates have been calling me Loverboy. Not a good look for a guy who's supposed to be a leader, but who among us hasn't felt the conflict between the team and life outside the sport? Maybe finding balance is a matter of putting the right things first at the right time.

"I know. It's not easy; I'm not saying it is. But the point isn't to make excuses for what's not working. The point is to find something new that will work. Where's your head? Are you focused? Can you do what I'm asking?"

"Yes. Absolutely. I can do it." I perk up. Maybe he's not going to shitcan me for our team's terrible performance and my poor leadership skills. I can only hope for another shot at righting the ship, but if I were him, I'd probably find a replacement. "I haven't exhausted all the tools at my disposal, and there's still time to get us back on track. I feel confident," I say.

I pick up a puck from the desk and use it as a stress toy, squeezing it when there's no give at all. I've had a stick in my hand and a puck at my feet since I was a kid, and this should be the high point of my career—team captain of a team with such a stacked roster that the Stanley Cup is practically ours to lose. Maybe that's a large part of the problem. We're taking things for granted when other teams are going hard because they have to.

Barrington rubs a hand over the thinning strands of gray atop his head. When he started coaching this team, he had a full head of dark hair. The sport is hard on everyone's bodies, even those who don't suit up. "Listen, I named you a captain because you're the best. You have more experience as a player than most of these guys, and I have confidence in you, but I have to ask, is everything okay outside of the sport? Your relationship taking its toll?"

I could tell him about the baby, pull him in as a father figure and ask him what the hell to do about a woman whose heart I broke in order to clear the decks so I could play hockey. I need to figure out how to do my job and also do everything to avoid breaking it again. I could talk to him. I...should?

No.

I can't let him see me as distracted. Or human, for that matter. I've clearly been prioritizing my personal life over hockey. I need to do better. I warned Trix that I may not be able to hack it as a multitasker. She knows this about me. She'll understand.

Almost as if on cue, my phone buzzes with a call from her. I send it to voicemail and turn off my phone.

All the team wants is a guy who can do a job, and I need to make sure I'm that guy.

"I'm good, Coach. Nothing to write home about," I say, flashing him a smile I hope seems convincing.

He watches me, blinking slowly like he's waiting for me to say more. I don't intend to, but the longer he stares at me like that, the more unnerved I feel. So I return his stare with a steely gaze, reassuring him that I'm a capable captain. I'm fully focused.

Now, I just need to do everything in my power to be just that.

CHAPTER
Twenty-Eight

BEATRIX

Me: Hey, how's it going?

Me: Hey, congrats on the win!

Me: No pressure, but send up a smoke signal and lemme know how you are.

Three messages, an hour apart in the evening when training is finished, with no response to any of them.

I'm not trying to be a pest. Or possessive. Or clingy.

But Ren has gone from attentive to absent.

I know he's stressed. He's in the thick of the season, and there are games all through the holidays, so he'll miss Christmas with my family and his mom. Still, he hasn't returned my calls or texts, and the radio silence for the past few days feels eerily familiar. Maybe PJ's concerns got in my head, because I'm telling myself this feels like college right before he dumped me.

We're different people now, and we're bonded by the child we'll be raising together, but still. He loved me in college, and I know how that ended. So just because he says he loves me now…

No. I need to get out of my head. We have plans tonight after he gets back to town, so we'll get into it then. Now I understand what he was trying to tell me the day we saw his mom—he's scared. Maybe that's all this is.

So I go about my day and check in on the contractors, who assure me that they can finish the inn by the deadline. For the first time in a week, I feel relieved. This is where I excel in the working world—managing projects, managing people, attending to details. In that way, I'm not so different from Ren. But when Ren plays hockey, he cuts out all distractions.

Maybe that's all that's happening here. Or maybe hockey is his only real love.

Stop it.

I try to get his mother's words out of my head, but it's hard. *Thank you, dear, for roping him in.*

Ren has never made me feel like I've trapped him, but maybe he's just too much of a standup guy. Or maybe I don't want to see it because I'm in love with him.

I pick up my phone to text him once more about where to meet for dinner, and it rings in my hand. It's Ren.

"Hey, I was just thinking about you. You good?" I ask, forcing levity and joy into my voice that I don't really feel. But he's working hard trying to rally his teammates and turn their losing streak around, so he needs positive energy. I can give him that.

"Yeah." The one word is followed by silence.

"Okay, good."

"Yeah. Decent. You?"

"I'm fine." Fine, except that I feel like I'm talking to an estranged aunt.

"So…"

"Yeah, so listen. I know I've been out of reach, but it's been hectic on the road, and I don't think I can make dinner. I need to eat with the team, keep our focus. It's the intangibles that're gonna get us moving, and I think we need bonding time."

"Sure, I get that."

I get it, but it hurts. I'm too attached. Vulnerable when I promised myself I'd never open my heart like this again, especially to him. Yet here we are. I love him more than I ever did before.

"Thanks."

"Okay, so…"

"You feeling good with the pregnancy?"

I feel the levity and joy leave me at his perfunctory question. "Yeah, I'm fine."

"Okay. I'm sorry, Trix."

"I get it. It's okay."

"I'll make it up to you, I promise. I just need to get us over the hump."

"Sounds good. Love you," I remind him.

"Love you too. So much."

I believe him. I know he loves me.

Just like I knew it in college.

Stop it.

I try to separate the two situations because we're in a very different place now, but I can't help the same feeling of dread washing over me that I felt back then when he started to pull away.

It's different now. We're different. He's in the thick of hockey season, and the team won the last game they played. Ren seems excited and nervous about it, almost like he's balancing on a razor's edge, not wanting to disturb anything about what's working well for fear that things will take a turn for the worse. I understand. Really, I do.

But I also worry. Maybe he loves me and he's doing the best he can, or maybe this is all too much for him. After all, he didn't ask for any of it.

I try to push negative thoughts from my mind, but it's hard to do.

CHAPTER
Twenty-Nine

REN

I give pep talks before every game, but I feel this one in my bones. Every pair of eyes in the locker room is fixed on me. I don't need to look from player to player to know it. The heat of their stares is palpable, and it feels good. It feels right.

No sound other than my voice in the room. No fidgeting. The players are listening.

And for the first time in weeks, I have something new to say.

"We've been caught in the trap of great expectations, and I'm not talking about the Charles Dickens novel. Actually, maybe I am." I shrug, pivoting to something I know a little bit about and hoping my teammates don't tune out because I sound like an English teacher. "Whether you've read the book or not, whether you've ever heard of Pip or Mrs. Havisham, the gist is this: we make assumptions about our lot in life and the positions of other people, and they can lead us astray. We have a roster that looks better on paper than almost any team out there. But is that enough?"

The question is rhetorical, and my Dickens reference may not be spot-on, so I wait to see if anyone's still with me. I hear a chorus of responses, some of them grudging. "It's not." "Not enough." "No."

"It's only a start. We absolutely have what it takes to beat any team on the ice in our league. Any one of them. Do we agree on that?"

I listen for agreement and hear another chorus of "Yes" and "Hell yeah."

None of this is much different from other pep talks I've given, and I don't sense the tenor of the room changing at all. The players are bored, waiting for me to finish so they can take the ice. I'm not getting through to them because I'm holding back, not giving them anything personal. Playing my own game, as though I don't trust them to keep up their end of the bargain if I open myself up. That has to stop now.

Lead by example.

Barrington dared me to do better, and maybe the problem is that I'm not digging deep enough. I'm not making this personal, telling them why it matters beyond the obvious need for a win. I don't have anything prepared, so I dig deep for some thoughts that have meaning to me.

What I realize is that I'm an asshole.

What I realize is that I've been trying to compartmentalize my life and prioritize hockey at the expense of Trix, and I hate myself for it. I hate that I've pushed her aside to "focus" on hockey when she's been nothing but supportive and understanding of the pressure I feel. She's been the one pushing me to be a better version of myself, and I've been the one falling short. And if I lose her because of it...

I banish the thought because I can't face that possibility right now.

Instead, I start talking to my teammates. This time, I'm speaking from the heart.

"Listen, in a few months, I'm going to be a first-time dad." If I thought the room was silent before, it's a vacuum of sound now.

"I haven't said anything because I was too busy trying to be a leader, trying to be a machine. But that's not gonna build our chemistry. That's me playing my own game, staying in my head." I look around the room. "Sound familiar? I'm betting we're each out there carrying around our own version of a story with one lead character." Shaking my head, I hear all the tiny lessons, the words of advice Trix gave freely to help me get past my fears about being a father. To show me I'm not in it alone.

"I'm scared shitless I'm gonna screw it up. Some of you've been there, you have kids. I've got nothing but respect because this feels like a mountain. I'm going to be coming to you for advice, trust me. And on the ice, I'll have your backs, every one of you. This sport goes deeper than the skills we have. It's personal. It's taking the most vulnerable shit in our lives and blocking it out, using it on the ice, letting the team carry it for you. You know your own stakes—getting more play time, making up for a fuck up in the last game, impressing a woman." There are some titters in the room. Expected. "Come on, isn't that why we all started playing sports in the first place? That, or so much unbounded energy that it was either play sports or get into fistfights on the daily? No? Just me?" A few more laughs. The guys are paying attention.

"We're taught that there's no "I" in team, but I disagree. It all starts with the personal. It all starts with a demon each of us has inside. We have to dig deep and find something worth fighting for. That's where the passion lies. It's basic, primal. Ego, big and surly. And we meet that challenge by lifting someone else up. Pouring all of our individual hopes and dreams into something we can only do together."

Something shifts in the room. The air gets lighter, easier to pull in with each breath. Instead of slumping on the benches, players are sitting upright. Even I feel empowered by the words because I'm not dreaming them up as much as letting them flow through me. I'm channeling what we need to believe in order to give everything we have to the team.

"We have what it takes to beat any team in the league. That's powerful. We just need to leave everything we've got on the ice. The best player out there becomes the worst player when he forgets that, and we've all forgotten it. We've all relied a little too much on our stats and our trade value and all the shit that doesn't help us. The team is the only way for the individual to shine."

I let that thought resonate, hearing it myself and knowing that something's shifted in me as well. I was part of the problem, too, thinking the team's record was mine to engineer. I'm only a part of it. Trix's words ring in my ears.

"You're not alone in this. That's the beauty. Realize that, and you'll succeed."

I feel like the grade-A jerk I am, giving a pep talk based on Trix's support of me and my career while I've been a shit to her. She gave me a second chance to be a better man than I was in college and what did I do? I gave her some half-assed text replies and told myself it was for the good of the team. Unacceptable to hide behind hockey because I couldn't figure out how to prioritize the woman I love in a stressful situation. I've got some heavy duty groveling to do.

I know I've been absent these past couple weeks. I need to apologize to Trix and double down on my commitment to her and the baby. I need to make sure she knows how important she is to me.

The thought of losing her again because I've been a shitty boyfriend makes me want to vomit.

I need to talk to her. I need to hear her voice.

There's some throat clearing in the room, and I realize I've been silent for the past thirty seconds. I look from face to face of the men on my team and return to the challenge directly in front of me. The energy in the room is restless now. The players are antsy to get on the ice and manifest whatever individual spark drives them. They're nodding and starting to feel a little bit of the magic we feel in anticipation of a game we want to win.

"It's not about the odds. I fucking hate the odds. Nothing gets in my head more than some bookmaker telling me ahead of time whether we're going to win or lose a game. How does that fucking guy know what's about to happen in a game we haven't even played?"

I don't wait for a response. "He fucking doesn't. We control the game. We control how we play and whether we work together as a team or whether we get bogged down in stupid shit that we decided to make important."

The players are getting restless, and it's a good thing. They're amped, and we need to get that energy out onto the ice. Coach Barrington needs them warming up and feeling the desire to win. So I wrap it up. "We are winners. Let's play that way."

My teammates bring it in for a cheer before disbanding to finish getting suited up to play.

Coach Barrington meets my eyes, and I see approval. It feels good. It also feels good to have my focus on hockey. This is our game to win, and this is my team to lead.

I'll call Trix as soon as I'm off the ice.

CHAPTER *Thirty*

BEATRIX

I fall asleep early and miss a call from Ren, but I wake up with two main thoughts. One, I shouldn't have eaten that second piece of pie. Sugar always messes with my sleep, and sure enough, I spent last night tossing and turning and having bad dreams. The ones I remember all involved some form of being chased by an animal or flying off into space. In one, I was floating above the roof of my house, attached to a helium balloon on a silk string. It seemed obvious enough that I needed to cut the string to free myself from the balloon, but when I untied it, the balloon fell to the roof, and I kept floating higher and higher.

Clearly, I'm getting nervous about being a mom. The dreams are about losing control, and parenthood seems like the best example of that.

The second thought I have this morning is that maybe my dream has something to do with Ren. I feel out of control there, too. I don't like the way we've been ships passing in the night, even though his voicemail was sweet. "Hi, honey. Sorry I missed you. Hope you get some sleep." Generic, but sweet.

Not sweet enough. Not when he's been treating me like I'm an inconvenience, someone he has to text because I texted him first. Someone he has to call to check in about the pregnancy like it's an obligation. In the past ten years of building my career and becoming self-sufficient, I've learned one important thing—I'm just fine on my own. And I can't go on waiting for the other shoe to drop, worried that Ren will leave me behind again. All the old signs are there.

I try to talk myself down because maybe the pregnancy hormones are making me overly-sensitive. Ren was probably exhausted after the game. He felt pressure to lead the team and not run off to call me. I get that.

But a part of me worries that he's trying hard to play a role because it's the right thing to do. Even if he loves me, being with me wasn't part of his plan. Maybe I need to set him free. Or at least have an honest conversation about where we stand. I'm not the twenty-year-old without a life plan. I can handle whatever comes my way, even if I don't know what to say to Ren right now.

I push the thought away, but it creeps back as soon as I leave my bedroom and pad down the hall in Ren's large pajama pants and one of his soft tees. Yes, I slept in his clothes. They're comfortable, and right now they fit better than mine do. They also remind me of Ren, and it makes me happy to wrap myself up in fabric that smells like him.

In my kitchen, I flip on a light and start the coffee maker, grateful that the smell no longer makes me sick. Even if it's decaf, I still like my daily fix. It's a ritual. I warm the milk in the microwave and wait for the coffee to drip slowly into the pot. Leaning on the counter, I practically doze off. My elbow slips to the side, and I'm jarred awake.

Decaf coffee isn't going to power me through the day, so I look in my pantry for something to give me some energy. Next to a box of bran cereal, a bag of Oreos screams out to me. "Eat all the chocolate!" I imagine it's saying. Slamming the pantry shut, I back away.

I don't dare eat a sugary breakfast after the pie wreaked havoc on me last night. I settle for a peach from a wooden bowl on the counter and try to stop worrying about what to say to Ren when I see him.

The coffee maker beeps, and I pour some coffee and milk into a metal tumbler. Then I swap out Ren's pajama pants for sweatpants and shove my feet into a pair of slip-on tennis shoes.

Walking around Buttercup Hill will help me clear my head, and I desperately need to be focused today if I'm going to get the last touches finalized so we can reopen the inn on schedule. And we *will* open on schedule. I haven't busted my ass for the past two weeks just so things can fall apart at the last minute. Every table at the restaurant is booked, and all the rooms at the inn are sold out.

I don't notice where I'm walking until I realize I'm standing outside the restaurant. But I'm not here for food. My office is upstairs. All roads lead to work for this girl, apparently.

"Hey." The deep baritone startles me with a combination of excitement and dread. I turn to find Ren walking up the path from the parking lot with that boyish grin on his face. His hair is slicked back from a shower, and he wears a loose pair of sweats and a long-sleeved tee that clings to the muscles I love to ogle. "Stopped by your house. Thought this was the next logical place to check. Glad I caught you."

His eyes sparkle like I'm the best thing he's ever seen, but I bristle when he wraps his arms around me and kisses me. I love the way it feels, but I can't lose myself to him the way I want to. All the pent-up emotions bubble to the surface and I feel a sob choke in my throat. Pushing it down, I swallow hard and banish the pinpricks of tears. Now that I've decided we need to talk, I want to get right to it.

"Ren…" I pull out of his grasp and back a few steps away. His smile fades in an instant, and he crosses his arms.

"Oh."

I shake my head. "It's just that I think we need to talk."

His head drops to his chest. I hate being the one to make his sparkle fade. "I know. I've been a shit. I'm sorry I've been absent. The team needed my focus, but I fucked up. I know that's not—"

"Stop. I get that hockey is important. And maybe it's good that you've been out of touch because it's given me some time to think."

I drop onto one of the benches outside the restaurant and inhale the heady scent of rosemary growing all around the building. It's always calmed me, and right now, I need that.

"I love your mind, Trix, but I'm worried about what it's been thinking. This doesn't sound good, honey."

The nickname is like warm chocolate, and I want it to drown the ache in my heart, but I try to keep my focus. "Ren, I'm struggling with how to feel about you, and we haven't even had the baby yet. When you ghost me like you have for the past few days, my mind goes straight to how you dumped me before. I know it's probably not fair, but I can't help it."

"That's not…" He shakes his head. "It's completely fair. And I'm sorry. I would never do that to you—or the baby."

"Exactly. Because you're a good guy. Because you follow through on commitments. But that doesn't make us a couple. It doesn't make it easy to go days without hearing from you. I think that in the whirlwind of emotions and intense feelings I have when I'm with you, I haven't been thinking clearly. And I need clarity."

"You hate the gray area. I know. But this isn't gray to me. I want to be in this with you."

I shake my head. "You're here for the baby, and that's already a lot to ask. I know you have guilt about leaving ten years ago, but I've basically hijacked your life. Barely hearing from you for the past two weeks was a wakeup call. I need to stop fantasizing about something that's probably not realistic and give you your life back." I've been wringing my hands, but I force them to still and drop them into my lap. I do my best to remain cool and calm on the surface, even if I'm crumbling underneath. Even if my heart feels like it's breaking all over again.

"I'm not asking for that." He kneels in front of me and takes my hand from my lap. "When have I asked for that?"

"Maybe not in words, but ghosting me to focus on the team kind of conveys the same thing, don't you think? We're a co-parenting team, and I'm counting on you for that. I'm grateful for it. But letting my heart hang in the wind is too hard for me, worrying that you'll want me one day and leave the next. I'm still a distraction for you, just like I was ten years ago."

He closes his eyes, and my heart aches for this man who wants to do the right thing. When his eyes open, they flash with intensity.

"I *want* to be distracted by you. I always have."

It's almost enough to make me cave. I want to be with him so badly that I nearly wrap my arms around his neck and promise never to let go. I want him so much that I almost cave and allow myself to believe his words. But I guess I don't have enough confidence that he'll want to stick around if I do.

"I know ten years is a long time, but having you disappear on me was a reminder that I can't put myself through it again. It was too hard to get over you the first time, and now I have to think about someone besides myself."

He shudders as my words slice him apart. Sharp, unyielding scissors. But he knows I'm right. There's a baby involved. A child. A tiny person who deserves the best father Ren knows how to be, and I'm a distraction that will only make it harder.

It wasn't until I saw how he commands the ice—and his team—that I fully understood it. Hockey is a part of him. It's not just a sport he plays. It's who he is. If I love him, the most selfless thing I can do is give him room to do what's right for him.

"Just think about it, okay? It doesn't make you a bad guy if you're honest with yourself. It makes you human. It will also make you a better dad."

Ren stands, understanding that he's not going to convince me of anything today. I'm asking him to do a gut check. I'm asking for clarity. I'm hoping it will lead him back to me for the right reasons. But if not, ten years has taught me something—I know I'll be okay.

CHAPTER
Thirty-One

REN

I pull my baseball cap down and take a seat at the corner of the hotel bar, where I can sit with my back to anyone coming in. The place has a nice dark wood bar with a mirror on the back wall and six barstools with leather seats. A few low tables are scattered around the room, with club chairs upholstered in purple velvet. It immediately makes me think of Trix and what she'd say about the textile choice. I'm betting she'd say the style works, but the color doesn't. Before I realize what I'm doing, I snap a photo with the intention of showing her.

No. She asked me to take time to think. Sending her pictures of velvet chairs is not going to prove that I want to be with her, not when she thinks she roped me into something.

It nearly killed me to walk away from Buttercup Hill the other day. I wanted to protest, but I know when I'm beaten, two goals down at the end of the third period. I'll pretend to think, even though there's nothing to consider. I don't need space. I need to close the gap between us for good.

My barstool gives me only a partial view of the flatscreen TV, but I don't need to see sports highlights when I just lived the real thing.

Tonight's win had a different feeling from the ones we eked out earlier in the season. It wasn't accidental. It wasn't luck. We played like a team, and we earned the win.

Now, celebrating in downtown Nashville with the team, I'm holed up in the half-empty bar, which is too bright for my liking. But I'll focus on the half-empty part. No one is in my face to talk to me about hockey. Or my life.

"I'll have what he's having." Coach Barrington loses his voice a little bit during every game, and tonight's rasp is per usual. It always comes back by morning.

"This is scotch, neat. You sure you want that?" I ask him, half hoping he won't take the empty seat next to me.

He nods at the bartender. "Make mine a double." He regards mine. "Just like his."

Swinging a leg over the barstool, Barrington makes it look harder than it needs to be. He's in his mid-fifties but he stays fit, working out in the team gym for an hour each day. His hockey career ended early with an injury at around my age, and he's been coaching ever since. I play the same position he did, so I've always felt a bit of kinship beyond our normal day-to-day.

"Good win tonight," he says.

"Felt good," I say, hoping that will be the end of the discussion.

"It was palpable, the rhythm. You're building unity. It's good to see."

I nod and take a sip of my drink. The bartender brings Barrington his scotch, and he holds it up to clink my glass. Neither of us toasts to anything, but the clink of the crystal draws its own conclusions.

On the bar, my phone vibrates with a text.

Trix: Great win. I watched

It's the first time I've heard from her since we spoke the other day, and even the generic congratulations feels like hope. My fingers itch to respond, but I still don't know what to say to her.

I flip it over without responding, embarrassed that Barrington might see Trix's name entered with heart emojis before and after her name. Like I'm a hapless high school freshman or some shit.

"Don't mind me. Feel free to answer your phone," Barrington says, raising an eyebrow as he sips his drink. Instead of responding, I take another drink from my glass. The whiskey burns my throat as it goes down, and somehow it feels right. Even with the win, I'm acting like an asshole toward Trix. Punishing her to punish myself.

"It's fine. I can deal with it later."

Barrington drums his fingers on the bar and looks up at the partial view of the TV. I'm not sure whether he's interested in the sports highlights or just trying to avoid looking at me. Doesn't stop him from talking to me, though. "Can I give you a word of advice?"

I can't say no. He's my coach.

"Sure."

"Don't neglect the people in your life." He's still looking at the TV. He can see slightly more of the screen than I can, but there must be something really absorbing going on. I glance up, but it's only a news crawl of scores and two talking heads discussing baseball with subtitles. Not interesting to me.

"You mean the players?"

"Did I say the players?" His gaze snaps from the TV to my face so quickly that it creates its own wind.

The back of my neck feels hot, and I slap a hand back there to wipe what will be sweat in about two seconds. Barrington is the nicest guy in the world, but when he wants to make a point, it's best to get out of the way and listen. Otherwise, he gets testy. It's a great quality in a coach, less so in a guy sitting on the next stool at a bar.

"Just thought maybe we were still talking about team morale."

"We're not. I think you've got that covered."

It's a relief, but he still sounds aggravated, so I haven't fully exhaled in about a minute. I pull the napkin from under my drink and fold it into squares just to have something to do other than sweat on the hot seat.

My phone vibrates again, but I ignore it.

"Goddammit, Renaldi, if that's your woman you're ignoring, please stop being a dumbass and answer her."

I blink heavily and think about my options. I can tell my coach to go fuck himself, which would not bode well for my career, or I can do what he's telling me. The second option falls much closer to what I want to do, but I don't trust myself not to lose my focus on the game.

"It's Trix," I admit, feeling like a naughty child who got caught with a stash of candy wrappers in his underwear drawer. And because I know Barrington won't let the conversation drop until I've told him everything, I tell him everything. "The short version is that I love her, and I think she's afraid I'm only with her out of obligation. Worst part is that I bailed on her ten years ago, and I've regretted it ever since. Now, here I am, not wanting to make the same mistake again."

"So don't make the same goddamn mistake, Renaldi. I don't need a degree in psychology to tell you that one, but I've got one."

This piece of information pulls me from my wallowing for enough time to push my chair back and take a good look at my coach. "You do?"

He nods and takes another sip of his drink. I do the same. We've both finished about half, and I'm already feeling the effects of the alcohol. Not drinking a drop for the past few months, combined with a hundred proof liquor, is making me a lightweight. The kind who's dangerously close to confessing way too much to his coach if he's not careful.

I look around the bar for something—anything—that I can use to distract myself from pursuing this conversation. I find only a couple at a table behind us, laughing and chomping tortilla chips with their margaritas.

Turning back to Barrington, I think I'm asking a question but that's not how it comes out. "You never said anything about it before."

He shrugs. "I don't advertise it, but it's not something I hide. Anyone who looks at my bio on the team website can find it." He lets that land before smiling. "I don't expect you to hang out and read bios on the team website."

"Still, seems like something a semi-observant human would know."

"Don't beat yourself up." Barrington signals to the bartender and asks for a bowl of nuts. It occurs to me that I've never done this before—sat with my coach in a hotel bar. Maybe he does this after every game, and it's just news to me. I wonder what else I don't know about him. Before I can ask, he waves a hand dismissively.

"What I studied or didn't study in school isn't the point because most of what I know was learned on the job. As a player and a coach."

I nod. "Yeah. Same here."

"Good. So you should understand that what makes a team powerful is player health, and I'm not just talking about physical fitness. If your head's a mess, you're a mess, do you hear me?"

"Yes." I take a long pull from my drink.

"So get it straightened out. Especially with a baby in the mix."

I nod.

"You said her name's Trix..." He looks up at the ceiling like he's imagining what someone named Trix would look like.

"Yeah."

"Pretty name. I don't need to ask if you love her because it's written all over your dumb face. You're nuts about her, so I don't understand why you're ignoring her texts." The bartender puts a small dish of peanuts in front of us and a second dish with green olives. Barrington pops a handful of nuts into his mouth and chomps down on them, talking as he chews.

"Because I don't know how to convince her I'm serious about the two of us. So I'm giving the team my total focus until I can get back and talk to her." I figure he'll respect my commitment to the team.

He rolls his eyes and eats a few more nuts. "That's not how it works. You don't get to put people in boxes and decide when to take them out and play with them. You integrate them into your life, or you lose them. I learned that the hard way many years ago, and I won't make the same mistake again. Neither should you."

"I thought you were married."

"I am. Third time's the charm in that department. Now that I've gotten it right, I'm not going to do anything to jeopardize my relationship. Not one thing," he says, slapping the top of the bar. The bartender looks up, but Barrington waves him off. "Just emphasizing."

"Not sure it works that way for me. I don't know how to do both, and I've always been a hockey player."

"Learn," he says. "Learn to do both equally well. I know you've got it in you, Renaldi. I didn't choose you as captain because you're a charity case. And I don't want your broken-hearted ass showing up for training after she dumps you for acting like an ass. If you think being in love's distracting, try heartbreak." Barrington finishes his drink and holds up a finger. "Scratch that. Don't try heartbreak. Just do the right thing. At least check your phone for crying out loud."

Flipping the phone over, I find another text from Trix.

> Trix: Don't want to freak you out, but I'm feeling some weird pains

While I'm reading that one, she pings me again with another text.

Trix: Julie is taking me to the hospital just to be safe

I show the text to Barrington as I feel the blood drain from my face.

"Take the jet. It can come back in the morning for the team."

"Are you sure?" I can't think straight. I don't know whether I should just text Trix back or get on a plane.

"It'll just be sitting there all night waiting to take us back in the morning. Go. Go now."

He doesn't have to tell me twice. I hop off my barstool and take off at a run.

CHAPTER
Thirty-Two

BEATRIX

"Try not to panic. Women have been having babies alone in corn fields since the beginning of time," Julie says as I wait for the medication to kick in. She stands on one side of me while a nurse comes in and out, running tests and checking my vital stats.

"I know you think you're making it better, but corn fields? Really?" A contraction tightens my stomach and jangles my nerves. It's too soon to have a baby, and I still haven't heard from Ren. I know I caught him at the tail end of a game and he probably hasn't seen my text. Or maybe he's back to his spotty communication after our last conversation. But as upset as I am with Ren, I don't want to have a baby without him here.

"Yes. Corn fields. You have modern medicine on your side, and I'm sure this is all going to be fine. It's probably false labor. It's really common."

"I hope you're right, Jules." I offer her a wan smile as she wipes sweat from my brow.

I've been in such a tailspin since the doctor told me to come to the hospital that I've just been nodding at Julie since she showed up at my house. With barely a word, she gathered Truman's supplies, and loaded us into her car, and dropped the dog off with her husband. Then she drove me here. For the first time in years, I didn't make all the decisions. It felt kind of nice.

I've been having contractions all week long after I told Ren to take time to think, almost like the baby heard us and is registering a protest.

Please get along, Mom and Dad. Please be a couple.

"Yes to the first part, little one," I tell the tiny bean inside me. "Jury's out on the second."

With the blue flowered hospital gown draped over my belly like a tablecloth attempting to hide Mount Everest, I give Julie a half smile that probably doesn't look convincing. In fact, I've done nothing but panic since I called her in the middle of the night when I noticed I was bleeding. With months to go until my due date, I should not be going into labor, if that's what's happening.

I intentionally kept my text to Ren vague so he wouldn't be worried until I have more information. Even though I'm still upset with how we left things, he has a right to know what's happening with his baby. So I've kept my phone nearby, figuring he'd call me when he saw the message. I have no idea what kind of post-game obligations he has with the team, but I do know that he'll complete every last one of them before taking his phone out and checking on the outside world.

I check my phone once more, and there's nothing on the screen. No missed calls, no messages. Zip.

The shreds of hope plummet as my heart deflates. I don't want to read into the silence, but I don't know what to think.

"Still nothing, huh?" Julie asks.

"Nope."

"He'll call. I have more faith in him right now than you do, so try to trust me." I look at her, noticing for the first time her black long-sleeved top and red polka-dotted skirt. "Were you wearing that outfit when you got here?"

She glances down, smooths the skirt, and laughs. "It's my

Minnie Mouse costume. Sometimes, I dress up when I read Disney stuff before bedtime. I just hopped in the car when you called and didn't remember I had this on."

That's when I realize I've taken her away from time with her own family. "Oh gosh, I'm sorry you're missing bedtime.

"Don't be silly. Ed loves it when he gets to put her to bed by himself. They have a whole routine, songs, books, a secret snack they think I don't know about…"

"Cute." I wonder if that's how Ren will be with our child. He certainly seems excited about being a dad, and he can be so sweet when he wants to be. I just need to make sure I fill in the gaps when he disappears, like he's done lately. Our child needs stability, not a dad who's afraid of committing to life outside of work.

Another contraction hits me hard, and I suck in a breath. That, coupled with my emotional state, leaves me half sobbing, half breathing. "Oh gosh, I'm a mess. What if I can't do this?"

It's the first time I've said those words out loud, but maybe that's because this is the first I've felt alone in what's coming next. I know I can be a great mom. I'm a born multitasker. I just got a false sense of hope that Ren and I were a real couple. And now…I'm adjusting back to the reality that's much healthier for me. I sniffle and wipe my tears indelicately with the back of my hand.

"Hey, hey, it's okay," Julie says, smoothing my hair like the fairy godmother I've forced her to be. "Like I said, just try not to panic."

"I'm not panicking. I'm fully freaking out. I'm going to be a single mom, and I don't know what I'm doing," I tell Julie, wishing my voice didn't sound like a whine.

I've been at the hospital for two hours already, and the nurses have given me a dose of steroids, which will speed up the baby's lung development in case I deliver early. I've also been given a dose of magnesium to stop the contractions, which are probably false labor, but we need to be sure.

"Feels like you're panicking," Julie says, noting my rapid heart rate on the monitor beside the hospital bed. "The nurses seem to think everything looks okay."

She's right, so I should feel a little consoled by that. I'm still waiting for my doctor to arrive and I'm doing my best to stay calm, but it's not exactly working. And I can't even fool Julie when she has access to my vital signs as proof. "Fine, I'm nervous. What if I go into labor right now? What if I'm having a miscarriage? Is everything going to be okay? And where the hell is my doctor?"

"The nurse said she's on her way." I don't remember that. I wasn't paying attention because of all the panic. One more reason why I'm intensely grateful to Julie for coming with me and keeping a clear head.

"Okay. Okay, that's good." I look again at Julie in that getup. She's been as perky as the real Minnie Mouse, and I'm the polar opposite. "Okay, stop looking at me like that. Find something to do," I order, taking my frustration out on her.

Julie knows it's not about her. She flips channels on the TV perched in a high corner. It's been set to a news show on mute, and I've ignored it until now. Without asking, she flips to ESPN, where the sports highlights play on a loop. I start to tell her to switch it off. The last thing I need is another reminder of the awful way Ren and I left things before he got on the plane for this game.

But I can't help the way my eyes shoot to the screen, scanning for clips of the Otters game from earlier today. Even though I told myself not to watch it, I know they won. Good news for the team and for Ren, who takes every downturn as a personal failure. As a type A personality myself, I get it. I just wish his devotion to his sport didn't come at the expense of everything else in his life.

"I think a part of me will always worry that he's going to bail on me again," I tell her, searching the screen for any sign of game highlights, any tiny glimpse of Ren. I'm no better than the groupie I was right after he left, searching sports news for photos of him, scrolling tabloid sites, not wanting to see him with other women and hating myself for looking.

Eventually, I got over him and stopped. Now, though, I won't be able to do the same because we're bound by the child I could lose right here, right now.

"Of course you're going to worry about that because you're in love with him," Julie says. "Same guy, same love. Only now, it could really be something. Of *course* it's going to hurt more if he can't come through for you, but I think he can."

There's a quick knock on the door, and then it swings open. I sigh in relief at the expectation of seeing my doctor's face.

Finally.

I need her. She'll know what to do. She'll calm me down if there's nothing to worry about. I need a full report so I can relay it to Ren, even if he doesn't seem interested in texting me back.

Instead, I get Ren. He looks as panicked as I feel as he rushes into the room wearing a long-sleeved Otters tee and sweatpants. He lets out a long exhale as though he's been holding his breath for a week. "Trix, Jesus. You scared the shit out of me. What happened? Are you okay?"

His eyes rake over me, searching my eyes for answers and settling on my enormous belly. He starts to reach a hand toward me but reconsiders and shoves it into the pocket of his sweats.

"How are you here?" First things first.

"I took the team jet as soon as I got your texts. But the Wi-Fi was jammed on the plane, so I couldn't reach you in the air." He comes close to me and picks up my hand. I feel a rush of warmth envelop my body just from that tiny touch. "What happened? Are you okay?"

"I had some bleeding and contractions," I tell him.

"Everything's *fine*," Julie adds, shooting me a look. It's a mixture of hopefulness and warning.

"As far as we know," I correct, wishing I could feel nothing when I look at Ren with his tousled hair and his long-sleeved shirt that can't hide his strong shoulders and arms.

Ren looks from me to Julie and back again. "Which of you do I believe? Is everything okay or not?"

Before we can answer, there's another rap of knuckles on the door, and Doctor Salinger enters in her blue scrubs and white coat. She looks a hell of a lot calmer than any of us in the room. Apparently, she's used to that because she doesn't skip a beat. "It's going to be okay," she says, reading my chart and then washing her hands.

Ren doesn't look convinced. In fact, he looks like he might faint. Doctor Salinger must notice the same thing because she wheels over a stool so he can sit on it. He looks steadier, but the color doesn't return to his face.

For a moment, it warms my heart to see how much he cares. Then I remind myself that he's just being a good dad. We are not a couple. My heart needs to settle down and stop looking for something it can't have.

The exam only takes a few minutes, after which Doctor Salinger assures me that the bleeding may come and go, but the amniotic sac is intact, and all the baby's vital signs look good. "You've been having Braxton Hicks contractions?"

I shrug. "My stomach tightens, and I feel pressure. Am I in actual labor?"

"When did it start? What can I do? How can I help?" Ren looks helpless and sweet asking this flurry of questions, and I have to remind myself I'm still upset with how we left things. This is the guy I want by my side. I just wish it didn't take a medical emergency to get him here.

"Calm down, it's going to be okay," the doctor tells him. She walks him through the medical protocols and what to expect if the drugs do their job. "These are Braxton Hicks contractions, totally normal in the middle of a pregnancy, though I recommend limiting vigorous activity because of the bleeding. For the time being, no brisk walks, no lifting weight at all, and let's see if we can get things to calm down. I could keep her here for observation tonight, but I think that getting a good night's sleep at home would be the best medicine. Just relax, Beatrix, as much as you can. Stress is not your friend."

"Okay," I say under Ren's concerned stare.

"Like I said, I don't see any reason to worry, but if something changes, call me right away."

The doctor makes some notes in my chart and moves from the room, leaving the three of us in an awkward silence. Ren looks at me. I look at Julie. She looks at Ren. Rinse, repeat.

"If you don't have any questions, I'll leave you two alone. Ren, you can get her home, yes?" Julie nods at him, then at me. I tilt my head at her questioningly, and she presses her lips together and points to Ren.

"She's saying we should talk," Ren interprets. "And she's right because I have some things I need to tell you."

"I'm also saying you should cut back on work." Julie points at me and lingers in the doorway for a moment, gazing at us. "I'm rooting for you, Ren," she says before closing the door. "I'm rooting for both of you."

Yeah. I'm rooting for us, too.

CHAPTER Thirty-Three

REN

"Are you sure you really want to eat that?" I gesture at the two double cheeseburgers sitting on a paper plate in front of Trix. It sits next to a milkshake and a double order of fries. Most guys on my team could only put away half that amount of food at ten at night, and they'd pay for it in the morning. Then again, they're not pregnant.

"I'm sure that the baby wants me to eat it." She dips a fry into a cup of ketchup and shoves it into her mouth. I ordered a chocolate milkshake so Trix wouldn't have to "eat alone," as she put it, but I haven't touched it.

She asked that we leave the hospital and go out for food before I told her what I came to say. "I don't know whether I'm going to like it or not, and I'm hungry. Can we get some food before you talk and I lose my appetite?" she asked.

"I really hope I don't make you lose your appetite."

We drove toward Buttercup Hill and stopped at a burger stand on the road about twenty minutes from home. It nearly killed me to drive next to her and not say all the things I'd been rehearsing in my head during the two-hour flight from Phoenix, but I did what she asked. Felt like the least I could do after the way we left things before my trip.

"Okay, can I talk now?" I ask as she takes a giant bite of the first burger. Her cheeks are flushed in the moonlight, and she looks angelic as she nods.

"Sure. I'm just gonna eat, if you don't mind."

"Honey, of course I don't mind." I run a hand through my hair, agonizing over the thought that I could possibly mind anything she might do. "That's what I need you to understand. You're the first person—the only person—who makes me want to take a step back from hockey. You're—"

She interrupts me by holding up a hand, which happens to contain two fries. "Stop. I don't want you to take a step back. It's your life, Ren. It always has been. I'm good with raising our child full-time and letting you do what you need to do." She nods and takes another bite of her burger. There's no agony etched on her face. She really is okay moving on without me and letting me be a drop-in dad.

"No fucking way."

"Sorry?"

"I'm not taking any time away from you or our child unless I'm on the ice. That's it. Any other time, I'm yours if you want me."

She puts down her burger and assesses me calmly. No judgment. She tilts her head. "I do want you. But I don't want you to sign on because the sex is fun, and you feel obligated to our baby, and then realize that hockey is your one true love."

"I know I've done a shitty job these past weeks of proving that I can have balance in my life. But you and our baby are worth figuring out how to do it. I stepped back from my captain role on the team. It'll give me some of my time back and take some pressure off."

"I don't want you to sacrifice—"

I hold my finger out, and she stops talking before it even lands on her lips. Tracing the outline of her mouth, I watch her eyes go glassy. "It's not a sacrifice if it brings me back to you. It's not. Trix, I haven't had a real relationship for ten years because I never got over you. I bought the winery because I was hoping it would lead me back to you. I always wanted more than just hockey in my life. I wanted you. Only you."

I cup her chin in one hand. She looks dumbfounded at my confession.

I suppose I would be as well, but it's been my reality for so long that it doesn't seem strange anymore. On the contrary, it seems like the most logical thing in the world to buy a property when you have the money to afford it. But I have to tell her the last part.

"I'd give it all up for you. My whole career."

Trix bends her head to kiss the palm of my hand. "I don't want you to do that. I don't want to be the only thing in your life. But I want to be the part you come home to."

A lump lodges in my throat, so I simply nod and kiss her temple.

"I told you when I came here that I want balance in my life. Hockey is not my only love. You are too."

She nods. "I want to believe you, but I'm nervous."

"You can't know the future. At some point, you're going to have to trust me. The same way I need to trust myself to find balance."

Taking a sip of my shake, I feel like gagging on the thick, sweet chocolate. "This is what you crave?"

She nods. "And I crave you. But not everything we crave is good for us."

Fuck.

"You're right, Trix. Not everything we crave is good for us, but I think we're good together. And I'm not going anywhere."

I take an envelope from my pocket and hand it to Trix.

"What's this?" She turns it over to see the seal of the hotel where I was staying in Miami. Inside is one piece of hotel stationery, which she takes in her hands and unfolds.

"You said I should write a letter. I did."

After reading the words on the paper, she holds it up to me. I see my scratchy pen scrawl from that night, reading, "Do you want to know why I bought a place in Napa?"

"Okay, I'll bite. Why did you buy a place in Napa?

"Flip the page over."

She does so and reads aloud. "Because I knew you lived there. And when I became a free agent, the first team—the only team—I looked at was the Otters. Because I hoped it would bring me back to you. In ten years, I've never stopped loving you."

Shock registers in the clear blue of her eyes. "You're serious?"

I nod. "Ten years. So you can think you hijacked my plans with a baby or whatever, but I'm telling you that you were my plan all along. You are the only plan worth dreaming about."

I pull in a deep breath of air and hold it in my lungs before letting any last bit of resistance drain from me. There was never anything to think about, no chance I was ever leaving, so I might as well tell her the rest.

"You came back." She says the words slowly, like she's getting used to them.

I nod. "I guess I don't want a one-note life that's focused only on hockey. I guess I was hoping for a complication."

She barks out a laugh. "Well, you sure as heck found one. Two, actually." She points to her belly.

We've been sitting on opposite sides of a concrete table under an umbrella, but I move from my bench to her side and tuck in close to her. I want to be closer to her when I tell her how I feel. I don't want a chance she won't hear me.

"Best decision I ever made. Bar none."

She looks up at me, those clear blue eyes that see everything and still find joy in wondering how the world works. "Bar none?"

I shake my head. "Best decision. Ever."

She tips her head against my shoulder, dusting my cheek with the loose tendrils of hair that have fled her ponytail. This is my happy place. I run a finger beneath her chin and turn her face up to mine. I want to see the serene blue of her eyes, and I want to kiss her lips.

I'm gentle at first, tentative because I want to make sure she really wants this. Wants me. She responds, gripping my face in her hands and pulling me tighter against her lips. I delve deeper, swirling my tongue against hers and sucking on her bottom lip until she gasps.

Leaning back, Trix puts her hand over her heart and looks at me with wide-eyed amazement. "I am never going to get enough of you," she says.

I shake my head. "Same. Not ever. I'm so sorry I made you doubt me."

We sit in silence for a while, and I pull her tight against my side. No one else is here. Our only company is three empty tables with red umbrellas. Trix lays her head on my shoulder again and I stroke her hair.

"Thank you for coming back," she says.

"It was fine. Team doesn't need to fly out until the morning." I start thinking about the logistics of getting to the next away game if I miss getting back on the jet later. But I'll deal with that once I get Trix home.

She reaches for my chin and turns my face toward hers, bringing me back to the present.

"No," she clarifies. "Not tonight. Thank you for coming back to me."

CHAPTER
Thirty-Four

REN

Two Weeks Later

I never like hearing the odds makers predict our chances of winning a hockey game before we've even warmed up on the ice. It gets in my head, and even when we're playing great, I can't stop thinking about whether we're "supposed to" win or not. To avoid hearing predictions, I stay off social media and avoid sports news in the days before games. Usually that works, but there's always the chance of overhearing something accidentally.

Today, I'd like some odds.

What are the chances that the surprise I have planned after PJ and Colin's wedding will be a mistake of colossal proportions, and what are the odds that I'll get the happy ending I envisioned when I convinced Archer to help me with my plan?

Yes, I pulled in Archer because I needed someone to do some advance recon, and scraping together a package of center ice seats for the remainder of our season was easy payment for his trouble.

"You really don't need to do that." He waved a dismissive hand when I offered, but I could see the itchy flinch in his hand, wanting to reach out and take the envelope from me.

"It's the least I can do for you, man. If I pull off what I'm hoping to, I'll keep you sitting in the good seats for life."

I was treated to one of Archer's rare smiles, which he was quick to explain. "The seats are a bonus. My sister's who I care about, so I'm looking out for you."

After dropping Tru at the doggie day spa, I pull up to Buttercup Hill, where a valet attendant takes my car and points me to where the wedding will be held on the back lawn of the restaurant. Trix finished the renovations on the inn a week ago. Julie made sure Trix kept her word and worked less, and they still got everything done a week ahead of schedule. Walking me through the rooms, she pointed out the fabric she was carrying the day I ran into her at the market. Hard to believe that was five whole months ago.

The place looks amazing, and I could see the pride on her face as she walked me through the new lobby, with its high-pitched ceiling, large hearth, contemporary clean lines mixed with antiques. Muted earth tones mixed with color. I have no idea how she looks at a blank space and sees potential, but this place meets its potential ten times over.

The restaurant itself is a California Craftsman with a wide front porch and weathered gray shingles. The windows are framed by white plantation shutters, and a wraparound deck on the second floor affords views in three directions.

I follow the crowd around the side of the restaurant to where rows of chairs are set up on the lawn, flanked by the hills that give the winery its name. A simple arch of flowers stands at the front of the space—at least, it looks simple. Because I know Trix, I know that every stem was chosen with care, every colored bud picked to contrast with the one next to it. all the tangled vines done so intentionally. It's beautiful.

But it's nothing compared to the woman standing to the side, greeting guests in a peach-colored silk dress hanging from tiny straps on her shoulders. Her hair flows down her back in loose waves, no tendril or wisp restricted from blowing in the light breeze. Her deep ruby lips offset her dark hair and piercing blue eyes, which land on me as soon as I come around the side of the building and walk onto the lawn. She smiles and starts walking in my direction.

"You look gorgeous." My whispered words near her ear make her flinch, and when I tentatively run my fingers down her bare arm, she shudders.

"Thank you." Her response is quiet, and she looks off into the distance, not at me. When my hand reaches her wrist, I encircle it with my fingers and rub the soft skin over her pulse with my thumb. I feel her relax, even though we're only touching at this one point.

Sliding my hand lower, I interlace our fingers and give her hand a squeeze. "Today's going to be great. You've got this."

"Do you think it looks okay?"

I know how hard she's worked to have everything perfect for PJ and all the guests. From where we stand, I see giant silver vases of pink and orange flowers framing the altar and tiny lights twinkling in the trees. With the setting sun, the vineyards look like a movie backdrop.

"No," I tell her. "I think it looks perfect."

She nods but she doesn't look convinced. "I need to go check on PJ," she says, looking at a point behind me where I assume her sister is getting ready inside the restaurant.

"Of course. You've always supported my career. Now it's my turn to support you. I'll be here."

That smile I love overtakes Trix's face. "Yeah, okay."

She starts to go, but I still have her hand, so I pull her against my chest, wrapping her in my arms. Leaning toward her ear, I whisper, "To be clear, if you weren't in the wedding, I'd drag you off to my room at the inn, caveman style." I feel her smile and she laughs. The tension seeps from her body, and she turns in my arms.

"And if I wasn't in the wedding, I'd go with you right now, Hockey Star."

"Do me one favor, will you?" I ask, not letting go of her.

She nods.

"After the ceremony, when everyone goes to the cocktail reception in the vineyard, will you hang behind for a few minutes? Meet me here?"

Her brow furrows. "I'm not sure I can. I need to make sure everything's set for the reception—"

I wait for her to finish. I know she'll have a laundry list of things to make perfect for her sister, so maybe my plan wasn't the best. But as soon as Trix says the words, she seems to reconsider them. "Actually, I have a staff of people who can tend to that, so… yeah, I'll meet you right here."

Trix watches our fingers untangle as though she's having the same second thoughts about letting go of me as I'm feeling toward her. She kisses me on the cheek before hurrying into the house.

In the garden next to the floral arch, a string quartet begins playing, signaling that it's time for the guests to take our seats. I choose one in the second row. I want the best view I can get of the woman in the peach-colored dress. And I want her to know I'm looking.

CHAPTER *Thirty-Five*

BEATRIX

"I pronounce you husband and wife." The minister barely gets the words out before a cheer goes up from the crowd squeezed into the chairs on the grass. Every one of them is filled, but no one is standing. I give myself a silent high five for estimating the exact number of last-minute no-shows and calculating the food and drinks perfectly for PJ.

Colin wraps his wife in an embrace, and my sister kisses him until a series of whistles and whoops from her guests brings her up for air. She holds her bouquet in the air and grins at Colin before moving slowly down the aisle. In her long white column dress and hair in a twist, she looks every bit the magazine bride. I watch them hug guests along the way until they disappear around the corner of the restaurant.

The rest of the wedding party couples off and walks back down the aisle, too. As maid of honor, I'm the last to go, on the arm of Trey, Colin's best friend from college. The string quartet plays "Isn't She Lovely," and I have to laugh at Colin's choice for his bride. It says everything a person needs to know about how much he worships her.

Trey and I walk slowly behind the rest of the wedding party. My arm is looped through his, but my eyes stay where they've been for most of the ceremony—pinned on the sly smile of Dominick Renaldi, who's been watching me like a wolf getting ready to devour his dinner. If I thought anyone else noticed, I might feel embarrassed, but standing next to the altar with my pregnant belly, I feel beautiful.

There isn't another person who could make me feel the way Ren does just by looking at me, and it's not because he likes the way I look. I mean, he does, obviously. He's made that clear, but what I feel when his eyes roam over me is that he appreciates everything I am, starting well beneath the surface. He's special that way, and I'm just nervous that it's too good to be true.

When Trey and I reach the end of the wedding area and move toward where the cocktail reception is taking place in the vineyard, I give him a hug. "Nice walking with you, Trey."

"Likewise. Thanks for making sure I didn't go too fast."

"Ha. Yeah, no runaway groomsmen here."

It was our inside joke that there's always one nervous bridesmaid or groomsman who walks down the aisle really quickly like they're on the run from the law. We each vowed to keep each other moving at a proper wedding pace.

"I'll catch up with you later. Try the sauvignon blanc. I promise you'll like it."

"Good tip from a winemaker." He gives me a high five and moves along with the crowd. Good guy. Easy. Nice looking. But he doesn't hold a candle to Dominick Renaldi.

I turn around to find him where he said he'd wait for me. The wedding crowd is filing out, so I can't see him at first. It takes a little navigating through the rows of white chairs on the lawn to get back to the spot where I left him earlier. And there he is, standing with a bouquet of flowers in his hands.

For a second, I think he's plucked them from one of the pots lining the ceremony space, but these are daisies. Nothing like the ones my sister insisted on—all deep pinks and dark oranges. These are my kind of flowers. Of course he remembers. This man has probably been planning this for ten years. It gives me a whole new appreciation for Ren and all the faith I need that he's in this for his own reasons.

Turning down a row of chairs, I make my way to him with a smile, touched by the flowers and expecting to see his usual easy-going grin in return. Instead, he looks serious as he holds up the bouquet of simple white blooms tied loosely with a raffia string.

"Hey." I push my hands through my hair for the first time since our hairdresser sent me to the family photo session with strict instructions not to touch a strand. "Whew. Glad we took the photos before the wedding. Now, I can relax."

Ren nods, but the concerned look doesn't leave his face. "Are you okay?"

He nods.

I pull a hair tie from where I've hidden it inside my own bouquet and start to twist my hair up and out of my face.

"No."

I startle at the gruff instruction, and I'm about to ask what the problem is when Ren takes the hair tie out of my hand. "Leave it down." Then, possibly worried he sounds too bossy, Ren adds, "Please."

"Okay."

I stand in front of Ren, whose expression now borders on tortured, waiting for him to tell me whatever he has to say. For an agonizingly long time, he's silent, and my brain kicks into gear. "What's wrong? Did something happen with the team? Do you need to leave?"

"No. It's not that, not at all." He rubs a hand over his face, and I pray he doesn't shove it into his hair because it looks so damn good and perfect in the tousled way it is. Then I kick myself for still being so dazzled by the way he looks that it's stealing focus from what he's trying to tell me.

"Ren, what is it?"

Seeming to remember that he's holding flowers, he presents them to me. "These are for you."

I put the bridesmaid bouquet down on a chair and take the proffered flowers. "They're my favorites. Thank you."

"I know." Slowly, he drops to one knee.

My mind goes to the idea that he must have lost something, and I start to bend toward where he is to help him look.

I bend down right into an open ring box, which he's holding out toward me. I'm hit by a wave of dizziness that has me clapping a hand across my chest. My heart flies into my throat and starts beating a million miles a minute.

"Beatrix..." Ren looks up at me and instantly bursts out laughing. "Honey, are you okay?"

"Am I... Ren, what are you doing?" I ask, taking a wobbly step backward. I'm really regretting the choice of two-inch heels right now, and I want to yell at Mallory for letting me talk her into them.

I must look a little wobbly because Ren yanks a chair from the closest row and brings it behind me. "Here, sit."

I obey because the only other alternative is to pass out. For the life of me, my brain can't compute what's happening. A minute ago, I was half convinced that Ren had changed his mind about me. About us. And now...

"What are you doing?"

He laughs again and pulls a second chair over to face mine. "Well, I had an idea."

Ren signals to the minister, who I notice for the first time sitting in the shade of a tree a few paces away. He has a book in his lap, and his foot crossed over one knee. The minister closes his book and walks over to us.

"He looked so comfortable. Don't disrupt him," I whisper to Ren, who shakes his head.

"Archer asked him to wait for us. That's why he's here."

I don't understand. "Wait for what?" The wheels whir off

again of their own will, and my mind starts thinking that maybe Ren wants him to bless the baby or stage an intervention before I become a mother who can't tell a breast pump from a boom box. My brain is still racing through ridiculous scenarios that require a minister when Ren again drops to one knee.

"Beatrix Corbett, I've already said this, but I want to say it again today. I am not with you because you trapped me with a baby. I'm not with you because you forced me into an impossible situation. I'm here for you. You are the reason I bought the winery in Napa, but what you don't know is that I did it six years ago."

I never knew what it meant when someone's jaw dropped open until this moment. My chin feels like it's on a hinge, my mouth gaping, no sound coming out.

"What?" I ask, finally.

"I bought the property six years ago. I did it through a trust, and it's mostly been sitting dormant. I hired a property manager to keep the fields watered and do the minimum to maintain the place. He's the one who hired the agriculturalist to plant the vines and fruit trees on the property. I mostly nodded and went on with my hockey career."

"Six years ago?"

"Yes."

"Really?"

"Yes. And I did it as a love-struck twenty-something, hoping he'd find his way back to the one who got away. So all that crap about trapping me, get it out of your head. I'm here because I love you. End of story. For ten years, my heart's ached for you, and there's no way in hell I'm walking away again. Zero chance. Zero. I give you my word right here today that I will be here for you always."

"Ren…" I say when he stops to catch his breath. "I do love you too."

He holds up a hand. "I'm not asking you to forgive me for ghosting you. It was wrong, and I regret it. And I can't promise that I won't fuck up sometimes because I'm a work in progress, but I'll give it my absolute best. I'm asking you to have faith in me—in our future—because the only future I can imagine has you in it. I'm asking a lot, I know."

It's my turn to laugh because I can't imagine him asking more than I already have of him. "More than me asking you to raise a child with me?"

He nods. "I'm asking for forever. I want you to be my partner, the love of my life, and my wife. And because I know you like efficiency, you can become my fiancée and my wife in one go. We can get married right now. If you want. Archer asked the minister to stay so he can perform a ceremony for us right here."

Again, he holds the ring box out to me. When I take a closer look at it, I notice the diamond solitaire isn't the only ring there. Beside it sit two plain, platinum bands. One for each of us.

I burst out laughing because I'm still not sure I'm understanding him right.

"Ren, are you serious? You want to get married right now? At my sister's wedding?"

Ren picks up my hand and brings it to his lips. "Now, or not now. Whatever you want, honey. I just wanted to give you everything and anything you could possibly want. If you want to pull off the ultimate multitasking day, you can be a bridesmaid, a fiancée, and a bride all in a matter of an hour."

When he says the words, I do feel a thrill of electricity hum in my veins, but for the first time, I know that being solely committed to my career is not my goal in life. Maybe it was, but it pales in comparison with what I see in front of me. The warm buzz of feeling I have is all for Ren and the possibility of spending my life with him.

"I love that you know me and my type A happy place," I tell him, squeezing his hand. "But the reason I'm saying yes—yes to everything you just said—is not because I want to be efficient. It's because I want to spend my life with you, Dominick Renaldi, so I say yes."

"You'll marry me?" He swallows hard as though the idea just

occurred to him. "Hell yeah. Sorry," he tells the minister, who nods.

"In the moment, people say all kinds of things. I'm used to it," the minister admits before his voice is drowned out by a cheer in the vineyard just outside of where we're sitting.

"PJ and Colin must've just walked in," I tell Ren. We listen and hear glasses clinking and the rising chatter of happy guests, and I strain to hear more. Ren reaches over and cups my chin in his hand, turning my face to look at him.

"Hey, I don't want to take you away from your sister's wedding. Maybe this was selfish."

I shake my head. "No, it's amazing, but you're right. This is her day, and we'll have our own day. I'll be more than happy being engaged to you for a while and spreading out the good stuff over a much longer time."

"Yeah?" he asks. "No multitasking?"

I shrug. "Not today."

We thank the minister for sticking around and make our way to the reception, Ren's arm draped around my shoulders. The voices get louder as we approach, and I get ready to dance with my fiancé.

"Wait," Ren says, halting our steps. He comes around to face me and drops again to one knee. "I screwed it all up. I never actually asked you to marry me."

Looking down at this man who's had my heart since I was twenty years old, I clap a hand over my mouth and shake my head. "Ren, you did ask." I pull him to his feet and put my cheek against his chest, nodding as I wrap my arms around him. "And I said yes. I will marry you, Dominick Renaldi. Yes. I'm yours. Forever."

Ren slips the engagement ring onto my finger and pockets the box with the wedding bands. "I'll save these for another time, but I'm holding you to it." He grins with that schoolboy charm I love, and my heart spills over.

With his arm draped over my shoulder again, we make our

way to the reception, where we both drink sparkling water to toast my sister's wedding and our engagement. I keep my ring finger hidden for the remainder of the night, so the celebration is only about PJ and Colin. But when Ren pulls me close and we dance to a slow song, he holds my hand right over his heart, and I never plan to let it go.

CHAPTER
Thirty-Six

BEATRIX

Four Months Later

It's the middle of the night, and one of Ren's practice tees hangs down past my knees. It's stretched tight over my belly but baggy everywhere else. I haven't slept for hours because of the contractions, but they're pretty far apart. My doctor told me I don't need to come to the hospital until they get closer together, but…

"I think my water just broke," I whisper to Ren, waking him from a deep sleep.

I'm expecting panic, both because I'm waking him abruptly and because it's two weeks before my due date. Instead, he rolls over and takes my hand. "There's a bag in the closet."

At first, I think he's in the middle of a dream. "Ren, I'm in labor," I say more urgently. He needs to wake up.

He sits up, still no panic in his face or his voice. "I know. This is it. Are you ready?"

"Are *you* ready? We need to go to the hospital. We need a

change of clothes and stuff for the baby to go home in. And we didn't install the car seat."

If he's not going to panic properly, I'll feed him the necessary lines.

"I practiced installing it a week ago. I can do it in under a minute. I'll get the bag. You… Is that what you want to wear?"

He's out of bed and pulling a shirt over his head. His gorgeous abs disappear, and I'm momentarily distracted by the fact that he's still naked from the waist down until he snaps his fingers in front of my face. "Earth to baby mama."

Walking over to the closet while calmly pulling on boxer briefs and sweatpants, he guides me to his dresser. "Pick out some sweats. The shirt's fine."

Numbly, I fumble through the drawers and take out another shirt. Ren shakes his head and opens a different drawer, where he finds a pair of gray sweats for me. By the time I pull them on, Ren has taken a large duffel from the closet and extends his hand toward me.

"What's that?"

"Clothes for us, baby stuff, snacks, crosswords. We're set for the hospital, and I just called an Uber. You ready?"

I stare at him, dumbfounded, as my heartbeat ratchets upward. This is really happening—we're going to be parents. But for the moment, I'm more interested in when Ren became a multi-tasker. "You called an Uber and found my clothes and produced a bag from nowhere…"

"Trix," he says, pulling me close and calming me with a deep, thorough kiss. "I promised you, remember? For as long as I live, I'll never break another promise to you. Never."

I nod, the last piece of doubt falling away. Until this moment, I didn't realize I was still holding on to it, but there it was, lurking in the recesses of my brain, worried about the future because I couldn't get over the past. But now it's time. "I know."

"I've got you," Ren says, draping one arm over my shoulder and slinging the duffel over his other arm. "And we've got this."

CHAPTER Thirty-Seven

REN

Trix closes her eyes when Taylor Swift sings the opening lines of "Lover." Attached to a small speaker near the hospital bed, my phone works through a playlist I made weeks ago.

"How did you know exactly which songs I'd want to hear? This is perfect," Trix coos, reaching for my hand without opening her eyes. She knows exactly where to find me because I haven't left her side for the past two hours.

Two long hours of labor, and there's no baby in sight.

"I've been keeping a list, actually." I don't mind divulging my secrets to winning her heart, at least some of them.

Her eyes pop open. "Really? For how long?"

"Pretty much since I saw you at Oxbow that day."

She shakes her head and gives me a lazy smile. "Who could've known that day that we'd be bound together?"

I don't waste a second answering.

"Me. I knew it then, and I know it even more now."

Trix squeezes my hand, and my eyes alternate between hers and the line on the monitor that keeps spiking each time she has a contraction. They're still over two minutes apart, but they've been getting closer together over the past two hours. I watch her face screw up as the contraction rips through her, and she sucks in a slow breath and lets it out in a whoosh.

Even with the epidural, she still feels them. I can tell by how hard she's gripping my hand. "Do you need more pain meds?"

I expect a nod or shake of her head, but Trix, in her usual fashion, has a long explanation. "The epidural is helping a lot, but you heard the nurse. I need to feel some sensation so I can push when it's time," she huffs out as she breathes through the contraction.

"Yeah. Is it time?" I ask, even though I know her guess is as good as mine until the nurse measures how effaced she is.

"You'd think," she grits out.

The contraction finishes, and Trix turns her head to smile at me. "Whew. Better. Is everyone still here?" She means her family.

It's three in the morning, and her siblings have all been sitting in the waiting area since we called to say we were headed to the hospital. "Last I checked. I can tell them to come back in the morning," I offer.

"They won't leave. They're stubborn like that."

A laugh barks out of me before I can stop it. Trix narrows her eyes at me, but then she rolls them. "Yeah, it runs in the family."

The door to the labor room swings open, and our nurse walks in. She snaps on a pair of gloves. "I saw you had another good contraction. They're getting closer together. Let's see how dilated you are."

I stay near the head of the bed while she measures with her fingers and meets our eyes with a satisfied look. "I'm going to call your doctor. You're fully dilated, plus one. Get ready to push when she gets here."

A nervous surge runs through me. It's like no pregame jitters I've ever experienced. Suddenly, all the stress about wins and losses pales in comparison to this moment. We're about to meet our baby. Trix is bringing life into the world, and I'm nervous as hell.

I sink onto the rolling stool, lean my elbows on my knees, and support my forehead with my hands.

"You okay?" Trix asks, side-eyeing me from the bed.

"Yeah. I'm good."

"You don't look good."

I can't do this to her. I mean, yeah, I feel like someone gut punched me, and if I was on the ice, I'd be looking for somewhere to take out my aggravation. But I'm here in the delivery room with the most amazing woman in the world, and I need to man up. I need to be there for her.

I swallow back the wave of nausea that hits my throat and sit up. "I'm good. What can I do for you?"

"Hold my hand. Now that this is happening, I'm nervous."

Wheeling over to her on the stool, I extend my hand and clasp it around hers. "You've got this. And I'm here. Whatever you need, for as long as you need it, I'm here."

"Once more, puuush," Doctor Salinger says, her hands shoved under the blue modesty sheet laying over Trix's lap. She's been pushing for over an hour and I glance at Trix's face, which is bathed in sweat as she pushes and squeezes my hand.

The guttural sound she makes with each push reminds me how helpless I am to help, other than to offer moral support and the bones in my hand, which, so far, she hasn't broken. It's up to her and the doctor to get this baby out. I hate feeling so useless.

"I can see the head. One more big push, Beatrix."

"I can't. I'm too tired. I can't do it," she whines. It's the first time I've ever heard her capitulate, and I suddenly realize I'm useless if I don't help her now.

Leaning in, I brush the hair back from Trix's forehead and kiss her there. "You can do anything, Trix. We both know it. Let's meet our baby. Can you push once more?"

Our faces are inches apart, and I stare into her eyes. She blinks back tears and sweat, but that bright blue sparkle starts to resurface. She nods.

"Once more."

"That's all I'm asking. Just one push. Last one." I look over the blue sheet at the doctor, willing her to make it true. I don't want to break my word, so she needs to catch this baby when Trix pushes.

"Okay, once more," she coaxes, while I let Trix crush my hand once more. I'm going to need to spend a week in physical therapy before putting on hockey gloves again, but it'll be worth it. One thousand percent.

With a guttural grunt, Trix gives it one more push, and the baby slides out. Looking over the sheet, I see our baby for the first time as the doctor holds her up. "It's a girl."

The nurse helps me cut the umbilical cord and then cleans our daughter up a little bit before bringing her to Trix. Staring down at the two most beautiful girls I've ever seen, I feel overwhelmed by my fucking good fortune. "She's beautiful." I choke the words out before a lump in my throat prevents me from saying anything else. Trix is staring at our daughter with such wonderment, I'm not sure she'll ever look away. But then she does. Her eyes meet mine, and she reaches up and wipes away a tear I didn't feel on my cheek.

"She's perfect," Trix says.

I simply nod, leaning over to kiss Trix on the lips and smooth the hair off her forehead. Then I kiss our beautiful daughter on the cheek. "She is. And I'm the luckiest guy alive because I get to love you both." We both know without discussing it that she already has a name—Daisy. And I love her more than I ever thought possible.

Trix pulls me close, and I hope she never lets go. "Love you too."

Epilogue

BEATRIX

Two Months Later

"Was that Ella Fieldstone?" PJ asks, coming up behind me as I say goodbye to a guest outside the inn.

"Yup. She's thinking about having her wedding here in a few months. We just toured everything. I think she liked it."

The inn has been booked solid since we opened, and we have weddings practically every weekend through the fall. If I thought I was good at multitasking before, having a husband and a baby and a busy job has pushed me to new levels. Gotta admit, I couldn't love it more.

PJ pulls out her phone and starts scrolling through social media as we walk toward the old brown barn. "She's engaged to Jimmy Angelo, the lead singer of Catalog Twenty. Do you know that band?" Before I can answer, she pulls up a song, and it starts blaring from her phone.

"Oh yeah, I've heard that."

"So, big celebrity wedding. That's exciting." PJ loves celebrity gossip almost as much as she loves wine country gossip. Almost.

The apple trees are almost all picked over, but it's too early for summer fruit. The trees we pass on the way to the barn are leafy but mostly barren. I spot one dangling apple and yank it from the tree.

"She hasn't decided yet. He'll probably want to see it too. Don't get too excited."

PJ shrugs. "Eh, he probably won't care. I think this is, like, like his third marriage, and he's your age."

"How do you know all of this?" I ask, deciding whether I'm offended that she made "my age" sound ancient.

She shrugs. "It's my job to know who's doing what."

"In Napa."

"No, everywhere."

We arrive outside the barn and follow Archer inside to grab coffee before our family meeting, which we're having outside because the weather is so perfect. Bluebird skies, flowers in bloom, ground squirrels running beneath the vines.

"Well, I'll let you know the second I know if Ella Fieldstone is a go, so you'll know what she's up to."

"What did you just say?" Archer's voice booms with his usual annoyance and disdain. He's the last person likely to be wowed by an actress. He spent the year after college living in Los Angeles and says he got his fill of "model-actress-whatevers."

PJ waves him away like a gnat. "Relax, Mr. Star-phobe. This doesn't concern you."

Dash comes in and grabs a mug. "Hey guys."

Archer doesn't answer. He shoves between PJ and me and pins his index fingers against his temples like he has a headache. "Did you say Ella Fieldstone?"

"Yeah. She just came to look at the inn for her wedding."

Archer shakes his head. "No. Absolutely not. She can't have her wedding here."

I feel my hackles shoot to attention. We each have our bailiwicks, and he can't tell me how to run the inn. "She can if her check clears."

"No, she can't."

"Why not?" PJ asks, scrolling through her feed again as though it will provide answers quicker.

"He hates her, that's why," Dash supplies, smiling innocently at Archer, who presses his lips together so hard they turn white.

"Why do you hate her? What did she do?" PJ asks me. I shrug.

"She's awful," he says.

Before we can pump him for more information, a car screams up the front drive of Buttercup Hill like it's running from the law. Dash looks up from the coffee machine and raises an eyebrow at me. "Someone expecting a fighter jet?"

"Seriously, do we need to install a speed limit sign?" I look down at where I have Daisy swaddled against my chest. Her soft brown hair is standing up in places, and I smooth it down. Bringing her to work with me is my new way of multitasking, and she seems to love it as much as I do, cooing softly until she falls asleep.

"Do we? Do we need to do that?" My voice goes up an octave as I coo at my sweet girl, whose eyes blink open at the sound of my voice before she falls back asleep.

"You're ridiculous," Archer says. "If you caught me doing the baby talk thing, you'd be laughing your ass off."

"Not if the baby was as cute as this one," I coo, just for emphasis. I'm treated to an eye roll.

"Just glad you're happy," PJ says.

"So happy," I sing.

In the months since she was born, the Otters have won their first playoff games, and Ren feels optimistic about their chances of going all the way. His playoff beard is already looking healthy, which only makes me want him more.

The pregnancy hormones have converted into maternal hormones, and I'm just as hot for him as ever. His game schedule is relentless, and so is Daisy's sleep schedule—in other words, she's not on a schedule at all, and I'm constantly tired. We haven't had extended time together at my house, where we're living, but that will change when the season ends. We'll be working on the renovation of his house and sleeping at mine until it's finished. As long as we're together at the end of every day, my heart will be full.

Then again, I'll be planning our summer wedding, so there will never be a dull moment.

Dash and I leave the staff lunchroom of the old brown barn to find the source of the noise, only to see our half brother Graham slam the door to his truck. Jax gets out the other side and stomps toward us with a sheaf of papers in his hand.

"We just came from the fire inspector's office." Graham waves the pages around.

"This again?" Archer comes down from his office, clearly alerted by the car noise. "And you should learn to drive, by the way."

"Sorry. I was in a hurry to tell you what they found." Graham starts pacing and shoving a hand through his hair.

"Dude, relax. Whatever it is, it'll be okay."

Graham starts shaking his head. Or maybe he's just shaking—it's hard to tell, given how wound up he is.

Jax shakes his head. "You're definitely not gonna think that when you see the findings. Someone was hired to start the fires, and he's already been apprehended."

"That seems like a good thing." I look down at Daisy to make sure all the commotion hasn't woken her, but she's still out cold, snuggled against me.

"Not when you see who hired him to commit arson." Graham nudges Jax, who hands the pages to Archer. "Unless we're reading something wrong, the one who paid him was our dad."

"Wait, what?" Dash asks, looking over Archer's shoulder at the pages.

"Yup," Graham says, pushing his hands into his pockets and finally calming down a bit.

Jax chimes in, sounding more reasonable. "That's what it looks like. He paid someone to set fire to Buttercup Hill. Then the wind took it next door. Bottom line, it looks like Dad tried to torch this place."

"But why? For insurance money?" I ask.

"Maybe it's his dementia. Maybe he didn't know," Dash says.

The air hangs heavy around us as we try to read over Archer's shoulder for any shred of explanation. Archer looks at the sky before throwing the pages in the air. "Fuck!" he shouts. "Like this day couldn't get any worse."

Almost on cue, my phone buzzes, and I walk a few paces away from my family to take the call. When I return, I share the news. "Ella Fieldstone loved the inn. She's a yes. Her wedding is going to be at Buttercup Hill."

Archer looks at me with a scowl, and I know the next few months are going to be very interesting.

Thank you so much for reading Beatrix and Ren's story—I hope you fell for the cinnamon roll hockey hottie!

For a glimpse into Beatrix and Ren's happily ever after, jump on my mailing list to have a BONUS EPILOGUE delivered right to your inbox! I'll only send you the best stuff—new release info, exclusive sales, and a monthly free romance from one of my author friends.

Ready for Archer and Ella's story? You can read it NOW!

Bonus Epilogue

BEATRIX

Two Years Later

There's no one at the tiny park outside of town, as per usual. "Don't you think we should take her to the big park so she can play with the other kids?" Ren asks.

Secretly, I think he likes the smaller park where no one seems to go. It gives him plenty of space to chase after our daughter, who most definitely has her father's athletic genes. Our little girl spent her first year cuddling with an oversized blue, plush hockey puck, and Ren had a tiny hockey stick in her hands as soon as she could walk. This park gives Daisy freedom to trot around with her inflatable hockey stick and use it to strike at acorns and leaves.

I love watching the glint in her eye as she charges toward a lightweight rubber puck and whacks it with everything she has. And I know Ren loves it even more. "What do you say, Daze? Do you want to go to the other park?"

"No, Daddy! I like this park!" Daisy screams past us, chasing something only she can see.

Ren's shoulders fall like they do every time he realizes he's outvoted by the women in his life. I almost feel bad for him.

Almost.

"Do you really feel like she doesn't get enough time with other kids?" I bump Ren's hip with mine, and he loops his arm around my shoulder. His gaze never wavers from our daughter, who is the mirror image, grinning at her dad like he hung the moon.

Who can blame her? I still look at my husband the same way more than two years after our engagement. I still feel the same way twelve years after our first date. The way I feel about Dominick Renaldi hasn't changed in all those years.

But oh, so much has changed. I feel more deeply and love more fiercely. I feel protective of our life together in a way I never imagined.

"Nah, not when she's this happy." He tips his lips down to meet mine. "Not when you're this happy."

"I am happy." Our sweet kiss deepens without either of us intending to have a public display in a park. It's only because of our daughter, who's toddling after the plastic puck, that we rein ourselves in. Not that she'd notice—her singular focus on her inflatable hockey stick rivals our focus on each other. We make a perfect family.

Secretly, a part of what I love about this park is the memory of the day I met Dash here and told him about my pregnancy. I still remember how freaked out I felt, and coming back here now with Ren and Daisy is a constant reminder that I'm grateful to both of them for tempering my Type A ways. Not that I don't still

I still pinch myself daily when it hits me that we're parents. And despite Ren's initial objections, we've waited over two years since our engagement to get married.

Today is the day.

Yes, today. This afternoon, to be exact. And I'm not even worried about it. No one could talk me out of planning it myself, so I know that every detail has been attended to, and I know that my team is setting everything up right now. The color scheme of pale pink, deep purple, and gray will offset the urns of daisies and the pale spring green of the vineyards. The canapes are being prepared by the kitchen at Butter and Rosemary, and I saw the chairs being set up on the lawn before we left for the park.

It feels fitting that we're spending the morning here with our daughter on a day when the old version of me would have thought I'd need all day to get primped and ready. I feel proud of myself, able to delegate tasks to my team and stay in the present with the two most important people in my life. I still remember the day that Ren told me he wanted more balance in his life, and I mistook that to mean he wanted to be a better multitasker.

My goal over the past two years has been to work less and be more effective when I'm there. That way I can leave it behind when it's time to have dinner with Daisy and cheer for Ren when he's on the road. And I can be fully present for our nightly phone calls from whichever hotel he's staying in—and he always gives me a video tour in case there are any design details I should note for future renovations.

Speaking of that, Ren's place is nearly finished. Given his travel schedule, he's entrusted me with most of the design decisions. When he comes home from a few days on the road, his eyes light up at whatever progress has been made in his absence. "The floors look great," he'll say. And even though the floors are the same and it's the window treatments that are all new, I appreciate his enthusiasm.

It's a perfect spring day, warm with bluebird skies marked by the occasional whisp of cloud. Perfect weather for an afternoon wedding.

Leaning against Ren's broad chest, I tip my head against his shoulder. He kisses my temple. "You want to get going?" he asks, his voice a low rumble that will always make me want to rip his shirt from his body.

I nod, loving that he knows me well enough to understand

that I'll start to get edgy if we don't head home so we can get ready. "Yeah. I'm excited to marry you." I look up at him, meaning every word. "I'm excited to be your wife."

He smiles, the corners of his mouth dimpling. His eyes soften as they roam over my face. "I'm excited too. Not that we need the piece of paper. You know how I feel about you. It's forever, Trix. I'm not letting you go."

Four hours later, I marvel at how right this feels, standing here with our daughter holding our hands between us. Then PJ scoops Daisy up and holds her on her lap in the front row, and Ren takes my hands. "You are my past, my present, and my future. All I could want in a partner and everything I love in a person."

What more is there to say? I can't top his words, so when it's my turn, I just add to them. "I love you, Ren, and I'm so happy to be marrying you. And I'm grateful to you for breaking up with me."

Ren flinches, and the small crowd of friends and family falls silent. His warm eyes encourage me to continue, a hint of amusement dancing behind his seriousness.

"If you hadn't, I might never have learned to pursue my own dreams. And now, I'm a better partner for it and a better person. It makes me more certain than anything that we belong together. I'm yours. Thank you for coming back for me."

I don't remember much more about what's said or who says it. All I know is that in a matter of moments, we're declared husband and wife, and Ren pulls Daisy from PJ's lap and wraps us both in an embrace. He kisses me. Then he kisses her. Then, we walk down the aisle to cheers from our favorite people.

Daisy gets restless immediately, so Ren puts her down. We watch her toddle into the reception area, where the canapes are waiting to be passed on silver trays, as I specified. At least half of the finger food is kid-appropriate—grilled cheese triangles, pigs in blankets, mini tacos. I still know how to put on a polished reception worthy of Napa Valley royalty when the occasion calls for it, but tonight, I'm going old school.

"Congrats, you two," Jax says, snatching an hors d'oeuvre from a tray. Inspecting it before dipping it in ketchup, he nods his approval. "Nice."

"Who doesn't love a mini hotdog?" Ren asks, draping an arm over my shoulder and rubbing his thumb over my bare shoulder. He takes one and offers it to me, but I shake my head.

"I'm holding out for a glass of champagne," I tell them. And because my staff is the best staff, a server shows up with a tray of flutes filled with bubbly golden liquid.

"To the newlyweds," PJ says, swooping in to grab a glass from the tray. A second later, Dash and Archer join us with glasses of their own.

"Cheers," Dash says. "Happiness always."

"Always!" Daisy overhears him and shouts it as she runs after the server with the tray of grilled cheese.

I look at Ren, whose eyes remain locked on me. He has a dreamy, relaxed expression that says he has everything he wants in the world. I can interpret it without having to ask whether I'm right.

Because I feel it, too. "Always," I confirm, not a doubt in my mind it's the truth.

Ren clinks my glass, and his eyes leave mine as he scans the distant vineyards for something I don't immediately see. Grabbing my hand, he nudges me away from my family. "Come. This way."

Unsure where he's leading me, I walk with him until we've left the small crowd of people all drinking, eating, and enjoying the gorgeous weather. The chatter and laughter recede as we reach the edge of the reception space and start walking between rows of grape vines. The sun is so bright that its rays paint the leaves a shimmery gold, causing me to shade my eyes so I can take in the vista before us.

"I'll never get tired of life on a vineyard."

"It's why I love it here."

"I've got a little surprise for you." Ren's deep voice sends a chill down my spine as though his words are hot flames licking at my skin. "I hope you don't have your heart set on being at the cocktail reception."

I'm about to ask what he means when we round the corner of a row of vines, and I see a shiny, red object in the distance. Is it…?

"You brought a tractor here?"

Ren's biceps bulge when he crosses his arms and nods, a smug smile dancing across his face. "You better believe I did. It's the first of many gifts I intend to give you on our honeymoon, which starts…" He looks down at the tank watch on his wrist. "Right now."

I wouldn't have imagined I could knock over a professional hockey player made of muscle, but that's what happens when I fly at Ren and jump into his arms. He ends up on his back in the soft grass with me on top of him. I feel giddy with excitement at the idea that he's brought a freakin' tractor here for me to joyride after our wedding.

"You are the absolute best person I've ever known," I tell him as my lips fall on his. Now, with no wedding onlookers or our two-year-old daughter in sight, we're in no rush to break the kiss. Moments bleed into minutes, and I revel in the beginning of married life. If this is what it looks like, I'm in for the ride of my life.

When we pull ourselves to standing and brush off the grass and dust, Ren intertwines our fingers, and we walk to the hulking red tractor. I'm game to hop onto the seat, but Ren leads me around the back, where I recognize his handwriting on a square sign reading, "Just Married."

"I love it," I tell him as he boosts me onto the seat. Then, I make some room. "Come on, cowboy. I'm riding on your lap, like we do."

He laughs, slings his leg over the seat, and pulls me onto his lap. "Like we do." Kissing my neck, he reaches around and turns on the motor.

And we're off.

Archer and Ella's book, LOVE YOU ALWAYS, is available now!

Acknowledgments

Readers, my sincerest gratitude goes to you. You make it possible for me to do a job I love, and I can't possibly express how much that means to me. Thank you from the bottom of my heart.

Jesse and Oliver, my favorite heartbreakers—I love you too much, and that will never change.

Thank you to the best beta readers, Leah and Amy, for having faith that this book had potential and helping me reach it. And Erica Russikoff, thank you for keeping me in line with your edits.

Thank you Echo Grayce for the gorgeous covers and the revisions without a complaint—I'm so impressed by your work and your kindness.

The team at Valentine PR is lovely and amazing—thank you, thank you.

Bloggers and bookstagrammers—thank you for embracing my books and exposing my writing to readers. I couldn't do it without your help. Glad to have you in my corner.

And to my fellow authors: I know you know. Love you too.

About the Author

Stacy Travis writes sexy, charming romance about bookish, sassy women and the hot cinamon roll heroes who fall for them. Keep the coffee coming, and she'll keep writing.

When she's not on a deadline, she's in running shoes complaining that all roads seem to go uphill. Or on the couch with a margarita. Or fangirling at a soccer game. She's never met a dog she didn't want to hug. And if you have no plans for Thanksgiving, she'll probably invite you to dinner. Stacy is the mom of two boys and two poorly-trained rescue dogs who keep her on her toes in Los Angeles.

Facebook reader group: Stacy's Saucy Sisters

Super fun newsletter: https://geni.us/travisNL

Tiktok: https://www.tiktok.com/@stacytravisauthor

Website: https://www.www.stacytravis.com

Email: stacytraviswrites@gmail.com - tell me what you're reading!

facebook.com/stacytravisromance
instagram.com/stacytravisauthor
bookbub.com/authors/stacy-travis
goodreads.com/stacytravis
tiktok.com/@stacytravisauthor

Also by Stacy Travis

The Summer Heat Duet

1. The Summer of Him: A Mistaken-Identity Celebrity Romance

2. Forever with Him: An Opposites-Attract Contemporary Romance

The Berkeley Hills Series - all standalone novels

1. In Trouble with Him: A Forbidden-Love Office Romance (Finn and Annie's story)

2. Second Chance at Us: A Second Chance Romance (Becca and Blake)

3. Falling for You: A Friends-to-Lovers Romance (Isla and Owen)

4. The Spark Between Us: A Grumpy-Sunshine, Firefighter, Brother's Best Friend Romance (Sarah and Braden)

5. Playing for You: A Sports Romance (Tatum and Donovan)

6. No Match for Her - An Opposites-Attract, Friends-to-Lovers Romance (Cherry and Charlie)

San Francisco Strikers Series - standalone novels

1. He's a Keeper: A Grumpy-Sunshine Sports Romance (Molly and Holden)

2. He's a Player: A Second-Chance Sports Romance (Jordan and Tim)

3. He's a Charmer: A Brother's-Best-Friend, Forced-Proximity, Sports Romance (Linnie and Weston)

Buttercup Hill Series - standalone novels

1. Love You More; A Single-Dad, Grumpy-Sunshine Small-Town Romance (Jax and Ruby)

2. Love You Anyway; A Small-Town Billionaire-Next-Door Age Gap Romance (PJ and Colin)

3. Love You Truly; A Fake-Fiancé, Small-Town Romance (Dash and Mallory)

4. Love You Too; A Small-Town, Accidental Pregnancy Sports Romance (Beatrix and Ren)

5. Love You Always: A Small-Town, Age Gap, Enemies-to-Lovers Romance (Archer and Ella)

Printed in Dunstable, United Kingdom

70007695R00161